MURDER
AMONG
FRIENDS

A totally gripping crime thriller full of twists

JANICE FROST

JOFFE
BOOKS

First published 2020
Joffe Books, London
www.joffebooks.com

© Janice Frost

This book is a work of fiction. Names, characters,
businesses, organizations, places and events are either
the product of the author's imagination or are used
fictitiously. Any resemblance to actual persons, living
or dead, events or locales is entirely coincidental.
The spelling used is British English except where fidelity to
the author's rendering of accent or dialect supersedes this.
The right of Janice Frost to be identified as author of this
work has been asserted in accordance with the Copyright,
Designs and Patents Act 1988.

**Please join our mailing list for free Kindle
books and new releases.**

www.joffebooks.com

We love to hear from our readers! Please email any
feedback you have to: feedback@joffebooks.com

ISBN 978-1-78931-551-6

To all my loyal readers.

ACKNOWLEDGMENTS

My sincere thanks to everyone at Joffe Books for everything you do to make my books the best they can be.

Also, my thanks to Stuart Gibbon of Gib Consultancy for his speedy and thorough answers to all my questions on police procedure.

PROLOGUE

The moment he walked into the shop he felt self-conscious. He told himself to chill. He had every right to be here. It wasn't like it was a female-only zone, like the women's underwear section in Marks & Spencer's. Not that he'd be seen dead in a shop like that. He wasn't looking for women his gran's age. He liked them young. Not too young, mind. He wasn't one of those perverts who fancied children.

A brunette fingering a slutty satin top caught his eye. Underage? That was an adult-rated top she was holding up to the mirror.

He took a deep breath. *I've got this.*

"That top would look amazing on you." He couldn't believe his luck when she responded with a giggle. Usually they gave him *that* look or walked away without a word. He'd even been told to fuck off.

"I'm not sure," she said. "I don't want to look like a slag."

"You're too pretty for that."

"It's expensive."

"How much?"

"Twenty-five quid."

"Try it on. I'll buy it for you." Eager. Too eager.

Suspicion clouded her eyes. "No thanks." He'd blown it.

"Bitch," he said, quietly, so that only she could hear.

"Get lost."

"I hope you get gang-raped." That shut her up. He smiled at her, enjoying the look of shock on her face.

Time to go. The security guy, whose radar he'd been trying to avoid, was making his way over.

"You alright, miss? Is he bothering you?"

He held up his hands. "I was just leaving."

If he ever saw that bitch again, he'd make her sorry she rejected him.

CHAPTER ONE

DI Steph Warwick nodded at the special standing on the opposite side of the road from the dead man. According to one of the regular PCs, her name was Jane Bell. She had been first to arrive at the scene. She was also on her first ever shift as a special constable.

Nothing like being thrown in at the deep end. Steph crossed the road.

"You okay?"

"I think so. I wasn't expecting something like this on my first night in the job."

"How come you're on your own? Rookie specials don't have independent patrol status."

"The regular PC I was assigned to had to rush off to the hospital after our shift. His wife's in labour. I was parking the car when I overheard a call about an incident at Greestone Stairs." She glanced at the corpse. "I'm afraid there wasn't much I could do for him."

Steph frowned at her. "You shouldn't have responded on your own."

"You'd think a passer-by might have stopped to help him," Bell continued.

Steph was irritated that Bell hadn't acknowledged her reproach. Even more annoyingly, she continued to ramble.

"I suppose most people would assume he was a drunk, or a spice zombie. I noticed some blood on the steps leading up from the archway. Maybe he was dragged up here."

"Or he might have dragged himself up and collapsed on the bench." Steph pointed out the hard-to-miss evidence for her theory, a bloody handprint on the handrail running alongside the steep path.

"Oh. Yes. Of course. I didn't notice that."

"Well, you'd had a bit of a shock. It's your first shift." Steph couldn't resist a dig. "And you're only a special."

"Right. Yes. That's true. Would it be okay if I stick around for a bit? My shift's over but I feel kind of responsible for him."

A murder investigation was outside the remit of a special, especially one with as little experience as Bell.

"We've got it covered. It's likely to be a long night. Think yourself lucky that you can go home now."

Bell's lips turned downwards in the manner of a disappointed child. Steph wondered how old she was. Mid-forties? About the right age for a mid-life crisis. There was no upper age limit for volunteering as an SC but these days more and more of those who joined were in their early twenties, using the specials as a springboard to a career in the regular force. Some people volunteered after experiencing crime first-hand as a victim. Others were inspired by the opportunity to give something back to their community, or because they got a buzz out of helping people. Which was Bell? If pushed, Steph would have bet on her being one of the do-gooders.

Steph surveyed her surroundings. A steep, irregular stone pathway approximately eighty metres long, Greestone Stairs connected the Lincoln Minster Yard with Lindum Hill, one of the city's busiest thoroughfares.

The stairs were reputed to be haunted. Now there would be one more ghost to add to the motley collection of hanged clerics, rolling bishops' heads and hovering orbs of light. Perhaps these spectres were huddled around the body already, eager to claim the young man's spirit as one of their own. It wasn't hard to believe on that cold January night, the steps sparkling with frost, a veil of freezing fog obscuring the view of the creepy stone arch farther down. Steph shivered.

She approached the corpse. The glow from a nearby Victorian-style streetlamp cast a fuzzy light on his upturned face, bringing his features into soft focus. Steph leaned in, noting the brown hair slick with bloody highlights, the pallid skin, the lifeless, staring eyes.

A CSI began taking photographs of the body. When he'd finished, Steph donned a pair of latex gloves and together they searched the victim's pockets.

The scene was illuminated, suddenly, by the headlamps of an ambulance parking further up the hill. Good. The man was dead all right, but only someone medically qualified could pronounce life extinct.

The CSI retrieved a plastic driver's licence from the young man's wallet. "Mark Ripley. Twenty-three."

No one said anything. So now the victim had an identity. They would be able to reconstruct his life bit by bit over the coming days and weeks. That made a difference to a lot of people, but not to Steph. She had a professional interest in getting to know Mark Ripley. That was all. What he was like as a person was of no interest to her unless it helped advance the case.

The wallet contained a plastic ten-pound note, some loose change, a credit card and a dozen or more loyalty cards for stores and cafés. His phone was in his inside coat pocket. It wasn't locked. A selfie on the screen showed a smiling Mark Ripley looking very much alive. Beside him was an attractive, dark-haired young woman. The picture had been taken at ten to midnight outside a cab office.

Steph's colleague, DS Elias Harper, looked over her shoulder. "Shame he didn't get in the taxi with her. Maybe he'd still be alive."

Steph nodded. She turned around and noticed, with a stab of irritation, that Jane Bell was still hanging around. She was inspecting the blood on the handrail. Probably still beating herself up over missing such an obvious clue.

Steph had nothing against specials. There were areas of policing where they could be of use — dealing with the fallout from binge-drinking on a Saturday night, chasing shoplifters, boosting police numbers at public events and demonstrations. A lot of regulars mocked these volunteers, or resented them, but she wasn't one of those. Like most cities, Lincoln was crying out for more officers on the streets. They needed all the help they could get.

But a murder investigation called for a trained detective, not a volunteer taking a break from the day job.

"Thanks for your input," she said to Bell. "We can manage from here."

"Isn't there anything more I can do to help? I could—"

"Your shift's over. Go home." Time was too precious and Steph's patience too short to be dealing with a needy newbie. Bell should have the sense to realise she was just getting in the way.

"Right. Okay." Still, the infuriating woman hovered, as though she hadn't grasped that she was being dismissed for a second time. Steph glared at her.

Finally, Bell got the message and walked away.

"Excuse me." It was a silver-haired man in a maroon quilted dressing gown. "I live in one of the houses on the terrace. Would you mind telling me what's going on?"

He wasn't the only one up. There were tell-tale lights and gaps in curtains in many of the houses round about.

"There's been a serious incident. We're dealing with it. Please go back inside, sir. We'll be speaking to everyone later in the morning. In the meantime, please let us get on with our jobs."

Unlike Special Constable Bell, the man didn't need telling twice.

CHAPTER TWO

Standing in front of the mirror in her special constable's uniform, Jane felt like an imposter. Or a little girl in dressing up clothes who believed they had the power to transform her into the real thing. Even though she wore the same uniform as the regular police officers and had the same powers and responsibilities, the feeling persisted. She was a fraud, a phoney. Sooner or later she was going to be found out.

Her feelings had only deepened after last night. She'd been well and truly shown up by that DI Warwick. How could she have overlooked the blood on the handrail? As soon as Warwick drew her attention to it, she'd realised how ridiculous her own theory was. Who kills a person and then drags them up a flight of steps to place them neatly on a bench?

Mark Ripley had crawled up those steps in the last agonising moments of his life, clutching the rail for support as he neared the top. Maybe he'd been hoping to reach the row of terraced houses where he could rouse one of the occupants and ask for help, but the effort had exhausted him. He'd seen the bench and stopped to rest, not realising he'd never rise from it again.

Jane closed her eyes. It was a tragedy. A terrible waste of a young life. The man had looked not much older than the kids she'd taught in the sixth form at Oliver Granger's. He was of an age with her own kids.

Jane thought back to the wet afternoon in April of last year when she'd made her first tentative enquiry about the selection process to become a special constable. Despite having read that age was no barrier, she'd been relieved to hear that mature applicants were valued for their skills and experience.

A telephone interview had followed a couple of weeks later, then some written tests, another interview, fitness tests, a medical assessment, security checks and, finally, a four-week training course.

She'd been more nervous than she'd expected when she turned up for her in-person interview, for only then had she realised just how much she really wanted to be selected. From that point on, failure wasn't an option. When the day of her attestation ceremony finally arrived, she'd felt a real sense of achievement, even pride, on being sworn in as a special constable,

Her training wasn't over. For the next two years she would work, under supervision, towards her IPS, or independent patrol status. During that time, she would be required to demonstrate her competency in a range of tasks. Only after successful completion of this phase would she be allowed out alone.

DI Warwick's condescending manner towards her had been a stark reminder of her inexperience, of her lowly place in the police hierarchy. Maybe Warwick was one of those regulars who looked down on volunteers. Especially the ones who'd worked only a single shift and had the temerity to ask if they could hang out at a murder scene.

Was she judging the DI too harshly? Warwick hadn't exactly been rude, just offhand, a bit arrogant. Definitely lacking in patience. Maybe she hadn't meant to come across as patronising. She was just doing her job. Jane liked to look for the good in people, but she was struggling a bit with DI Warwick.

Jane had volunteered to work for sixteen hours a month. Most of her shifts would be on Friday and Saturday evenings, like the majority of specials who had other lives and other jobs. She had her second shift that evening. It was hard to envisage how it could top the previous one. She'd been prepared for drunks and junkies and a bit of public disorder, but murder! No wonder she was feeling a tad nervous about stepping out in uniform for a second time.

She sighed. Perhaps the friends and relatives who'd questioned her decision to join up were right. Maybe she was mad to take this on at her age.

She'd expected some negative comments. Her son's opinion had been particularly grating. *Couldn't you just volunteer in a charity shop like most middle-aged women?* His ears were probably still ringing from her response to that piece of advice. Her daughter had merely shrugged and said, "Go for it, Mum, if it makes you happy." They'd been on Skype. Norah was obviously looking at something else on the screen while she was talking to her. Jane doubted she'd even heard what she said.

Her kids were part of the reason she'd volunteered. Both had left home and were living their own lives far from Lincoln. Hers had begun to feel empty. At forty-five and a widow of three years, she'd felt a need to hit the refresh button on her life.

She'd begun the process of reinventing herself the year Sam died by moving house. From the country to the town, the reverse of what a lot of people her age tended to do. She'd also downsized, swapping a four-bedroom modern family home in a village eight miles from Lincoln for a three-bedroom end-of-terrace cottage on Danesgate, right in the heart of the city and within walking distance of the castle and the cathedral. The estate agent's blurb had described it as 'requiring some modernisation.'

This hadn't put Jane off. A project was just what she'd needed to take her mind off being alone. She'd seen the house's potential immediately, and she was up for the challenge. Her husband, Sam, had been a builder, and his friends generously offered her 'mates' rates' on the bigger jobs.

Jane tackled a lot of the smaller jobs herself. There had been layers of wallpaper to peel off the walls and a fair bit of filling to do before she could redecorate according to her own taste. She'd scrubbed the floorboards in the bathroom with white vinegar and bicarbonate of soda to neutralise the smell of urine before two of Sam's ex-employees, Barry and Clive, installed new fixtures and fittings. All the other floors in the house she'd sanded down and restored.

She'd hired another of Sam's builder friends to build her a small conservatory off the kitchen. This was a delightful space for reading or enjoying a view of the garden.

The rooms in the house were spread over three floors. A window on the first-floor landing offered a glimpse of the cathedral towers, and was one of the reasons why she'd bought the house.

Her bedroom was on the second floor. The window there looked over her fair-sized garden to a view of the city skyline, these days increasingly dominated by uniform blocks of flats hastily erected as accommodation for the university's burgeoning student population.

From the house — she sometimes used the word cottage — it was only a few minutes' walk to Lincoln's famous Steep Hill, which led in one direction to the Castle square and the Cathedral Quarter, and in the other, down to the shops on the High Street. Steep Hill was lined on either side with an array of independent shops selling everything from craft beers to vintage clothes. Cafés, pubs and restaurants abounded. It was a privilege to live in this quiet but vibrant area of the city's historic quarter. Village life was all but forgotten.

Jane started up her laptop, looked up the website of the *Lincolnshire Post* and searched for news of the murder. It wasn't hard to find. Murder grabbed the headlines like nothing else, it seemed.

The victim was described as a twenty-three-year-old male student who had been found dead in suspicious circumstances. His name had not been released to the media, presumably, because his family had not yet been informed of his death. There was an appeal for witnesses to contact 101, or Crimestoppers if they wished to remain anonymous.

DI Warwick had cautioned Jane against speaking to the media. As if she would! She was perfectly well aware that it was up to the senior investigating officer, in consultation with the force press office, to determine when and how much information to make public.

Jane's involvement in the case was effectively over. She had her report to finish but after she'd printed it out and signed it off, the investigation would be out of her hands. She sighed. It hadn't occurred to her that she would feel constrained by the limitations of her new role. She envied Warwick and her young colleague, DS Harper, who would have the satisfaction of working the case to its conclusion.

Jane had spoken with a number of specials before applying for the force. They'd all talked about the sense of satisfaction the job brought. Now, she wondered if it would be enough, dealing with binge-drinkers and minor incidents. How much more satisfying to use your intellect to solve a crime instead. But you couldn't just wake up at the age of forty-five and decide you wanted to become a detective. The majority of police officers retired at fifty!

How old was DI Warwick, she wondered. Mid to late thirties, perhaps? That one time she had smiled at her colleague, faint lines had shown around her eyes and mouth. There were no streaks of grey in her hair, as far as it was possible to tell in the dim light.

Jane had a few hours until her next shift. She'd gone to bed around three- thirty in the morning after devouring a bowl of cereal and a cup of tea. Did that count as breakfast? It was ten o'clock now. She'd slept for around six hours and her stomach was rumbling.

Eating after her shift would have to stop. She'd soon start to pile on weight if she made a habit of having two breakfasts. Come to think of it, she'd eaten during her shift too. She and PC Sterne had shared a large bag of chips at 10 p.m. At this rate she'd end up failing her next fitness test.

She monitored the news updates on the *Lincolnshire Post* website throughout the day, in between cleaning the house and hoovering up all the bits of stray tinsel that seemed to be in every room. It was the sixth of January, twelfth night for some. Not for Jane. She always made sure Christmas was packed away by the fifth, just in case. No sense in risking a year of bad luck.

More details emerged as time passed, including the victim's name. That meant his family had received the heartbreaking news of their son's tragic death. Jane felt a lump in her throat.

Later, she was surprised to see an update stating that a special constable on her fledgling shift had been first on the scene. To her profound relief, there was no mention of her name.

CHAPTER THREE

Steeephanie . . . Her name was a taunting whisper inside her head, uttered by the voice of a dead man. This was the only way Cal could get to her now. In her dreams.

Lately, he was becoming more devious. He'd learned the art of disguise. Tonight, he was Steph's dead father. She saw through the illusion as soon as the apparition whispered her name. Cal was useless at voices. Her father's face dissolved before her eyes and Cal stood a table's width away from her, revealed as the monster he was. Steph recoiled. The monster lunged. Steph started awake, shivering in her drenched pyjamas, heart pounding in her ears.

They'd been doing this long enough for Steph to have acquired some techniques to beat Cal at his own game. One of these was lucid dreaming. The idea was to learn how to be conscious that she was dreaming and attempt to manipulate the narrative, dial down the threat Cal posed. Transform him into something benign, like a fluffy kitten or a floppy bunny.

But her tormentor was clever. He'd quickly caught on to what Steph was up to. Virus-like, he'd adapted. Now, he was the kitten. Or the floppy bunny. Anything or anyone she did not fear. Even by his standards, Cal had sunk to a new low tonight. She'd been sixteen years old when her dad had died. He was the only man she'd ever loved — Cal excepted.

Steph felt a profound sadness. It seemed obvious that Cal had devised this new strategy with the intention of forcing her to associate his vile apparition with the people she loved. She dreaded seeing his face every time she remembered the kind and loving father that John Warwick had been.

"You're dead, Cal! Go back to Hell where you belong." Shouting aloud made her feel better. It was a relief when Cal didn't answer back this time. But what it said about her state of mind was unsettling. She was shouting at a man who existed only inside her head.

Steph hadn't expected to dream at all. She'd put a lot of hours in over the weekend but not even exhaustion, it seemed, could guarantee a night free of terrors. It was 5.30 a.m. Dawn was still a long way off. Going back to sleep was no longer an option. Why give Cal a second chance?

Steph showered away any lingering memory of the nightmare. The coldness of the bathroom's stone floor had her dancing from foot to foot as she towelled herself dry. Even so, chills travelled, cramp-like, all the way up into her calves. One of these days, she'd get around to buying a mat.

Downstairs, now wrapped in a fleecy dressing gown, she made herself some porridge. As the hob warmed up it released a thin trail of smoke and the acrid smell of something burning. The culprit was a large blob of porridge spilt the day before — the last time she'd had a hot meal.

Home was a terraced house on a street off Burton Road, near the Ellis Mill, a tower mill dating from the eighteenth century and still in working order. Nearby Burton Road had a decent mix of shops, takeaways and places to eat and drink. The Bailgate with all its attractions was only a short walk away.

She read a crime novel while she ate her porridge. It was full of procedural errors. She thought of her gran, who'd been a nurse, tutting at *Casualty*. It used to annoy her at the time, but now she understood. They should get these things right.

Mark Ripley's death had been reported on the news the previous day. A lot of fuss was being made about a rookie special constable being first on the scene. As if that was the most interesting part of the story. Some eager journalist would be desperate to discover her identity and arrange an interview. Maybe Bell had been contacted already. You couldn't blame the press for trying, it would make a good human-interest story. But she'd reminded Bell that she shouldn't speak to the press. They'd have to make do with whatever crumbs the press office was prepared to share.

Thankfully, Jane Bell hadn't seemed the type to crave publicity. Steph couldn't now recall much about her appearance. She'd guessed her to be somewhere in her forties. It had been hard to tell much else about her in the gloomy light. She'd been wearing a bulky hi-vis jacket, which made it difficult to gauge her shape. Perhaps a bit on the dumpy side? Steph reckoned she had a couple of inches on Bell height-wise, a fact that should have been irrelevant, but for some reason, she found it oddly satisfying.

On Saturday, she and Elias had interviewed the man in the dressing gown who had come out of his house in the early hours of the morning. They and their colleagues had now spoken to the occupants of all the other houses in the area. An appeal had gone out for anyone with information to contact the police.

One woman, Isabella Porter, had been standing at her bedroom window around midnight. She claimed to have heard a scuffle coming from the direction of the Greestone Stairs. Unfortunately, she hadn't been able to see anything because her windows didn't overlook the stairs. She hadn't thought anything of it. There was often a bit of noise at that time on a Friday night from people taking a shortcut up or down the steps on their way home from an evening out. It might even have been a fox, or a cat. She really couldn't say.

A trawl of the city's taxi firms was underway in an effort to trace the young woman on Mark's phone. This had not yet yielded a result.

When she arrived at the police station, a new purpose-built edifice on Newport, Steph was greeted with some potentially good news. A young woman had turned up claiming to have information that might help the police with their investigation into the murder of Mark Ripley. Elias had shown her into an interview room, and he and Steph made their way there immediately. She had a hunch she was going to be the elusive young woman in the selfie and was eager to hear what the woman had to say. She was right.

"My name's Elle Darrow. I heard about Mark Ripley's murder on the news this morning and I was, like, how can this be true? I was only with him on Friday evening."

The young woman looked at Steph, eyes shining beneath lashes clumpy with mascara. Steph nodded encouragingly. She sensed that Elle Darrow was going to be a bit of a drama queen. A second later, her suspicions were confirmed. Elle fanned her face with her hands, eyes wide to stop her tears making her mascara run. A solitary forced (to Steph's mind) tear rolled down her left cheek. Elias handed her a tissue, which she refused.

"Take your time." Steph spoke gently, keeping a lid on her frustration. Attention-seekers were a pet hate of hers. *A young man's dead, for goodness sake. It's not about you.*

"I don't know why I'm so upset. I didn't even know him that well. We only spent a few hours together." She made a sound like a sob, though her tear ducts didn't get the message. "But there was, like, an instant connection. Do you know what I mean? A kind of chemistry between us?" She sighed, eyes drifting to Elias. "Maybe it was love at first sight."

Steph forced her facial muscles into an expression of sympathy. Her intuition about Darrow had been spot on. She was here for her moment in the spotlight, not because she'd cared for Mark. "Tell me about your evening with Mark."

Elle breathed in deeply. "Right. Okay. Sorry for being so emotional." She looked at Elias, lowered her voice. "Hormones. I've just come on."

Elias nodded. Too much information.

"Mark came up to me when I was in that new designer outlet shop in the Riverside Centre. It's called Opal. I was holding up a pair of super skinny jeans, and he said how they'd look great on me, so I said to him, 'why don't you wait while I try them on? You can tell me what you think.'"

She stared at her phone, no doubt itching to pick it up. "I wouldn't say that to just anyone. He was cute and charming and, like I said, I was really attracted to him. He was very complimentary about the jeans."

I'll bet he was. "So, you said you spent a few hours together," Steph chivvied.

"Yes. He asked if I'd like to go for coffee. We went to Starby's and talked for ages. He was so easy to get on with. We had loads in common. When it was time to go, he told me how much he enjoyed being with me. He said he knew a really good place to eat if I'd do him the honour of accompanying him. That's how he put it. Sort of old-fashioned and gentlemanly."

"When you were talking, did he tell you much about himself? Did you pick up any sense that he was worried about anything?" Steph asked.

"No. He didn't seem worried. He told me he was a student at Lincoln Uni. He's originally from Birmingham? Or Bradford? Somewhere beginning with a 'B.'" Mark was from Barnsley. "Actually, he didn't tell me that much about himself. I did most of the talking. He was a really good listener."

Steph imagined Elle would have relished the opportunity to talk about herself. She would be an easy pick-up, as Mark Ripley must have realised. All he was required to do was act the gentleman, show an interest, nod and listen. Was she being cynical in wondering about his intentions towards Elle? Had he genuinely liked her, or had he looked upon her as an easy sexual conquest?

"Where did you eat?"

"Lacey's. Do you know it?" Steph nodded. It was on a street off the top end of the High Street. Popular with the young crowd.

"And you stayed there all evening?"

Elle shook her head, "Only until nine. Then we went to the pub."

"Were you both drinking?" she asked.

"I drank more than Mark. He had a beer at the restaurant, then he switched to sparkling water. I had a couple of cocktails, well, maybe more than that. I kind of lost count. I was pretty drunk. Mark invited me back to his place, but I had to go home. I was working on Saturday and I had to get up really early. Mark was okay about it. We kissed while we waited for my cab to come. Oh, and we exchanged phone numbers."

"And took a selfie."

"Oh, yes. How did you know that? Oh, you must have seen Mark's phone." Elle picked up her phone. She showed them the picture. It was identical to the one on Mark's.

"We look good together, don't we?" There was regret in her voice. For what? The loss of a young man's life? Or the loss of a chance to be one half of a good-looking couple? Steph could take a pretty good guess at which.

"And when you said goodbye, when the cab arrived, was that the last time you saw Mark?" she asked.

"Yes. He ran along alongside the taxi for a bit, waving. It made me laugh."

Steph asked Elle for the name of the taxi company.

Elle agreed to get in touch if she remembered anything else. Before leaving the interview room, she checked her face in a handbag mirror, frowning at some imagined imperfection. Then she touched up her lipstick. Steph wondered how long it would be before she deleted Mark's image from her phone.

They showed her out. "I suppose we now know Mark's movements on the afternoon and evening leading up to his murder," Steph said. "We can put in a Data Protection Act application to view the CCTV footage for all the places they visited on Friday afternoon and evening. Shopping centre, café, pub."

Elias nodded. "I'll see to that, boss."

"Good. Anyone else come forward with information yet?"

They had heard from a few people who had known Mark at the university. He had attended a seminar on Friday morning. One of the students in the group remembered him saying that he was going shopping for a birthday present for his sister in the afternoon. He had missed a four o'clock lecture.

Elias shook his head. "Not so far, boss."

A little later, the cause of Mark's death was confirmed. He had suffered a subdural haematoma, most likely caused by hitting his head on a stone step. He'd been unlucky, not all head injuries are so devastating. His other injuries, sustained from being repeatedly kicked on the arms, legs and torso, would not have been fatal.

"It's possible his attacker didn't set out to kill him."

Steph considered Elias's comment. "If that's the case, it must have been a bit of a shock to wake up the next day and find out he's wanted for murder."

CHAPTER FOUR

Jane glanced at her fitness tracker. She'd bought it when she was preparing for the police selection fitness test and, initially, she'd found it fun. There was no doubt its morale-boosting messages had helped to motivate her. The reminders to get up and move every so often had been useful too. She hadn't realised she sat about quite so much. But the novelty had soon worn off. She was damned if a glorified wristwatch was going to bully her into exercising every twenty minutes. It would be relegated to the back of the kitchen drawer as soon as she remembered to buy a proper watch.

She'd arrived at Newport slightly early for her second shift. This evening, she'd been paired with regular Police Constable Tim Sterne. Her nervousness must have shown, for Tim immediately reassured her. "Don't worry. There's not much chance of a repeat of last night. I can't think of a time when anyone's dealt with a murder two nights in a row."

Their shift started at ten. Soon afterwards, she and Tim were called to deal with a disturbance at a fish and chip shop. A drunk man had ordered two large bags of chips. After covering them in ketchup, he'd begun throwing them at the staff while using obscene and abusive language. He'd also refused to leave the shop when asked.

Tim issued a warning as soon as they entered the shop. "Watch out! He's armed." A shower of chips landed at his feet. Jane ducked, then flinched as a pickled onion, big as a golf ball, whizzed past her ear.

"Oi!" Tim yelled. "Put that jar of pickled onions down!"

A member of staff raised his head above the countertop. The chip-thrower taunted him. "Hey! You! You the bloody cook? Should be bloody ashamed of yourself. Worst chips I've ever tasted."

He looked at Jane and Tim. "What are you two gawking at? If it's fish 'n' chips you're after, my brother-in-law's got a great little takeaway in North Hykeham. The Happy Haddock Plaice. As in the fish. Get it? It's a pun."

Just in case they'd missed it, he spelled it out — 'P.L.A.I.C.E. This P.L.A.C.E doesn't even come close." He ate a chip, then licked the vinegar off his fingers.

Well, Jane thought, *at least he's literate.* She wondered what the man's brother-in-law would make of his marketing strategy.

Things came to a head when the man slipped on a squashed chip and went down hard on his tail-bone. The jar of onions tipped, spilling vinegar over his crotch. Onions radiated out across the floor in all directions. Jane and Tim moved in.

Tim pulled the man to his feet. "How much have you had to drink, sir?"

"I'm not pissed. What are you here for anyway? I haven't done nothing wrong. Not my fault if this lot can't cook proper fish and chips. It's them you should be arresting. Bloody crime to serve up this greasy crap." He tipped what was left in the bags over the floor.

Tim wiped a dribble of tomato ketchup off the sleeve of his uniform. "We received a complaint from the staff that you've been verbally abusing them, assailing them with missiles and refusing to leave the shop when asked."

"Not me. You've got the wrong person. All I've got is chips. I haven't got any missiles."

Together Jane and Tim helped him to his feet. But he seemed to think they were assaulting him. "Get your bloody hands off me. I'm innocent." He lashed out in all directions, and Jane took a blow to the chin.

Tim had had enough. "Right, that's it. I'm arresting you for being drunk and disorderly, and for disturbing the peace. Hands against the wall." To Jane, he said, "Call for back-up and then help me cuff him."

"What are you arresting me for? I told you I haven't done nothing." He pointed at the manager, emerging from the kitchen. "He's the one who started it. He called me a bastard. That's a hate crime that is. It's him you want to be arresting."

"Shut it," Tim said. "As far as I'm aware, being illegitimate isn't protected under the Equality Act."

They grappled with him for the best part of ten minutes before they managed to cuff him. By then, a police van was pulling up outside the shop.

He continued to protest, loudly and obscenely, as they led him outside. Jane and Tim accompanied the van to the station, where the man was breathalysed and put in a cell to sober up.

"What gets me," Tim complained to Jane when they were back on patrol, "we could have been responding to a 999 call, a genuine emergency in the past hour, and instead we're tied up with an arsehole like that."

Jane sniffed her sleeve. "Fancy sharing a bag of chips? I can still smell the vinegar on my uniform. It's making me hungry."

Tim grinned. "Go on then."

The chip shop manager was so grateful for their intervention that he wanted to give them the chips for free. Jane shook her head "Thank you but we're not allowed." She searched her pockets for some loose change.

"Well, in that case." The manager shovelled another scoopful of chips into the carton. He also slotted the money she gave him into the charity jar on the counter.

Contrary to what the chip-thrower claimed, the chips were moreish. Maybe she'd keep using that fitness tracker after all.

The chip shop incident set the pattern for the rest of the shift. Jane and Tim dealt with one drunk and disorderly incident after another. At least the others were less troublesome: a middle-aged woman squatting on the Steep Hill to urinate, while her companions howled with laughter, a man who'd literally walked into a bar and required medical assistance, a group of lads brawling outside a club.

"When I said I volunteered because I wanted to help people, this wasn't quite what I had in mind," Jane said, holding a young woman's hair away from her face while she vomited into the gutter.

"I don't know," Tim said. "Think how long it'd have taken her to wash the puke out of her hair in the morning if you hadn't been on hand tonight. Great public service you're doing there I reckon."

At seven in the morning, her shift over, Jane couldn't wait to crawl into bed. It felt like she'd slept for only five minutes when she awoke to the sound of her alarm, accompanied by the cathedral bells chiming the hour. Normally she didn't work on Sundays but she'd missed a lesson with one of her tutees during the week because she'd had to wait in for a delivery. It didn't really matter, but Jane hated letting people down.

Her student, sixteen-year-old Thea Martin, had missed some weeks of school the previous term and was having a bit of extra tuition to help her catch up. When Jane first met Thea back in November, her parents had been around but Jane hadn't seen them since the end of December. They were staying in their London home, apparently, and would be gone for some weeks. It wasn't Jane's business, but she considered sixteen a little young to be left alone at home for weeks on end. There was supposed to be an older brother looking in on Thea from time to time, but his visits were few and far between.

Still, Thea seemed pretty self-sufficient. She ordered her shopping online and appeared to be fairly adept at cooking. "I can always call my parents if anything comes up that I can't deal with," she'd assured Jane when she asked how she was coping. Jane couldn't help but feel a bit motherly towards her.

Strictly speaking, Thea wasn't alone. There were the dogs, Buddy and Pearl, brother and sister labradoodles. But Jane couldn't see a breed with such a silly name being much use as guard dogs.

There was a chorus of loud barking when she rang the bell. She wasn't great with dogs, having been bitten on the arm at the age of ten by a vicious Yorkshire terrier. She still had the scar to prove it. It annoyed her when people laughed when she showed it to them. Okay, it was a bit on the small side, but Yorkies have teeth like vampires.

Jane heard Thea shush the dogs. She'd try to restrain them, but Jane knew they'd break free and jump all over her as soon as she crossed the threshold.

"You're late."

"Am I? I thought I was right on time."

"Joke. You're never late. Hey, how did it go then? Your special policing? Catch any bad guys?"

Jane felt a flutter of affection for Thea. Neither of her kids had bothered to text or phone to ask how her first shifts had gone.

"Not how I expected, if I'm honest." She told Thea about the body on the bench.

"Noooo! You're kidding me! On your first shift?"

"It's true. I couldn't make that up."

Thea whipped her phone out of her jeans' pocket. Within seconds she had a picture from the *Lincolnshire Post*'s website on her screen. "This the guy?"

"Yes, that's him. Twenty-three. Such a waste."

Thea didn't answer. She was staring at the screen, frowning. "He looks familiar."

"His name's Mark Ripley. He had his driver's licence in his wallet. That's how we were able to identify him so quickly." It felt fraudulent to include herself in the identification process. All she'd done was stand and watch Warwick and the CSI from the opposite pavement. "Do you think you've come across him somewhere?" She thought it unlikely that Thea knew Mark socially, given the age difference.

"Not sure. Maybe he's just got one of those faces. What did you think of my essay?"

Thea had emailed Jane her essay on *Measure for Measure* two days previously. "It was excellent." Of course it was. As far as grades were concerned, the alphabet stopped at A for Thea. Nevertheless, Jane had spent a little time going over the essay, highlighting some areas for improvement. Really it was just nit-picking, for there was little Thea could have done to make it any better, and they both knew it. "It should have been an A* really," Jane conceded when Thea asked why she hadn't given it the top grade. "I just didn't want you to get too big-headed. Here. Give it back." She changed the grade.

They spent the rest of the session analysing some poems. Thea's comments were less insightful than usual and she seemed distracted, restless. Finally, Jane gave up ten minutes early. "I don't think your head's in this today."

"I keep thinking about Mark Ripley, and where I might have seen him. I'll call my friend Stacey later. Maybe she'll remember. If she does, I'll text you."

Jane hoped Thea's friend would remember Mark. It might not lead to anything, but DI Warwick's remark about her being 'only a special' had jarred. It would be gratifying to prove her wrong.

CHAPTER FIVE

Phil Lavin was waiting for his mate, Adam Eades, to join him in the Cardinal's Hat, a popular pub in a Tudor-framed building at the top end of the High Street. It was reputedly named for Cardinal Wolsey, Bishop of Lincoln from 1514 to 1515. The building had housed a wool merchant's family, a fishmonger's and a bank in previous incarnations before being restored as an inn the 1990s. But Phil wasn't interested in the history of the establishment. His main concern was the urgent business he needed to discuss with Adam.

He'd ordered a platter of cold meats to share and there was a bottle of craft ale waiting for Adam on the table. Phil was already on his second bottle. He'd been feeling tense all day. He'd gulped down his first drink in seconds, hoping it would calm his nerves. While he waited, his attention strayed between scrolling the pages of the local newspaper on his phone to staring out of the window.

At last, he saw Adam striding up the High Street. Adam fancied himself a dead ringer for the actor Cillian Murphy. With his sculpted cheekbones and cool, blue-grey eyes, along with brown hair styled in a Tommy Shelby, he certainly looked the part.

"All right, mate?" Adam greeted him with a broad smile. He eased into the seat opposite Phil and reached for his bottle of ale. "Cheers."

"You know why I asked you to meet me, don't you?" Phil said, his voice low, despite the fact that there was no one nearby.

"I think I can guess but I don't know why we couldn't just talk about it back at the house."

"This is serious, Adam."

"I never said it wasn't."

"This is Mark. We knew him. How can you sit there and act like it doesn't affect us?"

"Because it doesn't. No way was Mark killed because of anything to do with the group." Adam emptied his bottle and waved it in front of Phil's face. "Same again?"

Phil grabbed his wrist. Adam shook him off. "Drinks first, then we'll talk."

Waiting for Adam to return, Phil chewed his fingernails, a habit he'd managed to quit three years ago after a lifetime of biting them to the quick. Then, realising what he was doing, he folded his arms tightly across his chest, hands tucked out of sight.

He caught a glimpse of his pinched face in a mirror on the wall beside him. Maybe he should try to relax, believe Adam when he said Mark's murder wouldn't have repercussions for them. Adam was right about most things.

Phil thought about the first time he met Mark Ripley. He'd been waiting for Adam in a bar on the Brayford. A couple of attractive girls were sipping cocktails at a table near his. Phil glanced at them, furtively from time to time, hoping they wouldn't notice.

Adam turned up with a companion whom Phil recognised from one of their seminar groups. "Phil, my man! This is Mark Ripley. Okay if he joins us?"

Mark didn't wait for a reply. "Hi, Phil. I saw you looking at those girls. Fancy your chances? Did you know that around eighty per cent of hot women are attracted to only around twenty per cent of the best-looking guys?"

"Yeah, that sucks." Phil had heard this before and wasn't entirely convinced it was true. Still, what did he know? His own record on picking up women was dismal.

"What can you do if you're not a hot guy that every woman lusts after?" Mark flexed his arm muscles. So, you've both heard of *The Game*, right?"

"The Neil Strauss book?"

"That's the one."

Phil was unimpressed. "Everybody knows about that, dude. It's way old."

"Then you know that what it boils down to is most of us guys just want to get laid, right? I mean, look at us! We're young, hot-blooded males. We're not looking for romantic love or a *meaningful lasting relationship*. We're not ready to *commit*." He spat the final word out as though it had a bad taste.

Phil looked around, hoping the women couldn't hear. Mark was one of those people who spoke to be heard.

"Why should men be denied sex because most females are too picky, or are looking for long-term commitments?"

Phil didn't think most of the young women he encountered were after that at all. Mostly they seemed to want to get a good degree and a foot on the job ladder. He hadn't heard any of them talk about marriage and kids. He didn't say this to Mark.

A trio of attractive young women walked past their table, all long hair and bare legs. They left a citrusy fragrance in their wake.

"Like what you see? Any of those gorgeous girls could be yours for the taking. All you need is confidence and a few handy techniques that can be learned easily." It sounded like he was talking about commodities, not human beings.

Phil snorted. "Yeah, right."

Mark inclined his head. "You're sceptical, I know. But believe me, I can teach you techniques and strategies that will guarantee you success with the ladies every time. You're a reasonable-looking guy, right?" Phil didn't answer. He'd noticed Adam hanging on Mark's every word. Didn't he find it irritating the way Mark was dominating the conversation?

Mark sighed. "Oh dear, oh dear. How can you expect women to like you if you don't like yourself? You need to acquire some self-belief."

He went on repeating his claims, like some professional pick-up guru. Or someone reciting a well-rehearsed script. "Believe me, learning about the art of seduction and how to practise it successfully will enhance your chances of getting women to have sex with you beyond your wildest dreams. If you'll let me, I can show you how to apply some simple strategies from the world of marketing to help you overcome any woman's resistance to your sexual advances."

Phil still had his reservations. It all sounded slightly off. "Sounds like you want to turn us into sexual predators."

"Not predators," Mark corrected. "Seducers. Think Casanova, Don Juan."

Phil laughed. "Machiavelli more like." But he had to admit he could use a bit of advice on how to get a girlfriend. It was all right for people like Mark and Adam. They were easy on the eye, confident. Even with Adam as his wingman, he'd never had much success.

"All right then," he said. "What are these techniques you're on about?"

Adam spoke up for the first time. "Actually, Mark's been talking to me about a business proposition and I suggested that you could come on board."

Phil thought it an abrupt change of direction, until, suddenly, he got it. "A pick-up coaching group. Is that what you're on about?" He realised Mark had been selling him the idea for the past ten minutes.

"Got it in one." Adam grinned at Mark.

"Adam told me you were smart."

Phil couldn't tell if Mark was taking the piss. "Are you asking me to join your business? Come on, Adam. You know my success rate with girls."

"You can help with other stuff, like recruiting clients, if you don't want to do the actual coaching. How about it?" Adam was obviously keen for him to say yes. Phil suspected Mark was only offering to include the geeky-looking friend to keep Adam on board.

"I don't know. It all sounds a bit dodgy."

"Not at all," Mark said. "You wouldn't be doing anything illegal. We talk about consent as much as we talk about seduction. We're not in the business of coercion."

"I don't think . . ."

Adam patted him on the shoulder. "Come on, Phil. What have you got to lose? You're a good-looking dude. We just need to work on your confidence. We're going to make a lot of money for minimum effort. You don't need to do anything you don't feel comfortable doing." He looked at Mark. "Right, Mark?"

"Right."

Phil thought for a moment. He was twenty years old and still a virgin. And, he had debts. Where was the harm?

Adam returned with the bottle of beer. Back in the present, Phil decided to drink this one slowly. He needed to keep a clear head.

"I can tell you're stressing out big time over this but there's really no need," Adam said. "Sure, the police will probably question us. We're Mark's mates. It won't take them long to establish that and, naturally, they'll want to talk to us. But not as suspects. We've done nothing wrong. I know you're worrying about what Mark was getting up to, but we weren't involved."

"The coaching . . ."

"Is not against the law. It was a business venture. One we tried out and decided not to pursue."

Phil relaxed for the first time, even managing a smile. "Because we were crap at it."

"Yeah, well. Wasn't as straightforward as it appeared, was it?"

"The police aren't stupid. They're trained in how to trip people up, how to manipulate them. And what if someone else tells them about the group?"

Adam's eyes flashed with sudden anger. "For fuck's sake, Phil. Grow a pair, will you? We did nothing wrong. It was all perfectly legal. And, yes, they'll probably find out about it but like I said, there's nothing wrong with teaching people useful skills."

"I know, but . . ."

"No buts."

"I was just going to say, what if they suspect us?"

"You've got to be kidding me. Apart from, *why would we*, we have a sound alibi, remember?"

"I know . . ." Phil bit back the 'but.' Adam was right. He was overreacting. This whole affair had him on edge.

Adam lifted a hunk of ham from the platter, tore it in two and offered the smaller piece to Phil, like he was the dominant male indulging a weaker member of the pack. Effectively that's what he was, an alpha. Just like Mark had been.

"So," Adam said with a slow smile. "How was the redhead?"

Adam was talking about the girl Phil had left the club with the previous evening. "Was she compliant? Any last-minute resistance? Did you talk her round?"

Phil kept his tone neutral. "Good. You were right about her tits. They were definitely on the small size." *Small but perfectly formed. Like everything else about Melissa.* Though of course he didn't say that to Adam.

Adam held up his bottle. "To Mark! He'd be proud of you. Onwards and upwards, mate. I reckon it's time you tried a blonde."

CHAPTER SIX

Jane thought she'd be more at home in her uniform after her first couple of shifts, but she still felt like an imposter. She wondered if that feeling would ever go away.

She was paired with PC Tim Sterne again for her third outing. After her busy shifts of the previous weekend, this Friday evening was comparatively quiet — to begin with. An hour and a half into their shift, they were asked to attend an incident at a house on one of the city's most notorious housing estates, the Cathedral. On the way, Tim listed the alarming variety of crimes he'd encountered there over the years. "Assaults, vandalism, burglary, stabbings, antisocial behaviour, domestic abuse, drug and alcohol-related offences, arson." His eyes slid to the left, gauging her reaction. "Rape and murder."

"Yes. I read the local paper," Jane said.

"That rag? Ha! They don't know the half of it."

In Jane's opinion the estate wasn't half as bad as people made out. A lot of the kids she'd taught at Ollie Granger lived on the Cathedral, and they weren't all delinquents. A lot of good stuff happened there too, but nobody bothered to write about that.

The despatcher had said that the incident was a possible domestic disturbance. A neighbour had reported hearing shouts and screams from the house next door.

There was no record of any previous callouts to the address, which obviously came as a relief to Tim. "That means it's unlikely to be a regular occurrence, thank goodness. Those are the worst, the ones who won't leave a violent partner until he's beaten them half to death."

The Cathedral Estate lay to the north of the city centre. It had been constructed during the interwar years in the spirit of the Addison Act's commitment to building 'Homes fit for Heroes.' Its design had been influenced by the garden suburb movement, evident in its narrow streets lined with grass verges, many with footpaths. Jane admired some of the earliest-built houses, which showed features of the arts and crafts style of architecture in their tall chimneys, deep eaves and swept roofs.

Nowadays, the estate was a mixture of council and privately owned houses. A few homeowners had individualised their properties, adding unattractive rendering that concealed some of the decorative features of the original facades. Jane winced at a house with some particularly ugly mock stone cladding, which rendered it completely out of keeping with the original red brick of the house next door. She heard a reproachful voice in her head. *Really, Jane Bell, you're such a snob.*

The area was well served by a number of amenities, including a children's play area, playing field, several shops, a library, a primary school, and churches of various denominations. Many of the public areas had a tired look, with evidence of vandalism and graffiti. Jane thought the estate had the feel of a once-great stately home that still showed signs of splendour amidst neglect and creeping decay.

Tim parked in a cul-de-sac whose houses were arranged around a circular green. They could see the number of the one they were after from the car. Before getting out, they activated their bodycams.

Jane felt a bit uneasy as they walked up the path. The door of the neighbouring house swung open. A woman dressed in pyjamas, Olaf slippers and a parka waved to attract their attention.

"It's all quiet now," she said, "but I swear she was screaming blue murder not ten minutes ago."

"Please go back inside, madam. We've got this now," Tim reassured her.

We've got this. Jane felt a surge of pride. The woman hovered in her doorway. No way was she going to miss a potential scene. Nor was she alone. Doors were opening all around the cul-de-sac.

Tim rapped on the door. When they had waited long enough, he yelled, "Police. Open up!" A couple of moments later, a heavily muscled man, dressed in jogging bottoms and a tight white vest, appeared in the doorway. Jane swallowed at the sight of his tattooed biceps. He seemed tanked up, hyper. He danced from foot to foot on the doorstep like a boxer warming up for a fight.

A flash of headlights signalled the arrival of another police patrol car. It made Jane feel more confident to know that help was at hand.

"Mr Tickle?" Tim asked.

Jane suppressed a smile, thinking of the *Mr Men* books she'd read to her children when they were little. This Mr Tickle looked more like Mr Angry.

"Yeah?"

"We've had a report of a domestic disturbance at your property."

"Not here, mate. That vindictive cow next door been making up stories again, has she?"

"A woman was heard screaming. Do you have a wife or partner at home with you, Mr Tickle?" Tickle looked uneasy.

"She's asleep."

"I'd appreciate it if you'd wake her up. We just need to check that she's okay."

"Why the fuck wouldn't she be okay?" Tickle shot an aggressive look at his neighbour. To her credit, she didn't flinch. "I'm not waking her up. She needs her sleep. And you can't come in unless you've got a warrant." He made to close the door. Tim wedged his foot in the jamb.

"We can if we have reasonable grounds to suspect that a person inside may be seriously injured."

Jane couldn't resist showing off her knowledge. "Section 17, Police and Criminal Evidence Act, 1984." Tickle scowled.

The PCs from the patrol car approached the doorstep. He was now outnumbered four to one.

"I suggest you stand aside, sir," Jane said. Tickle did more than that. He bolted.

"Cover the back door!" Tim yelled, and burst into the house in pursuit of Tickle. One of the two back-up PCs pushed past Jane, the other vaulted over a low brick wall and charged down the path to the rear of the house.

Believing that three of them would be enough to tackle Tickle, Jane went in search of his victim. She wasn't in any of the downstairs rooms. Jane felt a growing sense of dread for the woman as she mounted the stairs. She found her in the main bedroom, hunkered in a corner, bloodied and trembling.

"It's all right, you're safe now. We've got him."

At least she assumed they had, judging by the commotion coming from the back garden, dominated by Tickle's yells of protest. Jane did a quick assessment of the woman's injuries. Most of the blood on her face seemed to be from her nose. Then Jane noticed that she was holding her right side with one arm and that the other arm was hanging down limply at her side. She put in a call for an ambulance.

"Can you tell me your name?"

"H . . . Holly. Holly Carpenter." Her teeth chattered. Fearing shock, Jane grabbed a throw from the bed and wrapped it around Holly's juddering shoulders.

"Don't worry. Everything's going to be all right." Was it okay to say that? She knew nothing of the circumstances of Holly's life. The young woman could be one of those 'heartsink' cases Tim had alluded to, victims who suffer continued abuse from their partners but won't leave them. These women — and occasionally men — are often convinced that their abuser didn't mean to hurt them, that they would never hurt them again. Many might even believe themselves to be somehow responsible for the violence inflicted on them. Worse still, that they deserved it.

"Can you tell me what happened, Holly? Has he hit you before?"

"No, I . . . I've only been seeing him for a couple of weeks. I didn't realise what a temper he had on him. This is the first time I've been to his house. Soon as I got here, he started accusing me of seeing someone else. He'd seen us together on the High Street. It . . . it was only a colleague from work, but he wouldn't have it."

Jane felt a stirring of anger. "Right. What happened then?"

"When I denied there was anything between us and that we were just two work colleagues going out to buy a sandwich for lunch, he went off on one, called me names and then started hitting me." Holly winced and shifted position. She was still sitting on the floor. Jane helped her up.

"Can we go downstairs? I don't want to stay in here," Holly said.

"Are you sure you can manage the stairs?" Holly nodded. Together, they made their way down to the sitting-room at the front of the house. It took a while because Holly winced and paused at every step.

Jane settled Holly on the sofa and crossed to the window. She pulled the curtain aside and was just in time to see Tickle, hands cuffed behind his back, being jostled towards the back-up police car. She felt a stab of disappointment at not having been in on the arrest.

The ambulance arrived. A paramedic examined Holly and confirmed that she had bruised ribs and had probably fractured a bone in her arm. Holly thanked Jane and Tim for coming to her rescue. "You don't have to worry about me

36

going back to him. I never want to see him again. And I'll be happy to go to court if it helps get him put away."

The paramedic whisked her off.

"It's not such a bad job sometimes," Tim said. "This sort of thing can be quite satisfying. Taking a bastard like that out of circulation for a while. Hearing someone thank you like that. Almost makes it all worthwhile."

Almost? Jane hadn't felt such a surge of pleasure since she'd managed to get Liam Connery through his English GCSE with a pass grade. The only thing that could have given her greater satisfaction would have been to have given Mr Tickle a swift taste of restorative justice via a good kick in the balls.

They barely had time to grab a takeaway coffee before the radio crackled and another callout came through — a report of an assault taking place in an alleyway known as Butchery Court. Jane knew it. It was a cut through linking Silver Street and Clasketgate in the centre of town. She'd used it often, though she imagined it must be quite creepy after dark.

Jane asked if an ambulance had been despatched. It had. When they drew up at the entrance to the alleyway five minutes later, they could see a figure slumped against the wall and another standing close by, presumably the one who had called 999. Jane looked up and down the street and saw no one else. Hardly surprising, considering it was around two in the morning.

The victim was bent over, arms clutching his middle. More cracked or broken ribs.

"Do you know his name?" Jane asked the other man.

"Ryan Brown."

"Ryan. I'm SC Bell. Can you tell me how badly hurt you are?"

"Ribs. Kicked." His words were slurry. There were streaks of blood in his hair.

"He's got a head wound." Jane looked down at Ryan's splayed feet, the blood splattered over the paving stone. "Possible concussion."

Tim nodded. "Did you see your attacker, son?"

"Behind." He seemed confused.

"He came up behind you?"

"Yesh. Lucky." He didn't look very lucky. "Got shtartled."

"Someone startled you?" Jane looked to the other man.

"I shout," the man said uncertainly. Jane thought he sounded Polish.

"Shtartled," Ryan repeated.

"Did he take anything? Your phone? Your wallet?"

Ryan patted his pockets, shook his head, grimaced. Jane returned to Tim's question. "Did you get a look at his face? What he was wearing?"

Ryan shook his head slowly. He seemed distressed at his inability to recall anything about his attacker.

Jane rubbed his arm. "It's all right, it'll come back to you."

The sound of sirens in the distance made them all look up. "The ambulance is coming. The most important thing now is for you to get checked out."

When Ryan had been driven off in the ambulance, Tim spoke to the young Polish man. "Can you stick around for a bit to give us some more information?"

He looked puzzled. Maybe he hadn't understood. Or maybe he was afraid they thought he was Ryan's attacker.

Jane tried to reassure him about this, but he still looked uncertain. He began to speak. "I go work. I go home. I hear noise and stop." He mimicked the actions of walking and stopping, as though accustomed to backing up his speech with gestures. "I see man . . ." Air punches with his fists.

"Are you saying you witnessed the assault, sir?" Tim asked. The man frowned.

"You saw?" Jane pointed first at the man, then at her own eyes, then at where Ryan Brown had been.

"Yes, I see. I call. Shtartle man."

Jane smiled, turned to Tim. "Ryan said someone startled his attacker. This man is a witness, but we're going to need an interpreter." She looked at the man. "Polish?" A nod.

38

"I know someone who's a Polish speaker. He could be here in five minutes. He's a registered translator, police vetted. He could help us get some initial information now and come to the station tomorrow."

Tim looked dubious but agreed. Jane made a phone call to her friend, Jan Mazurek, whom she'd first met several years ago when his son was in her third-form English class at Oliver Granger. Jan had moved to Lincoln from Gdansk in the early nineties with his first wife, Joanna, and their infant son, Mateus. He was a stonemason employed on the gargantuan task of restoring Lincoln cathedral. He also volunteered as a translator.

He'd be asleep, she knew. But Jan was often called out at odd times to act as a translator for the emergency services. She called him. "He'll be here in five."

Jane stamped her feet. It was a cold evening. The one thing that had made her hesitate about volunteering as a special was that she would be spending most of her time outdoors. Winter was a season she preferred to experience at home, with the radiators on full blast.

She was clapping her gloved hands together to warm them when Jan arrived.

"Hah, you would not survive five minutes in Polish winter."

"Nor would you nowadays, Jan. I know why you only visit Gdansk in the summer."

"You are right. Tonight is brass monkeys. Why you call me out of warm bed? This better be good." Jan spoke near-perfect English, but sometimes he liked to exaggerate his accent. He also enjoyed using obscure aphorisms. He laughed when Jane told him no one knew what they meant anymore. It tickled him when he got the opportunity to explain English idioms to the English.

"A young man was attacked just inside that alleyway, Jan. This man witnessed the assault, but he doesn't speak much English. Can you interpret for us?"

"He is Polish?" As well as his own language, and English, Jan spoke fluent Russian, which he'd learned from his paternal grandmother. He was always having to point out that, contrary to common perception, the two languages weren't interchangeable.

"Yes. Can you start by explaining to him that he's not being arrested?"

"*Dobry wieczór.*" Jan used the formal greeting, 'Good evening,' rather than the informal, "*Cześć,*" that Jane was more used to hearing him say. Within minutes, he had established the young man's name as Krzysztof, or Kris. He was nineteen years old, and he came from a street in Gdansk only a few minutes' walk away from where Jan was born. Jane appreciated that Jan was putting the young man at his ease before moving on to discussing the assault he'd witnessed, but she could sense Tim's impatience to get down to business. Sure enough, he butted in. "Ask him what he saw."

It took some time for the questions and answers to be interpreted. Kris was returning from a late shift at work. He was a hospital porter. He'd been alerted to Ryan's plight by the sound of cries as he approached the alleyway. Ryan Brown was on the ground, shielding himself from his attacker's kicks. Kris acted out the whole scene as if he were in an action movie. It seemed that he was a naturally demonstrative person, not just when speaking English. Jane fought an urge to duck as he waved his arms around.

"He called out. Ryan's attacker was startled and immediately ran off. There was no confrontation between them," Jan explained.

"Can he describe Ryan's attacker?" Tim asked.

As soon as Jan put the question to him, Kris raised a hand an inch or so above his own head, then threw his arms wide.

"He says he was a white man, medium height, solid, like he works out."

"What about a description? Did he get a look at the assailant's face?" Tim asked.

Kris mimed pulling a hood around his face, making translation unnecessary. He then said something to Jan, his head lowered as if in shame. "He says he is sorry he did not pursue the man who attacked Ryan. It all happened very fast and he was worried about Ryan's injuries."

Tim nodded. "Tell him it's okay. He did the right thing."

Jane was disappointed that they'd learned so little about Ryan's attacker. Then, just as she thought that his statement was complete, Kris began speaking with Jan again.

"What's he saying?" Tim sounded tetchy. Jane suspected he was frustrated with how slowly the interview was proceeding. He was probably also peeved that he had been all but ignored throughout the exchange. Jan had looked at Jane whenever he translated Kris's responses, even when Tim asked the questions.

"He thinks the man was not old. From the way he moved. His gait? That is the right word?"

"Yes."

"Kris wants to know if he can go now. You want his contact details?"

Finally, the interview was over. Kris gave his details to Jan and headed off.

"Thank you, and thanks for stepping in, Jan." They were standing next to the police car. Jan kissed her on both cheeks. Tim rolled his eyes. "Kissing an officer on duty is an arrestable offence, you know."

"You want one too?" Jan puckered his lips. They all laughed.

Jan kissed Jane again. "You owe me." He mimed downing a shot.

"There'll be a double vodka with your name on it next time we meet."

The remainder of Jane's shift passed without incident. Tim dropped her off near her house on Danesgate.

Despite her exhaustion, sleep didn't come easily. Her body wasn't yet used to these nocturnal shifts. She lay on top of the bedcovers for a while, prickling all over with the discomfort of an incipient hot flush. It would be followed by clamminess and shivers as her body cooled. The flushes were a recent phenomenon. At forty-five she considered herself a little young to be perimenopausal, but her mother had 'gone through the change' younger than that.

She wished she could embrace this new phase of her life with enthusiasm, like those admirable women she frequently heard on *Woman's Hour*, those who became high achievers in middle age and had fabulous sex lives.

Periods were something she certainly wouldn't miss. It was all the other horrors that lay in store, like her bones losing density until they resembled the inside of a crunchie bar, brittle and pocked with air holes.

She found herself pausing at the skin care shelves in the supermarket to read the labels of 'anti-ageing' creams and serums. Their list of ingredients seemed to suggest an alternative periodic table of age-defying elements.

At least her age group was still within the target range of the manufacturers and marketers of skincare products, unlike the miserable wretches who were banded together in the sixty-plus category. It would seem there was no point in developing an age-specific product for them because, let's face it, who'd be looking at them anyway?

Jane sighed, plumped her pillow and turned it over. It felt slightly cooler against her burning face.

Outside, the city was stirring. She could hear the sound of traffic building up, the occasional wailing siren as an ambulance sped up Lindum Hill on its way to the County Hospital.

Ryan would probably have to spend the night at the hospital. A case of concussion could prove fatal if it resulted in a bleed to the brain. Ask Mark Ripley. Jane yawned. She wasn't a detective. She couldn't bring Mark Ripley's killer to justice, but last night she had made a difference. She had given something back by helping two people, Holly and Ryan.

A thought came to her as she was drifting off to sleep. Suddenly, she was wide awake again. Could Ryan have been attacked by the same person who murdered Mark? Would Ryan be dead too had Kris not cried out, scaring off his attacker?

Or, had Mark's murderer not intended to kill him? Mark had struck his head on the sharp edge of the stone step. Perhaps that had been an accident?

There were striking similarities between the attacks. Both victims were young men in their early to mid-twenties, both were beaten. She tried to remember if they looked alike. Jane had no difficulty recalling Mark's physical appearance. There was a copy of the *Lincolnshire Post* on her kitchen table downstairs, and Mark's wide-jawed, handsome face was on the front page, his intelligent blue eyes startling in their vitality. A world away from the dead, fish-eyed stare that even the streetlamp near his last resting place had been unable to spark with any life.

Jane felt the dead stare as an accusation. If only she could make it up to Mark by being involved in the quest to bring his killer to justice.

She reminded herself, again, that the investigation was out of her hands. Her part in it was over. Despite her earlier optimism about her new job, Jane felt the constraints of her role tightening around her like a straitjacket, stifling her instinct to become more involved. She sighed and turned over but changing position didn't make any difference. She was still wide awake, still unable to stop thinking about Mark's murder. Still 'only a special.'

CHAPTER SEVEN

Steph had tasked one of the PCs attached to the team with checking CCTV footage acquired from the Riverside shopping centre, the High Street and other venues from the day of Mark's murder, based on Elle Darrow's account of how and where they had spent the afternoon and evening after meeting in Opal.

PC Joey Fairbairn, bleary-eyed from hours spent staring at his screen, was now talking them through the sections he'd flagged up as relevant for them to see.

"This is the first time Mark Ripley appears on camera." Joey pointed Mark out amidst a press of people entering the Riverside Centre from the High Street. Mark headed straight for Opal.

"And there's Elle Darrow," Elias said. She was browsing a rail of jeans near the entrance to the shop. She picked a pair out and held them against her, checked the price tag, returned them to the rail and picked out a different pair. Suddenly, Mark Ripley appeared from her left and said something to her. There was no accompanying sound.

"He's telling her the jeans would look great on her," Steph explained. "She suggests he hang around while she tries them on so that he can give her his opinion." Even if she hadn't heard it from Elle, it would have been pretty obvious what the two of them were saying.

Mark waited outside the changing room while Elle went inside. His eyes strayed to another young woman holding up a black strappy top with glittery gold sequins. He glanced at the dressing room, then back at the young woman. If Steph hadn't already known that Mark had left the shop with Elle, she wouldn't have been surprised if he had abandoned her there and then for glitter-top girl.

The jeans did look great on Elle. She was wearing a crop top that showed off her wispy thin waist. She twirled and looked over her shoulder to catch Mark's reaction. His back was to the camera, but his approval was written all over Elle's delighted face.

"Just as well he doesn't know what fate's got in store for him," Steph commented. Mark had only a few hours left to live at this point. At least they'd been happy ones. She couldn't help wondering if he'd still be alive if he'd chosen glitter-top girl instead.

PC Fairbairn explained that he'd seen nothing untoward on the High Street footage of Mark and Elle leaving the shopping centre and proceeding south on the High Street. They picked the couple up again on CCTV footage that the police had obtained from Starbucks.

After ten minutes of observing Mark and Elle drinking coffee and clearly enjoying flirting with each other, Steph stifled a yawn. "Do we need to watch all of this, Constable? Because if nothing significant is about to happen, I suggest we speed it up a bit."

"Sorry, ma'am," Joey mumbled. He paused again a bit farther into the tape. Mark stood up from the table and headed for the toilet. Elle took a mirror out of her handbag. She turned her head from side to side, frowned and took out a lipstick, which she applied, pressing her lips together and pouting. Apparently satisfied, she put the mirror away and looked around at the other customers.

"This could be interesting." Elias said. Steph nodded. She'd already spotted the young man, cup in hand, surveying the room, looking for a table. It was busy, but there were some empty seats. His gaze settled on Elle.

He advanced on her table and signalled at the empty chair. Elle shook her head and looked away. The man seemed to hesitate. Just then, Mark emerged from the toilets and the man moved off, choosing a distant table.

"Poor bloke. Double whammy. She hardly acknowledges him when he speaks to her, and then the alpha shows up," Steph commented.

"Not happy, is he?" Elias was referring to the man's face as he turned away from the couple, his snarl of displeasure caught, clearly, on camera.

"Hmm. Guess no one likes being rejected," Joey said.

Steph was becoming restless. "Is that all you've got?"

Joey moved on. The couple had made an afternoon of it, ordering more coffee and chatting for a further hour.

"Did you study the customers around them? Any of them seem to be showing anything more than a passing interest in Mark and Elle? Anyone look suspicious?" Steph asked.

"Yes, ma'am. No ma'am." Moments later, they watched the couple turn down a stepped passageway between buildings. It led from the High Street down to where the River Witham flowed through the arch of the medieval High Bridge, a spot known locally as the 'Glory Hole.'

They walked along the riverside, passing under another, more modern road bridge with the words, '*Where are you going?*' painted over its arch. The other side, Steph knew, asked '*Where have you been?*' She'd never questioned why.

"They're heading for the Brayford," Joey said. Steph nodded. The popular Brayford Waterfront was lined on one side with bars, hotels and restaurants, on the other by university buildings. Brayford Pool, a natural lake formed by the widening of the River Witham, had been used by the Romans as an inland port and had remained important to the city's trade right into the twentieth century.

Elle seemed to be leading the way. She stopped outside an Italian restaurant and looked up at Mark, who nodded and followed her inside.

"Nothing worth mentioning happens in here," Joey remarked. "Darrow does most of the talking. At one point, he reaches across the table and takes her hand. She acts pleased when he does this. Look." He pinpointed the moment.

"Looks like they're really hitting it off," Elias said. Steph didn't answer. She was thinking of Elle's single tear when she'd been interviewed. Maybe she'd judged the young woman too harshly. After all, she'd only just met Mark. All she had to grieve for were possibilities, but her joy when he took her hand seemed genuine enough. Steph noted the time on the CCTV monitor. Mark had around five hours left to live. Had they both gone home full of expectations of seeing each other again, not realising that life had other plans in store for them?

"That's all we've got so far." Joey sounded apologetic.

"Thanks, Constable. Keep looking," Steph said. She motioned to Elias. "Let's go shopping."

They visited Opal, hoping to speak with any members of staff who had been on duty the day Mark and Elle met.

The manager identified Elle as one of their regulars. "Tries but doesn't often buy," she commented. "Except when there's a sale on." Steph wasn't sure if this was meant to be a criticism. If so, the same might apply to her. "I thought they were a couple. He was very complimentary about the jeans she tried on. You should speak to Ian Morrison. He's one of the security guards. He was probably on shift that day. He knows everyone."

Ian was on a mid-morning break. They found him in the control room, drinking tea with a colleague. Both were watching the CCTV monitors. Ian was middle-aged, ex-army, hard-faced but with a surprisingly gentle voice.

"Yeah, I recognise her. Nice girl. Always says 'hello.' Not all the customers do, you know. Most don't notice us. Until they need us, that is. The lad's not a regular, but I have seen him around. He's the one who was murdered, isn't he? I've got a good memory for faces."

Jane wondered if he remembered Mark because he'd seen him hitting on Elle. She was right.

"I'd been called into the store to deal with a mouthy customer upstairs in lingerie. I clocked Ripley talking to Elle on my way back down and I kept my eye on him. It's part of my job to make sure customers aren't harassed when they're using the centre." His colleague looked up from the CCTV monitors and nodded.

"Do you get a lot of that sort of thing?" Steph asked.

"Are you kidding? There's always lads sniffing around. You get to know the ones who're most likely to be a nuisance. And they aren't just the young ones, believe you me. I could tell that poor Mark Ripley wasn't one of them. See, you learn to read their body language. I can tell in seconds if someone's in the centre to shop or to get up to some sort of mischief." He tapped the side of his nose and gave a knowing wink. "Comes with experience."

Steph humoured him with a quick smile.

"Young Ripley looked innocent enough. None of that furtive glancing around the shop with a nervous look on his face in case one of us was onto him. He made a beeline for the handbags."

"Did you notice if anyone was watching Mark?" Her question took Ian by surprise.

"Interesting question," he said. "Not that I noticed." He glanced at the CCTV screens showing different views of the centre, inside and out.

"Our people are scrutinising your footage going back some, but I'd be grateful if you could take a look from around two in the afternoon on the day Mark was murdered. A pair of experienced eyes might spot something we've missed," Steph said, hoping the compliment would make him amenable to her request.

"Of course," Ian said. They waited while he found the right footage. "Here we go." They watched Mark walk towards the entrance to the shopping centre. Mark had told Elle Darrow that he'd gone into Opal to look for a handbag for his sister's birthday. He'd been browsing the accessories shelves when Elle caught his eye. After meeting Elle, he'd evidently forgotten his mission.

"He didn't follow her into the centre, looks like," Ian commented. "Sometimes they do that. Follow a girl in from the High Street and wait for an opportunity to pester her." He leaned in closer to the screen and pointed out a thin young man hovering near the entrance to the shop.

Steph hadn't noticed him in the footage Joey had shown them because she had been concentrating on Mark. It was like that video she'd seen in a training session once, about selective attention. The group had been instructed to watch a few moments of a basketball game and keep their eye on the ball being passed between three players dressed in white tops. They were instructed to count the number of times the ball passed between them. Three other players in black tops passed another ball among themselves. Steph and her colleagues had all counted accurately, and they'd laughed when the trainer asked if anyone had spotted the gorilla. Then he'd played back the video. Everyone had been astonished to see a man in a gorilla suit stroll right through the two sets of players, at one point even stopping to beat his chest. The invisible gorilla. The big thing you missed when your attention was focussed elsewhere.

"Hey! Looks like you were right. Someone was watching Mark," Ian said.

"I don't suppose you recognise him, do you?" Steph didn't expect he would, but she had to ask.

"As a matter of fact, you're in luck. He's another of our regulars. Comes in, hits on girls, never with any success, poor sod. Harmless enough though. Never gets aggressive." He gave a laugh. "I had to rescue him once as a matter of fact. Young lady whacked him one for staring at her boobies."

"What's his name?"

"Jason. Surname's Collins, I think."

49

"Thanks, Ian. You've been a big help."

"No worries. Anytime. Hey, let me know if you find who killed that young man, will you? I feel sort of involved now."

His words reminded Steph of that irritating special who'd been in attendance at Mark's murder scene. Everybody thought they were invested in the case, it seemed. She promised to let him know.

They left the shopping centre. Steph asked Elias to obtain an address for Jason Collins.

Elias contacted the intelligence unit, who came up with an address in minutes.

"Let's see if he's home," Steph said.

Jason lived on a council estate south of the city centre. It was in North Hykeham, which had once been a village in its own right but had long since been gobbled up by urban sprawl.

"Here we go." Elias pulled into the kerbside outside the Collins's modest but tidy-looking home. Steph had grown up in one just like this. Elias, though he tried to conceal it, hailed from somewhere much more upmarket. He was always being teased about his posh accent.

The door was answered by a middle-aged woman with limp blonde hair that was dark at the roots. Her over-plucked eyebrows suggested she'd been a teenager back in the seventies. She was dressed in leggings and a long top with a sequined pink heart on the front. A number of the sequins were missing, Steph noticed.

Before Steph had a chance to show her ID, the woman asked, "Are you police?"

"Yes. I'm Detective Inspector Warwick. This is my colleague, DS Harper."

"Good. I've been hoping you'd come today. I must say I was expecting someone in uniform, not the top brass."

"You were expecting a visit from the police?"

"Yes. I phoned this morning." Her expression darkened. "You sure you're police?" She opened the door wider and looked up and down the street. "Has he put you up to this?"

"We don't know anything about your call this morning. We're here to speak with your son, Jason."

"Jason?" She said it as if she'd never heard the name in her life. Steph checked the number on the door.

"You are Jason Collins's mother, aren't you?"

"'Course I am. Who's asking?" It was clear that she was still unconvinced that they were genuine police officers. Impatient, Steph waved her badge under the woman's nose.

"Is that fake? Everything's fake nowadays. Fake news. It's in the papers all the time." She glared at them as though they were personally responsible for all unreliable information.

"It's not fake," Steph said tersely. "Is Jason at home?"

"He's in bed. He works nights at Asda, stacking shelves."

A young man appeared at the top of the stairs, dressed only in boxers. "What's going on, Mum? I'm trying to get some sleep here."

"Now you've gone and woken him up."

"Jason," Steph called. "I'm Detective Inspector Warwick. Put some clothes on and come downstairs. I need to ask you some questions."

"What about?" Jason was halfway down the stairs. "I haven't done anything wrong."

"Suppose you'd better come in," Mrs Collins's tone wasn't exactly inviting. "I thought you'd come about the complaint I put in about that Pole across the street." Steph noticed Elias's gaze drift towards a telegraph mast on the other side of the road.

Thankfully, Jason reappeared before his mother could embark on a racist rant about her Polish neighbour. He was wearing grey joggers and a *Breaking Bad* T-shirt, the one with the drug dealer's chicken restaurant logo on the front. One of the chickens was missing its crown.

Jason glanced at his mum. He seemed a bit scared of her. "I haven't done anything wrong."

"Jason, have you been watching the news recently? Did you hear about the young man who was murdered just over a week ago?" Steph said.

"Yep. It was on the news, wasn't it, Mum?" Mrs Collins nodded.

"On the day he was murdered you were spotted on CCTV at the Riverside Centre. You were following Mark into a shop called Opal."

Jason looked puzzled. His mum was outraged. "What do you mean? Are you trying to say my son's a murderer?" She gave a shrill laugh. "He's a victim, that's what he is. Always the one who was picked on at school—"

"Mrs Collins, please let Jason answer for himself."

"I wasn't following him. I was studying him."

"Studying him?" Steph said.

"Yep."

"Can you elaborate a bit?"

"It's what you do," Jason said. "You pick someone who looks like an alpha and you study them. How they do it."

"How they do what?" Though Steph thought she knew.

"Pick up girls."

"Right. So, you were watching Mark to learn how to hit on women?"

"Yes." Jason looked down. Steph studied him for a moment. He lacked confidence, obviously, probably low on self-esteem too. He wasn't all that bright and no one but his mum would call him good-looking. She supposed his sex life was non-existent. She felt a surge of pity for him, then suppressed it immediately. Pity for Cal had got her into a lot of trouble.

"Where did you hear about this sort of thing, Jason? From your mates?" she asked.

Jason looked cagey. "Sort of." Steph waited. When he failed to elaborate, she gave him a nudge. "Did you read about it? See stuff online?"

"Online mostly."

"And you chose to follow Mark because you thought he looked like the sort of bloke who'd be successful at picking up women?"

"And because of what he said in the pub."

Steph raised an eyebrow. "You knew Mark Ripley?"

"I only met him once." Jason looked fearfully from Steph to Elias. "He came up to me in the pub and asked me if I wanted to join this group he was running. He said he could help me get a girlfriend."

"Go on."

"He told me he could teach me things . . . I can't remember the word he used, it means how to go about doing something."

"Techniques," Steph said.

"Yeah. He used that and another word that started with an 's.'"

"Strategies?" Elias suggested.

"Yeah, that's it. Said he was a pick-up coach. He said he'd even take me out on the High Street to practise. Going out in the field he called it."

"Right." Steph knew about this sort of thing. She'd seen videos where so-called pick-up coaches encouraged men to approach women in the street to practise the techniques they taught. The end goal was to obtain sex with a woman of their choosing, whenever they wanted it. It wasn't illegal to stop a woman in the street and attempt to chat her up, unless the woman was underage, but in Steph's opinion, street harassment should be made an offence. It was a nuisance, and it made women feel unsafe.

"So, is that what you did? Went 'out in the field' with someone who promised he could help you pick up women?"

"He's never had a girlfriend," Mrs Collins said. "He's started going to the gym to beef himself up so they'll fancy him more. Their loss if they can't just take him as he is, that's what I say."

Steph tried not to wince. She was sure Mrs Collins was well-intentioned, but her remark caused Jason to hang his head and stare at the carpet. Surprisingly, he returned to her question without prompting. "Yeah. Just that one time I met

Mark. He said he'd give me a free taster session. So we went outside. He went up to some girls while I watched from a distance. He got their phone numbers no problem."

"Okay. And then he tried to sign you up for more sessions — at a cost, I imagine?"

"Yes."

"Was Mark running the group alone, do you know?" she asked.

"I don't know. I never asked."

Mrs Collins butted in again. "You better tell them what they want to know, Jase. You don't want them thinking you had anything to do with that Mark's murder."

Jason scratched his arms, fiddled with the drawstring on his tracksuit bottoms, cracked his knuckles. "He never mentioned anyone else."

"Just out of curiosity, what did Mark want to charge you for his coaching?" Steph asked.

Jason quoted a sum that made his mum gasp. *Poor bloke,* Steph thought. *They must have seen him coming.* But Jason had been saved by lack of disposable income.

"I couldn't afford it."

"That's why you were following him? You thought you'd watch him in the hope of picking up a few more tips without having to pay?" Elias said.

Jason's head was practically between his knees. "Yep. I was in the shopping centre and I watched him. I swear that's all I did. He left the shop with a girl. I went the other way."

"We can check that. Did you recognise the girl he left with?" Elias asked.

Jason looked at his mum. "I went to school with her. Her name's Elle Darrow. She's pretty."

"Out of your league, son," Mrs Collins said crushingly. Jason nodded. "Are you finished now? Only Jase could do with putting his head down for a couple more hours. He's got another shift tonight."

"Yes, thanks." Steph stood up. They saw themselves out.

"I doubt he had anything to do with Mark's death." They were walking back to the car. "This pick-up coaching thing warrants investigating. I don't imagine Mark was running the group alone." Elias nodded.

Hours later, on her way home, Steph stopped off at the supermarket to buy some ready meals for her freezer. There'd be little time to cook while the investigation was ongoing. In the wine aisle, she chose quickly, selecting a bottle of red that was on offer. Just the one. She avoided stocking up on alcohol. It would be all too easy to make a habit of drinking. She'd done that for a while after Cal, until she'd realised it was just one more way in which he continued to exert control over her from beyond the grave.

There was a long queue at the self-service checkouts. Steph got her phone out while she waited her turn. A woman behind her was nagging her husband to return a couple of steaks. "Red meat's bad for your cholesterol, Bill."

Steph felt a stab of irritation at the woman's controlling attitude. Why did relationships inevitably mean one partner dominating the other, stifling them? Bill was a grown-up and perfectly capable of weighing up the risks. Let him make his own decisions, for pity's sake. She almost called out to him when he headed back, meekly, to the meat aisle, steaks in hand.

When it was her turn, she put her items through the scanner quickly and efficiently. Then she had to wait for the assistant to come over and verify that she was old enough to purchase alcohol. He was tied up with another customer for a few minutes and apologised for her wait. Steph grunted. His apology was meaningless, just something he'd been told to say to customers.

She'd spent too much to use contactless, so she stabbed in her PIN, irritated at the delay. Finally, she retrieved her card and made her escape. She was pushing her loaded trolley down the aisle towards the exit when a voice called out to her.

"Excuse me! DI Warwick!" Steph cringed. She recognised that voice.

It was SPC Jane Bell, holding something out to her. Her credit card. She'd stuffed it in her pocket after paying, meaning to return it to her card holder when she had a hand free, then forgotten about it. It must have worked its way out.

"Thank you," she said. "SPC Bell, right?"

"Yes. I didn't think you'd recognise me out of uniform and in the daylight. Well, artificial light." Steph was about to mutter her thanks again and hurry off, but Bell got in first. "How is the investigation into Mark Ripley's death going? I keep picturing him lying there on that bench. Are you making progress?"

"I can't really talk about an ongoing case," Steph said.

"No. I suppose not. I just thought . . ." Steph knew Bell had been about to point out that she was 'one of them.' But she wasn't. She was a special, not a detective, and had no right to make such an assumption. Maybe she'd stalled because she'd realised it. Steph took advantage of her hesitation.

"Thanks again for returning my card." She walked off at a brisk pace. Bell had had an empty trolley so there was no chance she was on her way to the car park too. Steph sincerely hoped that she'd seen the last of the annoying woman.

CHAPTER EIGHT

"I've remembered why that Mark Ripley looked familiar."

Jane looked up from petting Buddy and Pearl, who'd ambushed her at the door as usual.

"Oh, that's good."

"Finish making a fuss of those two and give me your coat. I've made hot chocolate."

With any of her other students, Jane would have suspected delaying tactics, but she knew that the two hours she spent tutoring Thea could easily be chopped in half with little loss of benefit to her student.

At last the dogs were appeased. Sighing and snorting, they curled up in a big ball of intertwined fur on the rug in front of the wood burner. Thea handed Jane a steaming mug of chocolate topped with fluffy marshmallows. "It's got honey and cinnamon in."

Cream too, if Jane wasn't mistaken. "It's delicious. Very decadent." She took another sip. "So, tell me about Mark Ripley."

"My friend Stacey reminded me. We saw him a few weeks ago when we went to the fitness club on Outer Circle Road. 'Hi! To Fitness?' Stacey's parents have family membership."

Jane nodded. She knew the place. A leaflet had popped through her door soon after it opened, offering her a week's free membership.

"We saw him in the café. We both fancied him."

Jane made exaggerated tutting noises. Thea giggled. "I know. What are we like? He was sitting at a table near ours with two other guys, both good-looking. Mark winked at us."

Jane nodded indulgently. She remembered being keen on a boy at school when she was around Thea's age. He was three years older than her and wouldn't have noticed her if she'd danced naked in front of him, but for that whole year the sight of him playing football at lunchtime was enough to send her into a state of euphoria for the rest of the afternoon. Maybe that's why she'd done so badly in maths that year. It was the first period after lunch. So, yes, she could relate to Thea's enthusiasm.

"Mark Ripley was twenty-three. Isn't that a bit mature for a pair of sixteen-year-olds?" Thea was small for her age, and in Jane's opinion, she didn't even look fifteen.

Thea snorted. "Once, when we were in Lincoln shopping, a man who looked about *forty* came up to us and asked if we'd like to go for drinks with him."

"I take it you declined?"

Thea rolled her eyes. "What do you think? We're not stuuuupid."

No, but you are young, and not nearly as worldly-wise as you think you are. "Good," she said. "Never, ever, go off with strange men. Best not to accept a drink from them either. You never know if it's been spiked."

Jane was surprised that Thea didn't come back with a putdown, a 'Yes, Mum,' or something like that. In fact, Thea was staring at her with something like affection. Jane felt flattered. It occurred to her that Thea wasn't used to someone being interested in her welfare. Her heart went out to her.

"Did you happen to overhear the names of Mark's friends?" she asked.

"No." Thea took a sip of her hot chocolate. It left a frothy moustache around her top lip. She wiped it with a finger and licked it off. "Sorry."

It was hard to concentrate on Thea's lesson after their conversation. As they analysed a poem, Jane's mind kept drifting, mulling over how she could follow up on the information she'd just received. She could visit the gym and show them Mark's picture, ask some questions. Maybe someone there might identify the two men he'd been with on the day Thea and her friend had seen them.

Finding Mark's friends, perhaps even speaking with them, would be a way of finding her way into Mark's world. She felt that she needed to get to know him better so as to stand a chance of uncovering the who, what and why of his tragic death. With that in mind, she drove straight to the fitness club after Thea's lesson.

Approaching the help desk, Jane wished she'd been in uniform. She'd have felt more confident about asking questions. Off duty and in casual clothes, she could be anyone. She'd have to use an indirect approach.

Before any of the beautiful young people on the desk could greet her with a, 'Hi. How are you? How may I help you today?' Jane started to speak. "I'm not a member. I had a leaflet through the door a while ago and I was just curious. Maybe one of you would have time to show me around?"

A young man stepped forward. "Hi, my name is Chase. We normally ask people to book ahead for a tour." He grinned. "But you're in luck. There's no one else booked in today, so I'd be happy to show you all the great facilities and equipment we have to offer. The tour takes about an hour, is that cool with you?"

Jane considered. A wasted hour was a small price to pay if it yielded some useful information. "Thank you, Chase. That would be great." She wondered if he'd be offended if she asked if they could start in the café.

Chase began by describing what the tour would involve. Jane listened patiently as he recited what was obviously a script that he'd memorised and delivered many times before. At the end he asked if she had any questions. *Yes, just not the type you're referring to.*

"Okay." Chase clapped his hands together with enthusiasm. "Let's start with the gym, shall we?" He made it sound like a random choice, as if every tour started somewhere different, when in reality the route was likely plotted with military precision.

They moved tortuously slowly around the gym, stopping at nearly every piece of apparatus for Chase to give a lengthy spiel on its purpose and benefits. Was it her imagination that he spent a particularly long time talking about the equipment for toning bums and tums?

There was no opportunity during the tour for Jane to ask the sort of questions she'd been hoping to ask. Chase droned on and on. Her remark that a lot of the equipment looked like the sort of stuff you'd find in a care home — mobility aids and gadgets for hoisting and lifting — failed to raise a smile.

He showed her the pool next. The water sparkled, blue and brilliant under an elegant suspension roof. Jane had to admit that this did look inviting. Chase called out to one of the lifeguards, "Hey! Dale! Can you come over a sec?" Dale was sitting atop the lifeguard's chair observing two young women swimming towards the deep end. Rather too attentively, Jane thought, but then again, he was paid to be vigilant. "This is Jane Bell. She's thinking of becoming a member. Dale's one of the pool attendants."

"And a lifeguard," Dale added.

"Want to give Jane a little intro to the pool, Dale?"

Jane thought Dale looked somewhat alarmed at the prospect. He turned a bright shade of red and muttered something about his supervisor usually doing that sort of thing. "That's cool, man," Chase said. "I can do it." Dale hurried back to the lifeguard's chair and resumed watching the bikini-clad women, even though they'd now got out of the pool and were heading for the changing rooms.

"Dale's a bit backwards at coming forwards, as my gran used to say about my dad," Chase said. He spent a few minutes talking about the pool, then they took a look at the sauna.

At last it was over. They were back where they'd started, at the reception.

"So, what do you think? Are you ready to sign up, Jane?" Chase asked.

"Maybe we could go to the café and you can go through the membership details with me over a cup of coffee?"

"Sure," he said, hesitantly, "but we usually do the paperwork over there." He pointed at a space next to the help desk where there was a cluster of tables and chairs, and a drinks machine. "Let me just check with my supervisor."

Jane thought his supervisor ought to be willing to ply her with free drinks all day if Chase could persuade her to pay the exorbitant fee for annual membership. The place hadn't exactly been crawling with clients. It had been eerily quiet throughout the tour.

Chase returned within a couple of minutes. "She says it's okay,"

It turned out that the most on offer was a complimentary regular coffee. Chase, of course, didn't drink coffee. He had a glass of water instead.

Jane looked at their surroundings. "It's pretty quiet here. Is it always like this?"

"No, this is very unusual. We're normally pretty busy." Perhaps thinking that she was seeking a quieter facility, he added, "It is possible to book at a less busy time. A lot of our, er, mature members don't like it when there's a lot of people about. They can be a bit embarrassed about their bodies. Not that that's an issue in your case. You look pretty fit to me."

Jane raised an eyebrow.

"I'm sorry if that came across the wrong way. I just meant you probably look after yourself. Take exercise, watch what you eat, that kind of thing." He floundered.

"I was just trying to gauge how popular the club is. As it's quite new, I couldn't find many reviews." *Probably because I didn't look.*

"Oh, I can assure you that our membership numbers are growing daily."

Jane saw her chance. "Yes, a young man I knew joined recently. His name was Mark Ripley."

"Oh!"

"You knew him?"

"He's the guy who was murdered."

"Yes." Jane wished she'd given some thought to how she would proceed before dashing in here. Winging it wasn't a skill that came easily to her. As a teacher, she understood the importance of thorough preparation. "Such a tragedy. How well did you know him?"

"I know a couple of his mates. He sometimes came with them, so I guess I sort of knew him, just not as well as I know Adam and Phil."

Chase looked down at the membership form on the table in front of him. His supervisor had probably given him a set amount of time in which to return it filled in and signed on the dotted line.

Jane considered bribing him. Her bank details for some information on Mark and his friends. Instead, without really thinking it through, she said, "Look, Chase. I haven't been completely up front with you. I'm a police officer. I'd like to ask you a few questions regarding Mark Ripley's murder."

"Straight up?" Chase shook his head. "Are you a detective?" Jane didn't answer. Let him make that assumption if he liked.

"What do you need to know?"

No request for ID. Really, he shouldn't be so gullible. Jane felt bad about taking advantage of him.

"What can you tell me about the sort of person Mark was?"

"He seemed okay. I've known Adam and Phil since school. We all went to uni together."

"You're a student?"

"Sports science. I work here part time."

"Do Adam and Phil work here too?"

"No. They work at the sports centre at the uni."

"Why do they come here then? I mean, aren't the facilities at the university just as good?"

"They come for football with some of our old mates from school. We hire the five-a-side pitch once a month. Adam and Phil invited Mark along to make up the numbers when one of our schoolmates broke his leg."

"Surnames, please? For Adam and Phil."

"Adam Eades. Phil Lavin."

"Were you shocked to hear about what happened to Mark?"

Chase shrugged. "To tell you the truth, Mark wasn't my sort of person. I got on with him okay but we weren't friends. I was shocked to hear he'd died though." After a moment, he added, "Tell you what else shocked me. Mark was a big guy. He knew how to take care of himself. His attacker must have been pretty strong."

"He fell awkwardly, hit his head on the sharp edge of a stone step."

"Yeah, I read about that."

"You said you played football with some friends from school. How well did Mark know the others?"

"Not at all, really. Adam and I would have a few beers down the pub with them after the game. Mark would sometimes come along, but I think he felt a bit of an outsider. He'd often head back to the uni before us."

Jane nodded. "Did he ever have a run-in with any of your friends?"

"No. There's no way any of those lads could have killed him. I've known them all my life. And, like I said, Mark didn't interact with them much."

"I just thought I'd ask," Jane said. Was it worth following this up? Before she could make up her mind, a woman dressed in yoga pants and a tight white vest burst into the café and advanced on their table. Her ponytail swished aggressively as she walked. Jane sensed trouble.

"Hi, sorry to interrupt. Chase, are you nearly finished? Only I need someone to hose down the men's dry changing room. I can take over here."

"This is Jane. She's a detective. She wanted to ask me some questions about Mark Ripley," Chase said.

The woman turned a gaze full of suspicion on Jane. "Why aren't you in uniform?"

"She's a detective. They don't wear a uniform," Chase said.

"Let's see some ID then."

Jane would have liked nothing better than to flash her ID triumphantly in the face of this officious woman. Unfortunately, it was at home in the pocket of her uniform jacket.

"It's in the car." Would a smile help, she wondered? She thought not. Better to meet sternness with sternness. She held the young woman's gaze until her eyes started to water. Then, something weird happened. The young woman's face broke into a wide smile. "OMG. I didn't recognise you, Mrs Bell. You look amazing! It's me, Crystal Clutterbuck! I went to Ollie Granger. Then I went to college and did a sports degree. I'm one of the assistant managers here now. I'll always be grateful to you for my C in English. I never got more than a D when I was in Mr Turnbull's class. My parents said it was the personal tutor they hired, but I reckon it was all down to you."

This was the first time that running into an ex-student had got her out of an awkward situation. Jane hoped it was the start of a new trend. Fortunately, she remembered Crystal. No one could forget a surname like that.

The question of ID seemed to be forgotten. Crystal referred to Jane's 'brave new career choice.' Twelve years had passed since she'd been in her GCSE class at Ollie Granger. Easily enough time for someone to have made the transition from teacher to detective, it seemed.

They spent the following ten minutes reminiscing about their school days. Crystal seemed to have perfect recall of details that Jane had long forgotten. Like Jane calling Harry Shore an arse in front of the whole class.

She didn't forget about signing Jane up either. Jane ended by agreeing to annual membership.

She'd cancel the bank transfer as soon as she got home.

CHAPTER NINE

Jane walked into 'Veganbites' café to the sound of Jan holding forth on the evils of Brexit. She chose a seat next to Jan's partner, Yvonne Howard.

"You're preaching to the converted, Jan."

Yvonne smiled. "Jane, thank goodness. Maybe he'll get off his soap box now that you've arrived."

"Sorry I'm late. A student had to reschedule for today instead of tomorrow, and he didn't leave until seven."

"No worries, you're here now." Frieda, the café's owner, asked Jane if she'd like a drink.

"Tea, please." It was on the table in front of her in moments.

Jane arranged her coat over the back of her chair. They had a full house this evening by the looks of it. Even Ed from out of town had made it. Not a bad turnout for a dreary January night with sleet slanting down on the back of a grim north wind. Even the floodlit cathedral had looked dreary when she'd hurried across Castle Square earlier. The weather had to be truly foul when it reduced the magnificence of an eleventh-century gothic masterpiece to a grey and barely visible blotch.

The members of the group were her friends and neighbours. She'd been introduced to most of them by Allie, whom she'd met when she'd been enticed into her fudge shop by the delicious aromas of vanilla and chocolate. The first words Allie said to her were, 'Bet I can guess your favourite flavour of fudge,' which, though appropriate to the situation, wasn't a claim you heard every day. Surprisingly, she'd got it right. "Most people go for rum and raisin, chocolate or vanilla. They don't really know that there are zillions of other flavours."

Jane thought that the hardest part of selling fudge must be getting people across the doorstep, overcoming that initial resolve to resist temptation. The aromas had worked for her.

Everyone wanted to hear about her part in the discovery of Mark Ripley's body. "Fancy landing a horrific thing like that on your first night," Karun said. Karun was Frieda's husband. They had recently moved to Lincoln from London, where they had met while Frieda was doing an audit of the restaurant where Karun worked. He was training as a chef in a restaurant owned by a celebrity chef. Frieda was an accountant. They now had a six-month-old baby called Neela. Together, they owned Veganbites, a vegan café on Burton Road and venue for the book group.

"A baptism of blood," Yvonne remarked. She shuddered. "Rather you than me, Janie. Can't understand why you want to do this community police thingy."

Allie corrected her, "Special constable thingy, and I totally get it. Jane's been a quiet, respectable schoolteacher all her life. Now she's going on a revenge spree to take out all the little pricks-turned-criminals who made her life hell at Ollie Granger."

Jane laughed. She looked around the table at this motley bunch of people, grateful that they'd welcomed her into their little community. She caught the eye of Ed Shipley. He was sipping his tea, so he crinkled his eyes by way of a smile. Ed was an artisan blacksmith. He lived in a small village six or seven miles from Lincoln where he had a cottage with a workshop attached. He'd had another life somewhere else before settling in Lincolnshire but he never talked about it.

Allie had got talking to him at his stall at the Christmas market the year before last and had invited him to join the group. At first, he'd only turned up occasionally, but now he came most months. Jane suspected that Allie regarded Ed as a prospective match for her.

Yvonne apologised for getting Jane's title wrong. "I don't suppose you can tell us about the investigation, can you?"

"Not really." Jane didn't add that she couldn't have talked about it even if she'd wanted to, because she wasn't a part of it.

"Finding a dead body isn't the only drama our Jane has been involved in recently." Jan explained about the assault on Ryan Brown. "How is that young man? Do you know?"

Jane recalled her visit to the hospital first thing on the morning after the incident. Tim Sterne had written up a report on the assault. Jane had had no need to have any further contact with Ryan, but she visited him for two reasons. One, she wished to check that he was recovering from his ordeal. Two, she hoped to ask him some questions when he had a clear mind.

Ryan had been pleased to see her. He told her that he'd intended to seek her out and thank her personally for her help. "You and your colleague." He accepted the box of fudge she'd brought for him with enthusiasm.

"You should really thank the young lad who scared off your attacker. His name's Kris Dabrowski." She told him that Kris had called the police.

"I heard someone call out, just after he smashed my head against the wall."

"Do you remember anything more than you told us last night?"

Ryan touched the back of his head where a patch of gauze covered his wound. He winced. "I don't even remember what I told you last night."

"To be honest, it wasn't much. Which is perfectly understandable."

"I'm sorry. I didn't get a look at him. I was walking along, then next minute, wham, I was on the ground. He must have been waiting for someone to come along." It was interesting that he regarded it as a random attack. It probably was. He hadn't been robbed, but only because of Kris's intervention.

"You don't think it might have been someone targeting you?"

Ryan shook his head. "I can't think of anyone who'd do something like that to me."

"Are they letting you out today?"

"Yes. I survived the night, so apparently I'm not at risk anymore. Got to wait until I'm discharged, and then I need to stay with someone for twenty-four hours or so, just in case. My mum's coming to pick me up." He looked up and down the ward, as if hoping to see her walk in.

"Do you mind if I ask you a couple of questions?" Jane was acutely conscious that she wasn't in uniform.

"Sure. Go ahead. Doesn't look like I'm going anytime soon." Ryan slumped back against his pillow.

"What were you doing before the assault?"

"I'd stopped for something to eat after a late lecture at the uni. I went to a Chinese buffet place on the Brayford. They do a happy hour there. All you can eat for six ninety-nine." Jane nodded. She knew the place. It was popular with students looking to fill up on calories at a reasonable cost.

"Did you talk to anyone there? Or were you aware of anyone watching you, or following you after you left the restaurant?"

Ryan blushed. "They sat me at a table for two. There was a girl, Kylie, from my new history tutorial group sitting at the table. We got talking." He smiled, shyly. "We exchanged phone numbers. I think she was glad to talk to me. She said that before I came in some bloke had been pestering her, trying to hit on her."

"Did she point him out to you? You didn't confront him, did you?"

"No. He'd gone by the time I sat down."

"Did you and Kylie leave the restaurant together?" Jane asked.

"Yes. We chatted outside for a bit, then Kylie was going to the cinema with a friend, so we went our separate ways." He gave a wistful sigh. "She said she'd call me."

"And this bloke who'd pestered her, she didn't mention anything about seeing him hanging around when you got outside, did she?"

"No." It suddenly hit him what she was hinting at. "Whoa! Wait! You don't think he was the one who beat me up, do you? That's messed up."

"I don't know. Probably not. Ryan, do you think you could ask Kylie to call me?"

"Sure. I'll text her right away."

* * *

"Jane?" Jan was waiting for her answer.

"Oh, he's fine, as far as I know. I visited him the morning after it happened. He was about to be discharged." Approving nods around the table. They turned to the book they'd chosen for this month's read.

Afterwards, Jane walked home with Allie, both of them sheltering under Jane's giant striped umbrella.

"Ed was looking at you a lot this evening. Did you notice?" Allie said.

"No."

"Honestly, Jane, you're hopeless. He looked quite worried when we were talking about your special constable stuff."

"Allie, how many times do I have to tell you I'm not interested in another relationship? I'm forty-five and I'm done with all that. I'm perfectly happy living on my own."

"So you say. And forty-five is no age." Allie was in her fifties.

"It's the truth."

"Ed's about the same age as you, I'd say, give or take a year or two."

"Stop it. I'm not interested." Which wasn't entirely true.

"Just saying."

They'd reached Allie's house. Jane gave her friend a peck on the cheek. "I know you've got my best interests at heart but you don't need to worry about me being lonely."

"Well, at least get a cat, or something." Allie had three grown-up kids, two cats, (one a little feral) a dog and a husband, all of whom adored her — when it suited them, in the case of the cats.

"I'm allergic to fur."

"Well, get one of those hypoallergenic dogs. A labrawhatsit."

Jane sighed. They'd had this conversation before. She loved Allie dearly but now she felt a prickle of irritation. Maybe it was this business with Mark Ripley and Ryan Brown playing on her mind. Or maybe Allie's observations about Ed had upskittled her.

"Give my love to Peter," she said, and hurried inside to put the kettle on.

Rain mixed with sleet battered against the window, loud enough to be heard above the noise of the kettle. When it had boiled, Jane heard a different sort of sound coming from the garden. She thought it might be the wheelie bin blown over by the wind. If she didn't go out and pick it up, the contents would be strewn all over the place by morning.

Jane swore under her breath. The last thing she wanted to do was go back out in the rain. She pulled on her wellies and an old coat that she kept by the back door and stepped outside. An icy wind stung her face and wrapped her hair around her eyes like a wet blindfold, so that she could barely make out where she was going. There was no moon and the lights of the city around her were smudgy behind a veil of sleety mist.

The bin was upright. Her soaking was all for nothing. She gave it a kick, cursing the weather. It didn't improve her mood.

She stood for a moment, wondering what had caused the noise. Probably one of Allie's cats, though they didn't usually come out on nights like this.

The wind was howling. She'd have to prevent the bin being blown over later on. No amount of noise would entice her out again. There was a brick she used to weigh down the lid when it was windy. It was dark, but she had a rough idea of where it would be. She bent over and swept her hand over the ground around the bin.

A sudden noise from behind startled her. She swivelled, jarring her back. A shape, dark and menacing, loomed over her, shadowy in the icy rain.

Her first thought was that she now knew why she couldn't find the brick — it was in the person's hand. There was no time for a second thought before everything went dark.

CHAPTER TEN

Steph's fear seemed exaggerated now that she was sitting, coffee cup in hand, at a window seat in the new vegan café on Burton Road. She'd ordered a vegan breakfast and as she was the only customer, hoped she wouldn't have too long to wait. It was already seven fifteen. By now, Elias would either be pounding the streets of outer Lincoln on his run to work, or already installed at his desk.

She'd had another disturbed night. Cal again, this time starring as himself. He was fickle like that. Just as she'd become wary of anyone familiar who appeared in her dreams lest they be Cal in disguise, he'd suddenly turn the tables on her. There was a need for constant vigilance.

She'd tried turning him into a kitten, but he was getting wise to this technique. He morphed into a hellish tiger and raked at her skin with razor-sharp claws, baring his fangs and moving in to sink them into her jugular, like a voracious feline vampire. She'd awoken to find blood trailing down her arms where she'd scratched at them with her own nails, and a phantom pain in her neck from an imagined bite so real that she touched the place and was surprised not to feel a sticky residue of blood on her fingers.

The nightmares always made her hungry. She'd ordered baked beans, mushrooms, tomatoes, vegan sausages, hash browns, and a couple of slices of toast. She hoped the food was as good as the coffee. She didn't mind that it was vegan. Food was food, animal or vegetable.

"More coffee?" The woman had crept up on her. "We do free refills for our regulars."

"This is the first time I've been here." Steph looked at the dregs in her cup. "How many times do I need to come to be a regular?"

"Well, at the moment you're neither a regular nor a non-regular. I'll give you the benefit of the doubt."

"Thanks. It's great coffee. You'll definitely be seeing me again. And I'll tell all my friends about you, though the vegan fare might be a bit of a hard sell with some of them." She thought of PC Joey Fairbairn, who started every day with a bacon McMuffin from McDonalds.

"It's a win–win situation," the woman said. "Americano?"

"Sure. Thanks. You can just stick it in here." Steph proffered her mug.

"That's okay. I'll get you a fresh one. I'm Frieda, by the way. Me and my husband Karun own the café."

"Nice place. I like the décor." The walls were painted duck-egg blue, a soothing colour. Frieda hovered. Steph supposed she'd better be friendly and give up her name too. "I'm Steph. I live near the mill. You're practically on my doorstep."

"No excuse not to be a regular, then."

Steph smiled. She was glad when Frieda moved away. She hoped she wasn't going to be one of those people who liked to chat to the customers when it was quiet, otherwise she'd have to forgo the free refills in exchange for some privacy elsewhere. Steph didn't always feel in the mood for chatting, especially if Cal had been in her head the night before. She worried that people would see him in her eyes.

"Here we go." Frieda placed the refill on the table. "Breakfast is just coming." She looked over to an open door by the counter leading to the kitchen. If it were a non-vegan place the aroma of frying bacon would be wafting through the café. "Oh, here it is." Frieda waved at the dark-skinned man holding a steaming plate aloft. "Over here, Karun."

"This is Karun," Frieda said, unnecessarily.

"Nice to meet you, Karun."

They left her in peace. The food was excellent. Shame she had to gobble it down so quickly. She would come back, so long as they left her alone. The café had a calming atmosphere, maybe on account of it being empty. Still, she hoped business picked up for Frieda and Karun. They seemed like a nice couple.

Steph finished eating and went to the till to pay. She stuck a pound coin in the tips jar on the counter. She'd had two refills. Frieda seemed a bit less smiley now. "You okay?" Steph asked, tentatively. She didn't really want to get into in a lengthy conversation. Frieda gave her a strained smile.

"I've just had a phone call about a friend of mine who's had a bit of an accident. Well, more than that, really. She was attacked last night, in her own back garden."

"Oh. Is she all right?"

"I'm not sure. She's in hospital. Allie, our mutual friend is with her. She found her. Well, her dog alerted her. Apparently, he stood barking by poor Jane's gate when Allie took him out for his last walk. She found Jane lying on the garden path, barely conscious. Allie said she'd been hit over the head."

"What was she doing out in the garden?"

"She went outside after hearing a noise. She thought the wheelie bin had been blown over, but it was still upright. That's all she remembers. Maybe it was a burglar."

That was a possibility, a potential burglar taken by surprise when the occupant came outside. Steph decided she'd look up the incident reports that had come in this morning, just to satisfy her own curiosity. She could tell Frieda about it next time she came in for coffee.

"Poor Jane. It sounds like she got caught up in the sort of thing she could have been investigating."

Steph's interest was piqued. "Your friend's in the police?"

"A special constable. Only been doing it a few weeks, but you'd never guess what happened on her very first shift."

Actually, she could. "She found a body." The victim must be Jane Bell, the rookie SC she'd met on the night of Mark Ripley's murder. Small world.

Frieda stared at her. "Oh! You must have heard about the incident on the news."

Steph considered lying. She didn't like too many people knowing what she did for a living. "No. I was there that night. I'm a police officer. A detective inspector."

"Wow. Hey, that's pretty weird, isn't it? I'm fascinated by connections and coincidences. There are forces at work in the world that operate beyond our level of understanding."

Oh no, not one of *those*. Steph should have taken the veganism as a hint. "Right. I need to get to work." She prepared to leave the café, turned back, and for some reason beyond her own understanding, added, "Look, I'll see what I can find out about the attack on your friend. I'll let you know what I learn."

Forces beyond our understanding she muttered irritably, as she hurried along Burton Road. There was nothing weird about it. She'd been on duty the night Mark was murdered. Bell had also been on duty. She lived off Burton Road. Frieda owned a café on Burton Road. They were both acquainted with Bell. Lincoln wasn't a particularly big place. The only coincidence was that she happened to be in the café when Frieda's friend called about Bell's misfortune. Things didn't happen for a reason. They just happened. It was all random. Her meeting with Cal was random. Her meetings with Bell were random, and she'd been hoping that there would be no more of them. It was absurd to think that they had been brought together by anything other than blind chance.

"Screw you, Cal." Bad days always seemed to start after one of his nocturnal visits. A passer-by gave her a look. She thought she heard him mutter, 'Weirdo'. Enraged, she turned around and glared at him, whereupon he scuttled across the road and turned the corner.

By the time she reached the station, Steph felt slightly calmer. Elias was already at his desk exuding running-induced endorphins.

"So, I've been doing a bit of research on the so-called 'art of seduction,' and the world of pick-up artists." Straight down to business. Steph approved of that. She'd once worked in an office where a sizeable part of every morning was taken up with small talk. The 'Good morning, how are you today?' was taken as an opportunity to open up and offload. Steph regarded a polite, 'fine thanks,' as the only answer that question required. She cocked her head, ready to hear more.

"I've been looking on various forums dedicated to the topic of male-female relationships. The thing a lot of them share is a degree of misogyny. There's a lot of vitriolic stuff out there, as you'd expect. I could read some of them out, but they're pretty offensive."

"I'm not easily offended, but don't waste your time. Vile and obscene comments directed at women are all over social media. I can easily imagine. The people who post comments like that don't have much imagination."

Elias looked up from his screen. "Maybe a woman killed Mark. In revenge for him spouting toxic crap like this about her. If he ran a pick-up group, chances are he had misogynistic views. He might even have been abusive to the women he dated. Or, if not the woman, maybe her boyfriend or her brother decided to teach Mark a lesson and went too far."

"Obviously we can't ignore that possibility," she said. "The post-mortem report indicated that Mark had hit his head on the stone step. His attacker could have pushed him, causing him to stumble backwards, then kicked him when he was down. It wouldn't have taken a lot of strength to do that. I could easily shove someone over." From the look Elias gave her, he didn't doubt it. "Speaking of knocks on the head, do you remember that annoying special we met at the scene of Mark's death? Jane Bell? She was attacked last night in her back garden. I was speaking with someone who knows her this morning. I'd like to take a look at her witness statement."

Elias frowned. "I don't remember her being annoying."

On checking, Steph was surprised to discover that the assault on Bell had not been reported. It seemed odd that a serving special police officer would fail to report an attack on her own person. She must be aware that she could have been targeted by someone she'd crossed in the course of her duties. It shouldn't be ignored.

Elias made an odd remark. "Could her attack be linked to Mark Ripley's death in some way?" The thought hadn't even occurred to Steph. She dismissed it immediately.

"Not at all. I just thought it might be related to some other incident she's been involved with. Plus, if she's upset someone to the extent that they'd go after her and bash her over the head, it might suggest she's not competent to be doing the job." Elias raised an eyebrow but didn't comment.

Lincoln County Hospital was located on Greetwell Road, opposite the prison. It wasn't uncommon to see inmates from there in the waiting areas, and as Steph walked in the main entrance, she saw two prison escorts sitting either side of a young man in handcuffs. She nodded at one of the officers, whom she recognised.

Jane Bell was on the assessment ward. According to the nurse, she was likely to be released later in the day. A large woman with stylish white hair and red-framed glasses sat in an orange plastic chair by her bedside, reading a detective novel. Steph recognised the cover. The woman saw her look and smiled. "I've already guessed whodunnit."

"I did too. Pretty much from the first page. I've come to speak with Jane." Steph showed her ID.

"Oh! Is it about what happened to her last night? How did you find out? Jane was adamant she didn't want to report it to the police. My husband and I even had to drag her here under protest."

"I had breakfast at Veganbites this morning."

"Frieda told you?"

"Yes. I've met Ms Bell before. I was the detective on duty the night she discovered the body of Mark Ripley."

"Nice of you to come and see her." There was a slight chill in the woman's tone. What had Bell said about her?

Concern for Bell hadn't been her motivation in coming to the hospital. Still, the sight of her badly grazed cheek, and the shaved patch of scalp with its stitches, almost stirred her to feel sorry for her.

"I'm Allie Swift, by the way. Jane's next-door neighbour-but-one."

"You're the one who found her?"

"Yes, well, it was all down to Dudgeon, really. My bull terrier. He started barking as we walked past her gate and wouldn't budge. He's very fond of Jane."

"How long had she been lying there when you discovered her?"

"Only a few minutes, we think. Jane went out into her garden around eleven after hearing a noise outside. She thought one of her wheelie bins had fallen over. She went out to pick it up and wham! I took Dudge out around eleven. It can only have been a few minutes between us leaving our house, Dudge standing barking by Jane's gate and the two of us going into the back garden to discover Jane lying across the path. Lucky she was wearing her jacket, or she might have ended up with hypothermia. It was freezing last night."

Steph thought that unlikely, given that Jane had not been outside for long. "Did you notice if the door to her house was open?"

"Sorry, I didn't. I was in a bit of a panic over Jane. I called Pete. When he arrived, we helped Jane to our car and drove straight here. Pete went back to Jane's afterwards. He said that the back door was unlocked."

"Did he go inside?"

"Yes. I told him he was an idiot. Jane's attacker might have been in there."

Steph thought that the attacker had probably made himself scarce, if he'd even entered the property in the first place. There must have been quite a commotion with the dog barking. "He should have got in touch with the police."

Allie rolled her eyes. "Tell me about it. But on the way to the hospital Jane kept saying that she didn't want us to do that. Poor Jane. She doesn't deserve any more bad luck."

Allie's words were an invitation. Steph wasn't interested in hearing Bell's life story, but Allie told her anyway. "Jane's husband died in a tragic accident three years ago." She gazed at her friend with true affection, causing Steph an irrational stab of jealousy.

"So, had anyone been in the house?"

"No. Pete said it looked undisturbed. Presumably the door was unlocked because Jane had left it like that when she went outside. Pete thought maybe the burglar had got the wind up after he struck Jane and ran off. Most burglars aren't into violence, are they?"

Steph ignored the question. "I'd like to talk to her about last night."

Allie looked hesitant. "Maybe we should ask one of the nurses." Ignoring her again, Steph stepped closer to Jane's bed.

"Jane Bell? Are you awake?"

Allie bristled. "Quite clearly she isn't." But Jane stirred, screwed up her eyes as if in pain. Allie stood up but Steph got in first.

"Ms Bell? It's DI Warwick here. We met at the scene of Mark Ripley's murder, remember?"

Bell squinted at her. She nodded. Allie hovered by her bedside, protectively.

"Thanks, Allie. I'm sorry if I was a bit of a pain last night," Bell said. Allie squeezed her hand.

"Just so you know, I didn't alert the police." Allie glared at Steph.

"I was in your friend's café this morning when Mrs Swift called with the news of your attack. Surely, you must be aware that an incident like this should be reported."

"I was going to report it."

"Can you run through what happened last night?"

Jane looked at Allie. "I'd been out for the evening. At book group. Allie and I walked home together. We parted around a quarter to eleven, I think. I took off my wet things, then went into the kitchen to make a cup of camomile tea to help me sleep. That's when I heard a noise from the garden. I thought it was the bin being blown over by the wind, so I went out to pick it up before the rubbish ended up all over the place. It was dark, sleeting, and visibility was poor."

Steph listened, impatient. She wasn't interested in the weather.

Jane touched the side of her head. "I was bending down looking for the brick I use to weigh down the lid of the bin when I heard a noise behind me. I looked up and saw someone standing there holding the brick. Then, everything went black. Next thing I knew, Dudge was licking my face and Allie was calling my name." She smiled at her friend. "And panicking."

"Did you get a look at your attacker's face?"

"No, it was dark. He had his hood up. I only caught a glimpse of him for a second and my eye was on the brick in his hand more than anything."

"How sure are you that it was a man?" Steph asked.

Jane pulled herself up against the pillows and took a sip of water from the glass on the cabinet by her bedside. "Not sure at all, actually." She looked slightly embarrassed. "It was sort of instinctive to say 'he.' That's bad, isn't it? Stereotyping like that."

"A lot of the time you'd probably be right. But it's better to say if you're not sure."

"I'm not sure. They were bulky, but I didn't get much impression of their height."

"You've done a few shifts as a special now, haven't you? Have you come across anyone while on duty who might bear a grudge against you?"

Jane shook her head. "I don't think so. There was the man at the chippy, I suppose. But he was just drunk and mouthing off. He wasn't charged. He spent a night in custody sleeping it off." Steph listened to a story about a man in a fish and chip shop assailing the staff and police with pickled onions and chips.

"I've had worse things thrown at me," she remarked when Jane had finished. Steph guessed that Jane hadn't envisaged being involved in a semi-farcical scene such as that when she volunteered. A lot of people joined the specials for a bit of excitement. It soon became clear that, though there were plenty of adrenalin rushes, there were often, also, long periods of routine plodding, punctuated by bizarre and sometimes downright surrealistic incidents. A memory of chasing two chickens around a car park sprang to mind.

"Anything else?"

A nurse with a trolley approached the bed. "No," Jane said to Steph as the nurse wrapped a blood pressure band around her left arm. She yawned. "Not that I can think of right now." She seemed drowsy. Probably full of painkillers. Steph made to go. Jane Bell roused herself and asked, "Have you got any leads on the investigation into Mark Ripley's murder yet?"

Steph prickled. "I can't discuss an ongoing investigation with you. As I think I told you that time in the supermarket. Please report this incident at the earliest opportunity." She walked away. *Idiotic woman. Does she really think I'll take pity on her and throw her some morsels just because she's in a hospital bed?*

Pity was a weakness, she reminded herself again. It had got her nowhere with Cal. But the reality was, there was little she could have shared with Jane Bell.

CHAPTER ELEVEN

Jane was sitting in the passenger seat of Allie's car being driven home from the hospital when her phone beeped. It was a number she didn't recognise. She read the text message and frowned.

Hi, my name's Kylie Bright. Ryan said you'd like to talk to me about the man in the Chinese buffet. When's a good time to speak?

Of course! Ryan Brown's new friend. Jane hoped her still thumping headache was the cause of her initial confusion. She recalled the conversation she'd had with Ryan at the hospital. When she'd spoken with him, she'd never dreamed she'd be the next victim of a bonk on the head. There seemed to be a lot of it about lately.

Her instinct was to text straight back and arrange to meet Kylie Bright immediately. Unfortunately, the pain in her head had other plans. She'd been instructed to rest, take some paracetamol and avoid strenuous activity.

"Another well-wisher?" Allie asked. Word had got around.

"Yes," Jane lied. She couldn't wait to get home. Allie hadn't been keen on her returning to her own house and had wanted her to stay the night with her and Peter.

"Are you sure you won't reconsider coming to us? Won't it be upsetting for you to go back there after what happened?"

"I have to go back sometime. It might as well be sooner rather than later."

"You know, Pete and I were just saying that maybe you could borrow Dudgeon tonight."

"Allergic, remember?"

"I know, but Dudge is short-haired. And he adores you. He practically saved your life."

Jane resisted the urge to snap at her friend. She told herself it was her aching head making her ill-tempered, not Allie's harping on about her wellbeing. She pictured the stocky little brindled Staffie barking frantically by her gate and felt awash with affection for him, and for her friends.

"I know and I'm really grateful to him. I'm going to buy him a big, juicy bone from the artisan butchers in the Bail at the earliest opportunity. But I don't want him moving in with me." She'd aimed for a light-hearted tone, but realised she sounded a bit on edge.

Allie insisted on seeing her inside. Despite her earlier fortitude, Jane shuddered as she stepped over the threshold. It was a bit unsettling to think that a stranger could have been here, going through all her personal belongings, even though there was no sign of a burglary. "It's cold. I'd better put the heating on for a bit."

Allie fussed around, made her a cup of tea. At last, there was nothing more she could do and she left, reminding Jane to call her for any reason, however trivial.

Finally, Jane was alone in the stillness of her familiar, now warm house, installed in an armchair in her sitting-room with the TV on. After five minutes or so, she turned it off. She tried reading a book but couldn't concentrate because of the headache, which the painkillers had merely pushed into the background. She felt drowsy, but it was late afternoon and if she dozed off now, she'd have difficulty sleeping when she went to bed. The last thing she needed was to lie awake half the night worrying every time she heard a sound from the garden.

She should call the kids, tell them what had happened, but she didn't want to worry them. They were both in London. Patrick was training to be an accountant and Norah had landed a traineeship at the BBC. Jane had never expected them to stay in Lincoln after they graduated. Sometimes she envied Allie with her family all living close by, but mostly she was content with the way things were. Perhaps she'd tell them later, when there was no need for either of them to feel the need to rush home.

It had been a thwarted burglar, she was sure. Jane thought about what the detective had said about someone bearing a grudge against her. The question had taken her by surprise. Until that moment it hadn't occurred to her that her attacker might have been someone she'd encountered in the course of her duties as a special constable.

It crossed her mind that perhaps she should have mentioned the attack on Ryan Brown to Warwick. Perhaps also her visit to the gym. But why? The attack on Ryan probably didn't have anything to do with Mark's murder, and as for Adam Eades and Phil Lavin, Warwick must have interviewed them and everyone else in Mark's immediate circle by now. Also, she didn't wish Warwick to know that she had been making her own enquiries.

Despite her intention to stay awake, Jane dozed off. She woke with a start at around six in the evening. Her mobile was ringing. Damn! She'd missed the call. Seconds later, a text came through. Kylie Bright again.

Hello. In case you missed my previous text, my name's Kylie Bright. Ryan says you'd like to talk to me about the man who spoke to me in the Chinese restaurant. Are you free now? Could meet you in the Lion and Snake in the Bail in 10 minutes?

Jane moved her neck gingerly from side to side and was relieved that the pain in her head had subsided. She turned on the lamp beside her chair. She'd fallen asleep in daylight and awoken to darkness. She hadn't intended to go out again today and didn't really feel up it, but she had no idea when this Kylie Bright might be able to meet with her again, so she texted her back agreeing.

On her way upstairs to freshen up, she paused on the landing to admire the view of the cathedral's floodlit towers. A thousand years of history was contained within its limestone walls. It was about as permanent a structure as it was possible to find in a modern city. Jane tried never to take her view for granted.

She took the steps up to the next level two at a time and instantly regretted it as pain seared through her skull. She crossed the landing to the bathroom more tentatively. When she peered in the mirror, she was surprised to see that, apart from looking a bit washed out, she seemed none the worse for her ordeal of the night before.

Satisfied that she looked presentable, she went downstairs and pulled on her boots and a warm coat. It was still perishing out there.

The Lion and Snake was only a few minutes' walk away. It was located in the historic Bailgate near the castle and the cathedral. On the road outside the pub, a series of brick roundels marked where the colonnades of the Roman forum had stood when the city had been known throughout the empire as *Lindum Colonia*. Jane sidestepped them, as though they were cracks on the pavement to be avoided in case they brought bad luck.

The pub was reputed to be haunted by at least two ghosts, one a shy Roman soldier who resided in the cellar. The other, known as 'the Granny with the bun' roamed the upper floors of the building. Jane was sceptical about the stories of hauntings in this ancient part of the city. Hoping that she herself didn't look too ghostly, she scanned the pub for a young woman sitting alone. Someone tapped her on the shoulder.

"Excuse me. Are you Jane Bell?"

"Yes. Kylie?" She reminded Jane of Thea a little, slight, fair, fragile.

"I've got us a seat over there." Kylie pointed to a chair with a jacket draped over it.

86

"Can I get you anything from the bar?" Jane asked.

"A glass of wine?"

"Sure. Red or white?"

"White, please."

"Go grab that seat."

Jane joined her a few minutes later. After some indecision, she'd opted for mineral water, not wanting to risk reviving her headache. "You must have been a bit shocked to hear from Ryan that he'd been attacked right after he left you."

Kylie gulped down some wine. Her cheeks were flushed. Perhaps this wasn't her first glass. "I was. Especially when he suggested it might have been the guy who was pestering me in the restaurant."

"What do you remember about him?"

"He was sitting at a table on the other side of the restaurant from me, but he had to pass my table to get to the drinks machine. He gave me a smile on his way back from getting a refill. I smiled back, hoping he wouldn't stop by my table. Of course, he did. He paid me some lame compliment. I didn't quite catch it, but I think it was something about my hair."

"Then did he move on?"

"Yes. But he was back a couple of minutes later for another coke." She rolled her eyes. "I knew he was going to hit on me again. Doesn't it just piss you off when guys do that? Why can't they just leave us alone when we're on our own in public places? Anyway, this time, he asked if he could join me, and I said no. It made me feel bad, which is stupid, right? I mean he was the one putting me in that awkward situation in the first place."

She took another gulp of wine. "As soon as I made it clear I wasn't interested, he started to get a bit abusive. First, he called me a stuck-up bitch."

Jane wasn't surprised. She'd had similar experiences. There were plenty of men who took rejection personally. Whether through arrogance or low self-esteem, out would pop their latent misogyny. "I've been called worse than that," she said in sympathy.

"Well, it did get worse, actually. His comments got more . . . sexual." She lowered her voice. "He called me a whore and told me I needed a good . . . I'm sure you can guess what came next. I told him if he didn't leave me alone, I'd call someone over."

"Did he get the message?" Jane asked.

"Yes. I watched him go up and pay for his food. After he'd gone, I felt kind of shaky. I'm not sure if I was just angry or a bit upset as well. Maybe a little of both." She shrugged.

"No one should make you feel like that."

"I know. It's not the first time this sort of thing has happened to me. I didn't deal with it so well last time, but I've learned since then."

Jane waited in case Kylie wished to tell her more, but she didn't seem to want to talk about the experience. "Can you describe this man to me, Kylie?"

Kylie sighed. "He was white, medium height, sort of solid — beard, dark hair, dark-rimmed glasses. To tell the truth, he looked like a lot of guys. I'm not sure I'd be able to pick him out in a line-up. He was sort of, *ordinary*. Mr Generic."

"Try to form a picture of him in your mind. Was there anything about him that stood out?"

"Well, he was sort of creepy. I mean he wasn't bad looking, but there was something sort of off-putting about him. I'm sorry I can't be more specific. It was more how he made me feel than anything. Even before he started being abusive." She frowned. "Do you know what I mean?"

Jane nodded. "I think so." But a feeling wouldn't help identify the man. Kylie made him sound invisible.

"Do you remember how he paid?" she asked.

"Cash. I saw him take it out of his wallet." That was disappointing. No hope of tracing the transaction. Perhaps someone who worked at the restaurant might remember him.

"How long had he been gone before Ryan arrived?"

"Five, ten minutes."

"And Ryan didn't make you feel uncomfortable? He said the waiter seated him at the table next to you."

"No, Ryan doesn't give off any creepy vibes. He's very open and genuine."

Jane said nothing. There were probably a lot of unwholesome characters around who appeared open and genuine, charming even. Jane had read and watched enough crime stuff to be aware that dangerous psychopaths could fool even those closest to them. Then again, she hadn't felt any bad vibes issuing from Ryan either.

"Actually, I spoke to him first. I recognised him from my history tutorial. We hadn't actually spoken before. He says a lot of insightful stuff in class." Kylie reached for her wine. By now her cheeks weren't simply flushed, they were pink with embarrassment. Maybe her attraction to Ryan had preceded their encounter in the restaurant.

"Sorry I wasn't much help describing the man who harassed me. He might be a student. A lot of us go to that buffet place for the happy hour. I could look for him around campus and try to get a better description if I spot him. Maybe even get a name for you. What do you think?"

Jane knew she should tell Kylie to steer clear of the man, just in case. He could be dangerous. She hesitated.

"Obviously I'd do it subtly," Kylie said. "Without actually approaching him or anything."

There was nothing wrong with that, was there? It wasn't as if Kylie would be putting herself in any danger.

"Okay," Jane said. "But be careful. Don't challenge him."

"I won't." Kylie smiled. It probably seemed a bit exciting to her. They chatted about other things for a bit, and Jane asked Kylie if she'd come from far to study at Lincoln. Kylie told her she was from York but her grades hadn't been good enough for her to study there, so she'd chosen Lincoln. "Which is a shame," she said, "because if I'd got into York, I could have stayed at home and saved a lot of money. I'm broke. Just before you came in, I was asking the manager if they were hiring."

"Actually, I might be able to help you there. Some friends of mine have just opened a vegan café on Burton

Road. They're looking for some extra help. I'll give you their number. Tell them Jane Bell told you about the job."

"Oh, yes please. That'd be great. Do I have to be vegan?"

Jane smiled. "No. I'm not and they let me in."

Kylie gulped down the rest of her wine. "I've got to go now. I've got an essay to finish. It's got to be submitted by noon tomorrow so I might have to pull an all-nighter. Thanks for the job alert."

"No problem. Thanks for meeting me. I hope you meet your deadline."

Jane sat for a while after Kylie had gone. A man drinking alone at the bar smiled and tilted his pint at her. Jane looked away, thinking about what Kylie had said. She was right, some men just couldn't leave women in public places in peace. Would the man think her rude? Perhaps he was just being friendly. She'd done it herself, smiled at someone across a crowded bar, or on a bus, or waiting in a queue. Wasn't it just making a connection with another human being? A moment of shared humanity? That happened seldom enough in this era of mobile phones and avoiding eye contact with strangers. Surely there wasn't always a darker subtext to everyday exchanges with our fellow human beings?

Jane sighed. She'd met her late husband in a bar. He'd come up to her and paid her a cheesy compliment, made her laugh. She'd felt no sense of threat from him. If she'd shunned him, he would have just walked away, not pelted her with obscene abuse. But how to tell the difference between a Sam and the type of man who'd harassed Kylie? Despite what Kylie had said about 'creepy vibes,' feelings weren't a reliable measure of another person's level of threat.

Her glass was empty. As she zipped up her parka, she glanced back at the bar. The man who'd smiled and tipped his glass at her was gone. Jane placed her glass on the beer mat beside his froth-ringed pint glass. As the barman scooped them up, they chimed against each other.

CHAPTER TWELVE

When Jane arrived for a Saturday morning lesson with Thea, she noticed the dogs were surprisingly subdued. "They're exhausted," Thea explained. "I took them for a really long walk earlier."

"In the dark?" Jane wondered how early Thea meant. It was only nine now. A heavy, grey sky gave the impression of lingering darkness.

"Oh yes! I love going across the fields in the dark mornings. I wear my head torch."

"Is that wise?"

"Oh, take your police officer's hat off, Jane. It's perfectly safe with Buddy and Pearl bounding along beside me. No one would dare take them on."

"Hmm." When had Thea started calling her Jane? It had been Ms Bell to begin with. Jane didn't mind. Now that she was out of the classroom, setting boundaries with students seemed less relevant. Thea was a bright, confident young woman and Jane regarded her as an equal in all but age and experience.

After an hour and twenty minutes, she asked if Thea had any questions about the text they'd been studying. Thea shook her head. As Jane began putting away her things, she sensed Thea watching her.

"You have a daughter, don't you, Jane?"

"Yes. And a son."

"How old are they now?"

"Norah's twenty-one. Patrick's twenty-two."

"You were pretty young when you had them. Were you strict with them?"

Far too young, Jane thought. Patrick had been an accident but once he arrived, she and Sam decided they didn't want him to grow up without at least one sibling. Norah had been born eighteen months later.

"Depends what you mean by strict. I set boundaries. There was discipline. I hope I taught them to be good people."

"My parents let my brother and I do pretty much whatever we wanted. Most kids would envy that, but it's a form of neglect, don't you think, not caring what your children are up to?"

Jane looked up from zipping her bag, realising that Thea wanted to talk. "We had childminders," Thea continued, "the kind who come to your house, like nannies, I suppose. Some of them were quite strict, but not because they cared about us. It made their job easier if they taught us to do what we were told."

Jane avoided saying something trite, such as, "I'm sure your parents loved you really." She'd learned early on in her teaching career that for a lot of kids, parental love was not a given. She squeezed the young woman's hand. "If you ever need to talk about anything, Thea, you can talk to me, you know."

"Thanks, Jane. Do you fancy a cup of hot chocolate?"

"That would be nice." She had things to do, but they could wait.

At Ollie Granger, Jane had often worried about the welfare and wellbeing of some of the kids she taught. She'd had young people come to her with horrific and heartbreaking tales of bullying, cruelty, sexual abuse. The first time a child had rolled up her sleeve to reveal the slanting scars of self-abuse criss-crossing her forearm, Jane had been shocked. By the time she left Ollie Granger, she'd become so inured to the sight that she feared she'd become desensitised.

She ended up chatting with Thea for over an hour. When she left, Thea waved her off. She struck a lonely figure standing on the drive, a dog on either side of her.

Jane wasn't going straight home. She'd decided to have brunch at Veganbites. Knowing Frieda and Karun would be concerned about her following the burglary, she could put their minds at rest over some good food. If it wasn't too busy in the café, Frieda might be able to sit down and chat for a little while. Before coming to Veganbites, Jane had always considered vegan food slightly unappealing. Karun's cooking had caused her to reconsider, although she still had her doubts about whether all that soaking and boiling of pulses made them any more digestible.

She parked in a small housing estate near the Museum of Lincolnshire Life, a gem of a place that she'd visited many times, both with an army of schoolkids in tow and with her own children when they were young.

Housed in a Victorian military barracks, the museum was a treasure trove, its displays crammed with objects showing the social, military and industrial history of the county from the mid-seventeen hundreds to the present day. There was a tank on display there that had seen battle at Passchendaele. Jane always pointed it out to her cohort of year eight students studying First World War poetry. The tank had been built by William Foster & Co, a local firm that produced agricultural machinery. After the war, the Royal Commission on Awards to Inventors credited Sir William Tritton, the managing director of 'Fosters of Lincoln,' with being a co-inventor of the tank.

Jane had once won a tiebreaker at a local pub quiz night for knowing the security code name used for the tanks during their construction: 'water tanks for Mesopotamia.' Not a lot of people knew that. Not on that particular quiz night at the Dragon at any rate, when nearly everyone was in their cups.

The café was half full, or half empty, depending on your disposition. Frieda and Karun really did need help for the busy times. Jane hoped they'd take Kylie Bright on. Their one-and-only employee was taking an order from a man Jane thought she recognised as one of the museum employees, the one who always complained about the kids from Ollie Granger's being the worst-behaved of any of the schools to visit the museum. She sat as far from him as the modest proportions of the café's interior would allow.

"I'll be with you in a moment," the waitress called over with a toss of her abundantly thick and shiny hair. Jane wondered if she were vegan. She had once read that a vegan diet made your hair fall out and your nails crumble. It must have been a myth.

"It's okay, Francesca, I'll serve this customer." Frieda was half-in, half-out of the kitchen, holding a plate of noodles. The chalk board above the counter had announced that Pad Thai was one of the specials today.

She stood up in readiness for a hug. "Ouch!" Frieda gently touched the stitches on the side of Jane's head. "That's worse than I imagined. Have your lot got anyone yet?"

"Not as far as I know."

"Karun and I have been beside ourselves with worry."

"Yes. Allie said." Jane changed the subject. "How's little Neela?"

"She's great, a real little character. She's with my mum and dad today." One of the benefits for Frieda and Karun of moving to Lincoln to set up their business had been the eagerness of Frieda's retired parents to provide occasional childcare for their only grandchild.

Frieda held out her mobile phone for Jane to see a video of Neela stuffing a banana into her mouth. "Luckily I had my phone on hand to capture the moment."

Jane doubted that Frieda's phone was ever anything but on hand. Updates of Neela's progress seemed to appear on Facebook by the hour.

"How lovely. She's beyond cute."

"That police officer, DI Warwick, was here again the other day to let us know she'd seen you at the hospital. She assured us you were recovering well. Do you see much of her when you're out policing?"

"I've seen her a total of three times. At the murder scene on my first shift, briefly when I bumped into her in the supermarket, and again when she came to the hospital. She's a detective. I'm a lowly volunteer special. There's not really much reason why our paths would cross."

"Suppose not. She lives near here, I think. I've seen her walk past in the mornings. The morning after your assault was the first time she came in here. She seemed impressed with our coffee. Said she'd be back. She's very intense, isn't she?"

"Why do you say that?" Jane had never mentioned to anyone but Allie that her first impressions of DI Stephanie Warwick hadn't been entirely positive. On the three occasions they'd met, she'd found her offhand, slightly arrogant. Jane supposed they were simply too unalike to get on.

At the supermarket, Warwick had been chilly, considering Jane had returned her credit card to her, almost as though she begrudged being in her debt. At the hospital, Jane had been too groggy to notice much about her, other than that she'd been displeased that Jane hadn't thought it important to report her assault. Any excuse to find fault with her, it seemed.

"It was just my impression. She doesn't give much away. I also thought she seemed a bit upset that morning, and that she was making an effort not to show it. She looked like she hadn't slept in a week. I suppose investigating a murder takes it out of you." Frieda passed Jane the menu that she'd had tucked under her arm. "To tell you the truth, I felt a bit sorry for her. I know she's a detective, which means she can probably look out for herself, but she seemed to have an air of vulnerability about her. Brittleness even."

This was typical Frieda. She loved to analyse people, but she wasn't always right. In Jane's opinion, she was way off the mark regarding DS Up-herself Warwick. "I'll take your word for it," she said. "But if that woman has a vulnerable side, I've yet to see it."

"You don't like her?"

"Not a lot."

Frieda looked surprised. "I thought you saw the good in everyone."

"Only if it's there in the first place."

A couple of young women who had been hovering outside looking at the A board, made up their minds to come inside. They held the door for a man in a worn leather jacket carrying a violin case. Jane recognised him. He sometimes played pieces by the likes of Bach, Mozart or Corelli in Castle Square or on High Bridge. Jane often threw some loose change in his violin case. He'd taught music at Ollie Granger's when she started there. The story was that one afternoon he'd walked out on his unruly year nine class and installed himself in the staffroom, where he'd played violin solos until the Head called his wife, who eventually coaxed him out. He'd never returned to the school. Frieda waved to him and called out, "Hi, Mr Kendrick." To Jane, she said. "I'd better get back to work. Are you having the noodles?"

"Of course." Jane grinned. She was fairly predictable in her choices.

Francesca brought her order over a few minutes later. As she ate, Jane considered what Frieda had said about DI Warwick. The person Frieda described was almost unrecognisable as the one Jane had met. She considered herself a fairly good judge of character. Had she misread Warwick? No, she concluded. Frieda was simply wrong, though she had to admit somewhat grudgingly that Warwick was very good at her job.

She struggled to visualise her. The first time they'd met it had been dark, the second time had been brief, and the third she'd been a bit out of it. Warwick's eyes were her most striking feature, green, that rarest of eye colours. Only three per cent of people have green eyes. Jane's daughter, Norah, was one of them, which was probably why Jane recalled that detail about Warwick.

In a moment of perfect synchronicity, Jane looked out of the window and saw Warwick crossing the road, heading straight for Veganbites. Their eyes met as soon as she entered the café. Warwick hesitated before acknowledging Jane with a nod. She proceeded to the counter, where she ordered a coffee to take away.

On her way back to the door, refill cup in hand, she stopped by Jane's table. "I see you reported your assault at last."

"Yes." Jane had done it the previous day.

"Has anyone been to see you?"

"Yes. A young man called Joey. He found the brick they used to hit me over the head under some bushes at the bottom of my garden. He took it away with him."

"For forensics to look at."

"Yes. Can I have it back? It's useful for keeping the lid on the bin." She was irritated to see a glint of amusement in DI Warwick's eyes. Perhaps it was a slightly weird request. It wasn't even a whole brick, only a half one, but it was fit for purpose. Jane twirled some noodles around her fork, conveyed them to her mouth, ate, all without looking at DI Warwick.

"I'll arrange for it to be returned to you when forensics are finished with it. Have you had any more thoughts about whether someone might have targeted you? Someone you might have clashed with while on duty? I wasn't sure you were taking in everything I said at the hospital."

"I took it in."

"So? Anything?"

Jane considered. It was the perfect opportunity for her to tell DI Warwick about the attack on Ryan Brown, about

Mark Ripley's friends at the gym and the man Kylie had encountered at the Chinese restaurant. For some reason, she held back. "Nothing comes to mind."

"Right." Warwick sounded sceptical, which made Jane glad she hadn't said anything. The last thing she wanted was Warwick laughing at her theories.

After she'd gone, Jane finished her meal and shoved her bowl aside.

"Want me to take that away for you?" Francesca hovered by her side. Where on earth had she materialised from? Jane handed her the bowl. She looked up and saw the music teacher studying her, a sympathetic expression on his face. She half expected him to take out his violin and scrape out a plangent melody.

Frieda was making her way towards her, her face showing a mixture of concern and undisguised curiosity. "Have they caught him?"

"Who?"

"The man who attacked you, of course. Isn't that what DI Warwick was talking to you about?"

"No, they haven't caught the perpetrator. Not likely to either, unless they get something from the brick that was used to clobber me."

"Ah! The weapon. Bound to get some good forensic stuff from that."

"Hmm. Maybe. It's likely I surprised a burglar and he panicked, that's all. Maybe his prints will be on the brick and, if they're on record, he'll be identified. I won't hold my breath."

"You're sure he's not your pickled onion man?"

Jane shook her head. "He came back to apologise. He said he doesn't usually drink that much. His mates had been spiking his drinks. He tried to give me some vouchers for the Happy Haddock Plaice, his brother-in-law's fish and chip shop. Of course, I couldn't accept them."

"Karun's experimenting with a new mock fish pie recipe."

"I quite like the old one."

"You know Karun. He doesn't know the meaning of 'if it ain't broke, don't fix it.'"

"What do I owe you?" Jane asked.

"It's on the house."

"No. It's not. You two will never turn a profit if you keep giving everyone free meals."

"We're doing okay," Frieda insisted. "By the way, I hired that young woman you put in touch with me, Kylie Bright. She'll be helping out at Yvonne's birthday party. She seems like a reliable sort. Thanks for recommending her."

"No problem. Pleased I could do you both a good turn. I'm sure she won't let you down."

CHAPTER THIRTEEN

Jane's landline rang. It was Allie. She only lived two doors away but she often called if she felt like a chat. This time, the pretext for her call was a reminder about Yvonne's surprise birthday party that evening at Veganbites. "I hadn't forgotten," Jane said.

"Sorry, Jane, I just thought it might have slipped your mind, what with that blow to your head."

"I don't have amnesia, Allie."

"Okay, I'll leave you to whatever you're doing. See you later."

Jane immediately regretted being snappy with Allie. The truth was, she was tired of people asking if she was okay. It brought back memories of when she'd lost Sam. Everyone in the village, even people she'd never spoken to before, stopping her in the street or at the local Co-op to offer their condolences. She'd been glad to move house and get away from it all. She'd never enjoyed being the centre of attention.

She made a cup of tea and settled down to catch up on some marking for her distance-learning students. Thoughts about Mark Ripley's murder kept intruding.

At noon, unable to concentrate any longer, she texted Kylie Bright. Kylie called her straight back.

"I don't have anything to report. There's a couple of guys I've seen who could be the man who harassed me in the restaurant, but that just kind of proves how hard it is to be certain. He was just too generic."

"Okay." Jane couldn't disguise her disappointment. Kylie must have picked up on her tone and apologised again.

"Sorry. I'll keep trying."

"I appreciate that, Kylie. But, please, stay safe."

"I will. Hey, you'll be seeing me this evening!"

"Frieda told me you got the job at Veganbites."

"Yep. Starting this evening."

"Good luck."

"Thanks. See you later."

The rest of the day passed slowly. Jane wished she was on duty that evening instead of going to the party for Yvonne. Maybe she should volunteer for an extra shift during the week. Getting ready distracted her for a while. After a shower came the decision about what to wear. Ed Shipley would be there, she knew. Though she was reluctant to admit it to Allie, Jane was attracted to Ed. She found him rather intriguing. He hadn't always been a blacksmith, but no one seemed to know what he'd done before. He wasn't Lincolnshire-born either, not a true 'yellow belly,' as Allie would say.

Jane had lived in London for a few years. It was where she'd met Sam. She suspected Ed hailed from the capital, but she wasn't good enough with London accents to pinpoint where. She suspected his air of mystery was part of the attraction.

She chose a navy shift dress, then worried that it was a bit too short for a woman of her mature years. Wasn't the hemline supposed to be just above or on the knee after forty? Or was it fifty? Fifty, surely. Maybe she should wear leggings instead of tights for the sake of modesty? Sod it. It wasn't all that short. She added a few pieces of silver jewellery, applied a bit more make-up than usual and considered herself ready.

She locked her door and checked it twice, the second time running back down after she'd already climbed the steps up to the pavement. Maybe the assault had affected her after all. Not a bad thing if it made her more security conscious.

She knocked on Allie's door and waited for the barking to start. "Come on in out of the cold," Peter said from the hallway. He had one hand on Dudgeon's collar to restrain him from jumping at her. "Allie's just getting changed." He rolled his eyes. "Again."

Jane made a fuss of Dudge — after all, he'd probably saved her life. Pete presented her with a glass of wine. Allie came downstairs ten minutes later, full of apologies. "I was going to wear that black dress I wore to your birthday meal back in October but when I put it on, I decided it was a bit on the tight side. All that over-indulgence at Christmas has gone straight to my tummy."

Jane had thought the dress looked a little tight back in October, but she didn't say so. Instead she said, "You look gorgeous. As always." Which was also true.

"I know. It just takes a bit longer these days."

"You can say that again," Peter muttered.

It was a ten-minute walk to Veganbites. Allie, stumbling in her heels, took Peter's arm across the cobblestones on Castle Square. They continued walking along the Bailgate, turning onto Westgate by the remains of the Roman well dug by the Ninth Hispanic Legion. In 2010 the well had received a heritage makeover as part of a restoration project in the Bailgate. It hadn't been much of a success. A glass panel had been placed over the top to protect it, but no one had foreseen that condensation on the underside of the glass would stop people from seeing the fifteen-metre-deep brick walls underneath. More money was spent on installing a humidity control system. Jane thought it a shame that people could no longer throw a penny in for good luck.

Despite the many pubs and restaurants lining both sides of the street, Westgate was quiet. Only the Strugglers Inn showed much sign of life. A huddle of smokers gathered on the pavement under its infamous sign showing a prisoner 'struggling' against his captors on his way to the gallows. An alternative legend attributed the origin of the pub's name to the image of the condemned man struggling on the end of the gallows rope. The nineteenth-century inn was now better known for its cask ales.

The door of Veganbites was closed, the blinds drawn, as they always were after five. Frieda and Karun had ambitions to open their café in the evenings, but not until they had grown the business and could afford to employ more staff. They did occasionally cater for evening functions, but tonight's party was all about friends.

A warm glow seeped out from the places where the blinds didn't quite meet. It hugged them as they stepped inside after doing Karun's secret knock. Really, it would have been easier to call him on his phone, but everyone humoured him, knowing he enjoyed the intrigue.

The interior of the café looked magical. Tealights in pretty pink and gold Moroccan tea glasses were arranged at intervals around the room. Silver foil balloons spelling out "Happy Birthday" decorated one wall and a curtain of fairy lights shimmered over another. Rose gold balloons bobbed at ceiling height. Jan, Frieda and Karun had gone to a lot of trouble. It wasn't a special birthday, but Yvonne was a special person. In the year since her last birthday she had undergone surgery for breast cancer, then endured months of chemo and uncertainty before hearing good news. She'd borne the news of her diagnosis and the treatment with cheery stoicism. This party was everyone's way of showing how much they admired and loved her.

"It's lovely!" Allie said. "Must have taken you ages."

Frieda beamed with pleasure. "Francesca helped. She has a real flair for this sort of thing. She and a young student called Kylie are waiting on us this evening, so that Karun and I can relax with you guys." She glanced at her watch. "Actually, she's a little late. No doubt she'll arrive soon. Help yourselves to a glass of champagne."

The other guests arrived within minutes, all except Jan and Yvonne. The plan was for Jan to bring Yvonne to the café about twenty minutes after everyone else so that they could all surprise her.

All couples, Jane thought, she and Ed excepted. Frieda would probably sit them next to each other, an unsubtle hint that they should get together. She was convinced Frieda was in on Allie's plan.

It was nearly time. At a signal from Karun, Jane placed her glass of champagne on the table. She smiled when she noticed her place marker next to Ed's, just as she'd predicted. She joined the others behind the door as they waited for Jan and Yvonne to arrive.

"Surprise!" Their collective shout was a roar. Yvonne was showered with confetti. She wiped it away, eyes shining with tears and what appeared to be genuine surprise. Jan must be good at keeping secrets. Yvonne looked beautiful, Jane thought, sophisticated, with her post-chemo pixie haircut.

She caught a glimpse of her own, untidy chignon (she had tried for sophistication) in the wide mirror above the table. Its reflection also revealed Ed, watching her from across the room. She looked away quickly, worried he'd see her watching him watching her.

Jane nipped to the ladies' and by the time she came out, everyone was seated around the table. She smiled at Ed as she sat down next to him.

"How's the head?" So he'd heard.

"Fine, thanks. I have a thick skull." She looked at him, expecting to see a smile, but his expression was stern.

"Was it something to do with your work as a special?"

"I don't think so. I haven't made any enemies as far as I know."

Jane looked across the table at Allie and was appalled to see her friend give her a wink. Thank goodness Ed hadn't noticed — he was busy refilling their glasses.

"Did you find it difficult, walking away from that young man's murder, knowing your involvement ended at the very beginning of the investigation? I think that's what I'd find hard about being a volunteer constable," Ed said.

Jane was surprised to hear her own misgivings about the job echoed back at her. "Actually, yes. It can be frustrating."

"Well you're used to analysing books, aren't you? Digging deeper. Looking for the subtext. Studying the psychology of the characters, following patterns and connections. I imagine skills like that must be useful in investigating a crime."

Jane smiled. It wouldn't have occurred to her to make a link between investigative police work and reading literature.

She noticed that Karun's seat was empty. He was probably getting the starters ready for Francesca and Kylie to serve. A few moments later, however, he, Frieda and Francesca began serving. There was no sign of Kylie.

"What happened to your other helper?" she asked Karun as he placed a plate of tofu halloumi and roasted vegetables in front of her.

"She hasn't shown up."

"Oh! Did she give a reason?" Jane felt a spike of annoyance at Kylie for letting her friends down.

"No. We've heard nothing from her. No worries. It's not a big problem. We can manage without her."

"I feel responsible after recommending her."

"Well, you shouldn't. It's just one of those things," he said.

"Problem?" Ed enquired. Jane explained.

"Not your fault at all. How well do you know her?"

"Hardly at all, actually. I met her in connection with work."

"You tutor her?" Ed asked.

Jane hesitated. "No, not that work. My other work."

"Right."

Before he could follow it up, Jane said, "Tell me about your job." She was aware that Ed wasn't just a blacksmith, he was an artisan blacksmith.

"My father was a blacksmith. He taught me all the skills of the traditional blacksmith trade while I was growing up. It was a good grounding. But I also went to art college, and I did a business course. I knew I'd have to treat what I do as a business if I intended to make a living from it. I needed to learn how to market myself, as well as all the other business skills that didn't come naturally to me."

"I've seen your work. It's exquisite. And Jan told me you won a gold medal from the Worshipful Company of Blacksmiths, no less."

Ed laughed. "Sounds like a cult, doesn't it? It allowed me to put some letters after my name, which is good for business. FWCB, Fellow of the Worshipful Company of Blacksmiths. Bit of a mouthful. And not all my work is arty. I do boring, functional work too. Gates and railings, for example."

Jane suspected that even Ed's 'boring, functional work' would be produced with a flair for design and detail. "And business is good, I hear — from Jan, that is." Jane hoped Ed wouldn't think she'd been looking him up. She had of course, though everything she'd found was connected with his business. He seemed to have no other online presence.

"Yes. It means I have to spend one day a week in my office and another day out and about visiting clients and delivering orders. Then there's time spent on design. I used to push myself hard, work every hour of the week, and at weekends, but I try to take weekends off these days. You get to a certain age and suddenly you realise there's more to life than just work." He smiled. "Even when you love what you do."

Jane was thinking of asking him if he'd always been a blacksmith when they were interrupted by Jan standing up to toast Yvonne. After his emotional speech, which left most of them dewy-eyed, the main course arrived. "Have you heard anything from Kylie?" Jane asked Francesca.

"Not a word. I don't think Frieda and Karun will be giving her a second chance. It's not difficult to text or call to let them know why she couldn't make it, is it?"

Jane frowned. She didn't know Kylie well enough to be a judge of her character, but she hadn't got the impression that she was the type to let people down. She hadn't identified the man who'd harassed her yet, but she'd given Jane no indication that she was about to give up. The reverse, in fact.

Jane felt a slither of anxiety. She shuddered. Ed asked if she felt cold. Unlikely, given that the café was glowing with warmth, as were the cheeks of most of the guests, though the latter might also be attributable to the wine.

"I'm fine."

"Are you sure?" Ed asked. He seemed very attentive, a fact that hadn't been missed by Allie, whose right eye flickered in a half-wink.

"Absolutely." But she wasn't. Her head was full of Kylie. Why hadn't she turned up for work, or even called? She decided to set her mind at rest by sending her a text. She took out her phone. "Excuse me. There's something I forgot to tell my daughter."

After sending the text, she could check her phone every so often and, with luck, hear that Kylie had found some other activity that she considered more attractive than waiting tables. A date with Ryan, perhaps.

The evening wore on. Jane's phone remained resoundingly silent, save for a text from her son with a picture attached of him pulling a silly face. At some point, around ten, the champagne must have relaxed her, for she forgot about Kylie in her enjoyment of the company of Ed Shipley and her friends. The café was bathed in warmth, friendship and good humour.

After the meal, the tables were pushed aside, and they played charades. Charades was a favourite of Jane's. They played in two teams of four and Ed was on Jane's team.

Other games followed, then there was music and dancing. Somehow, it was getting on for one. Jane felt flushed and light-headed. She had a sense that she'd been concerned about something earlier but as she couldn't remember what it was, it couldn't be all that important, could it?

At around one fifteen, there was a loud knock at the door. Someone said, jokingly, that it was the police, come to warn them to keep the noise down.

It was the police.

But they hadn't come about the noise.

CHAPTER FOURTEEN

Karun opened the door. "You're lucky I answered. You didn't do the secret knock." He giggled.

Jane giggled too, until she recognised the stern-faced woman thrusting her way past Karun into the café. Everyone fell silent. It was as if DI Warwick had brought some of the night's chill inside with her. She was shadowed by a younger man, DS Elias Harper.

There was no preamble. Warwick's eyes swept the room and came to rest on Jane.

Ed looked at Jane. "Jane, do you know these two?"

"Yes. They're police officers. Detectives." She searched Warwick's face for an explanation.

"Sorry to intrude on your celebration. Special Constable Bell, is there somewhere we can talk privately?"

"You can use the kitchen," Frieda offered. She showed them through.

Warwick closed the door on the subdued partygoers. "How drunk are you?"

Jane avoided the question. "What's this about?"

"How well do you know a young woman, a student at the university by the name of Kylie Bright?"

Jane's heart lurched with anxiety. "Why? Has something happened to her?"

"You called her earlier in the evening. Yesterday evening, to be precise. Later on, you sent her a text asking if she was okay because she hadn't shown up for work. Did you have a reason for believing that she might not be okay?"

"I . . . Please, just tell me she's all right." Jane cringed at the way her words sounded — thick and slurry. She thought she saw disgust flicker in DI Warwick's eyes.

"I wish I could, but it would be a lie."

DS Harper cleared his throat. "Kylie Bright has been found dead. We think she was murdered."

"Oh no!" Jane covered her mouth with both hands.

"Oh yes." She recoiled as Warwick took a couple of steps towards her and was immediately angry. Why should she feel intimidated? Hell, Warwick couldn't consider her a suspect, so why the hostility?

"What was your phone call about, and why were you so concerned about Kylie's wellbeing earlier this evening?"

"I . . . she was trying to track down a man who harassed her in a restaurant last week. I was worried she'd found him and . . ." Jane lost her train of thought. Her brain was processing in slow motion. She tried to go back to the start. "I was called to the scene of an assault on a young man, Ryan Brown, while on duty just over a week ago."

Steph ran her fingers through her hair. "I'm not quite getting this. Was this Ryan Brown the person who harassed Kylie Bright?"

"No. They'd only just met. We . . . I wondered if Ryan's attacker might be the same man who harassed Kylie. Ryan was attacked after he left the restaurant with Kylie."

"Kylie witnessed the assault?"

"No, but Kris did. But he couldn't give a description because he didn't speak English very well. Jan helped with that."

"Kris? Jan? Who the hell are they?"

Jane frowned. "Kris is a hospital porter. Jan's a stonemason. He works at the cathedral."

Warwick and Harper exchanged confused glances. "I don't think we're going to get much sense out of her until she sobers up," Warwick said. "I'm going back to the scene. You stick around, talk to her some more, see if you can piece together some sort of coherent narrative. Probably a lost cause." She turned her steely gaze on Jane. "Try to concentrate and give us a joined-up picture of what you're talking about. If I find out you've caused this young woman's death by dabbling in things you don't understand, there's going to be hell to pay." She stormed out the door.

After she'd gone, Karun came into the kitchen and asked how much longer they were likely to be. To Jane's relief, DS Harper replied, "Not long."

"Allie and Pete are going to wait and walk home with you, Jane." Karun told her.

"No, please tell them to go. I'll take a taxi if I don't feel like walking."

"I'll see Ms Bell home," DS Harper said.

Mistakenly thinking that he meant immediately, Jane stood up. Harper waved her down again. To Karun he said, "Can you get her a coffee?" He looked pleased when Karun asked if he'd like one too.

"Ms Bell, I know that DI Warwick was a bit abrupt with you. She's had a long day, and now this, a new murder added to her workload. We came rushing here hoping for a lead after finding that you'd left a message on Kylie Bright's phone. She was frustrated and disappointed that you were unable to tell us anything meaningful."

Jane supposed that was a polite way of telling her she was too pissed to make much sense. It wasn't just the champagne. Her mind was struggling to process the shock of Kylie's murder. She felt a stab of anger at DI Warwick for insinuating that her actions might have been to blame for Kylie's death. It was followed, immediately, by another stab — of guilt. She should never have encouraged Kylie to seek out the man who'd harassed her in the restaurant, particularly as she'd had a suspicion, albeit unfounded, that he might be violent.

Karun handed her a mug of coffee. "Okay?" Jane nodded. "Here you go. He thrust another mug at DS Harper and went back into the café.

"Can we go right back to the beginning again?" DS Harper said.

It took about fifteen minutes of stopping and starting for Jane to relate the story of Ryan Brown's assault and his connection with Kylie Bright. Every time she faltered, she had to start all over again.

DS Harper seemed to have infinite patience. He didn't get angry when she lost the plot or garbled something nonsensical or out of context. Finally, he seemed satisfied that he had a version of events that might satisfy DI Warwick's demand for a 'coherent narrative.'

Jane's mouth was dry. The coffee had tasted bitter, and she'd let it get cold. She noticed DS Harper savouring every sip, as though it might be his last for a very long time.

"Can I go home now?"

"Yes, you may."

They went back into the café. Many of the candles still flickered with a faint, guttering light, casting gloomy shadows on the walls. Someone had turned off the twinkly lights. One or two of the balloons bobbed on the floor, almost deflated. Only Frieda, Karun and Ed remained. Jane wasn't sure what she felt about Ed still being there.

"Okay if I walk you home?" he asked.

"I don't need an escort."

"I know that. I thought you might like some company."

Jane agreed. The alternative was to have the police escort her.

DS Harper gave an odd little bow. "I'll see myself out. Thanks for the coffee."

As soon as he was out the door, the questions flew.

"What was all that about?" Frieda asked.

"That DI Warwick seemed like she was on the warpath," added Karun. "Was it you she was upset with? Is it something to do with your special constable work?"

Jane explained as best she could, leaving out Kylie's name. She ended by saying, "DI Warwick was upset because she's already overworked, and this new murder investigation is likely to be added to her caseload. They just wanted to ask me a few questions because I sort of knew the victim. They found a message on her phone that I left earlier today. I mean, yesterday. I'm sorry, I can't disclose any more details. You'll hear about it soon enough."

Frieda gave Jane a hug. "When you said you were going to volunteer as a special, I thought you'd be dealing with shoplifting and the like, not murder. Do look after yourself, sweetie."

Jane and Ed set off on foot. Jane noticed Ed's van parked a short way from the café but didn't comment. To tell the truth, she did feel like a bit of company after hearing about Kylie, and a walk would take longer than a car ride.

"Another murder," Ed said. "It wasn't this student who was supposed to be working for Frieda and Harun this evening, was it?"

"How did you . . ?" Too late. Jane clamped her hand over her mouth.

"A wild guess," Ed said.

"I called her before the party, the police saw my name on her phone and thought I might be able to help. I couldn't. I could barely put a proper sentence together I was so drunk."

"I'm sure they appreciated whatever help you were able to give."

Jane thought of DI Warwick's parting words. "I doubt it," she said. With a sinking feeling, she realised that Warwick could make things very difficult for her.

Ed was a comforting presence, but when they reached her house, she hesitated to ask him inside. He took the decision from her.

"I've got a breakfast meeting with a client in Horncastle in the morning, so I'd better go home and get some sleep."

"Thanks for keeping me company."

"My pleasure. Any time."

There was a moment's awkwardness, then Ed bent to kiss her on the cheek. "Take care, Jane. Call me if you're in any sort of trouble."

Jane wasn't sure what to say, so she just nodded.

Inside her cosy house, the door locked securely behind her, she reflected on the events of the evening. She had no right to feel safe. Kylie was dead, and it was her fault. She wished she could do something to help, but she could do nothing. She drank a large glass of water, swallowed a couple of paracetamols and went to bed.

In the morning, she received a call from the police station informing her that a complaint had been issued against her by Detective Inspector Stephanie Warwick. An inquiry was pending. In the meantime, she was suspended from duty.

CHAPTER FIFTEEN

"That woman is a bloody loose cannon. How she ever got through the selection process is a complete mystery. Are they so desperate to put boots on the streets these days that they'll appoint any idiot who can scribble an X on an application form?"

Elias was quiet while Steph ranted on for a bit longer. He'd just returned to the murder scene with the news that Jane Bell seemed to have been carrying out her own investigation into the murder of Mark Ripley, and that for some reason, she'd associated Mark's death with an assault on a friend of Kylie's called Ryan Brown.

Steph glared at him. He didn't flinch. She'd noted before that it never worked when she attempted to exert her authority over him. She couldn't stop herself responding with sarcasm. "Oh. Right. You think so, do you? Well, why don't we put her in charge of both of our murder investigations? Maybe she can solve them for us while we have a little holiday."

He was probably wondering why she was so incensed by Jane Bell. Her dislike of the woman had begun even before she'd found out what she'd been getting up to behind her back. Perversely, the fact that there was no real basis for it made her dislike Bell all the more.

Steph regretted her sarcasm. It was unprofessional and showed her in a bad light. She wasn't sure what opinion of her Elias had formed in the time he'd been working with her. She didn't particularly care whether he liked her or not, but if she wanted to maintain his respect — which was vital to their working relationship — she'd need to try harder.

The mood swings she'd been enduring lately had to be something to do with Cal. He was seldom out of her thoughts, and his nocturnal visitations were depriving her of sleep, making her edgy and irritable day and night alike. An unsettling thought occurred to her. What if she was starting to blame Cal for her own shortcomings and failures?

"So," she said, "her half-baked theory is that this unknown man who harassed Kylie Bright in the restaurant assaulted Ryan Brown because he had better luck than him hitting on Kylie? And she's got a suspicion that said unknown man is the same person who attacked and killed Mark Ripley. *Because why?*"

"I think it's more of a hunch than anything. She saw similarities between the victims. Mark and Ryan are close in age. Both were students. Both were beaten. I know Mark died, but we don't know for certain that the perp set out to kill him. Mark could have been pushed and was unfortunate enough to strike his head on the sharp edge of the step. On the other hand, it's possible the perp did set out to kill him and would have killed Ryan too if a passer-by hadn't called out to him. Bell was present at Mark's murder scene, and she responded to the attack on Ryan Brown. I think she's just made a link between the two in her mind. She's inexperienced."

Steph recalled something else Elias had mentioned. "You said Bell asked Kylie to find out the name of the man who harassed her, even though she suspected he could be dangerous?"

"I think it was more that Kylie volunteered."

"And Bell didn't discourage her. She put that young woman at risk. I'm going to make damn sure she doesn't have an opportunity to do that to anyone else. She won't be masquerading as a police officer again if I have anything to do with it."

"You intend to get her dismissed?" Elias said.

"I'll do my best. I'll put a complaint in. That'll get her a suspension, if nothing else. And it will keep her nose out of our investigation."

Steph took a deep breath in and exhaled slowly, watching her breath form a misty white cloud in the freezing night air. She stamped her feet, wishing she could send life-resurrecting tremors through the ground to Kylie Bright's lifeless body. But Kylie continued to lie, cold and dead, on the glistening Yorkstone setts.

"I've been thinking about Jason Collins," Elias said. "He watched online videos on picking up women after seeing Mark Ripley modelling how it was done. He wasn't very successful at putting what he learned into practice, but he didn't blame anyone but himself for his lack of success. Could we be looking at a more aggressive and embittered version of Collins? Someone who takes rejection and failure very personally and turns his rage on men and women alike? Women when they reject him, and men who succeed where he fails? Both Mark and Ryan were attacked soon after 'picking up' a woman. Maybe the perp knew Mark because he had approached him too, just like he approached Jason Collins, claiming he could help him become irresistible to women. But Mark failed him as a coach. Seeing him with an attractive woman like Elle Darrow could have pushed the perp into violence."

Steph felt a stab of irritation at Elias's insight, which was essentially a sort of endorsement of Jane Bell's theory about a connection.

She didn't comment. Instead, she surveyed the surrounding area. Kylie's body had been discovered on Motherby Hill, a narrow, precipitous footpath, notable in historical terms because it followed the line of the lower walls of the old Roman city walls. It linked the lower part of the city with the upper, ascending steeply from West Parade to Drury Lane. It was reasonably well-lit, but there were some shadowy areas, and it was likely to have been quiet at the time of evening when Kylie set off. The rush hour would have been over, and it was still a bit early for people to be going out. Moreover, it was a Tuesday evening, not the busiest night of the week for socialising.

"She should have stuck to Spring Hill." Steph was referring to an alternative route to uphill Lincoln via a reasonably busy main road. "Most people would do that after dark, instead of coming up a lonely lane like this. Perhaps she was running a bit late and favoured the shortcut. My guess is he followed her from the university to the foot of Motherby Hill, then ran up Victoria Street and along the little path leading off Alexandra Terrace. Then, he waited for her here, where the two paths join." Steph pointed to the spot, a few feet from where they were standing.

Elias didn't know the area as well as Steph. She waited while he looked it up on Google Maps to see the lie of the land. "I agree. But he took a bit of a risk."

"Because of the houses?" Steph looked around. It was true there were some buildings overlooking the path, but they were set back and separated from it by a high wall. "He could have pushed her against the wall, then forced her head down, repeatedly, onto the cobblestones. I doubt anyone would have been able to see. And he would have been quick. It doesn't take long to smash someone's skull against stone."

"Mark's head came into contact with stone too. And according to Jane Bell, Ryan Brown's attacker bashed his head against a brick wall. Maybe after the perp learned about Mark's fatal brain bleed, he realised that he'd discovered an effective way of killing. We don't know if Ryan's attacker would have killed him if someone hadn't intervened." Elias looked at Kylie's body. "There's some doubt over whether the perp intended to kill Mark, and whether he intended to kill Ryan. But in Kylie's case, there's no doubt about his intention — he meant to kill her. If we're talking about the same person, it could indicate an escalation."

Steph grimaced at the unsavoury possibility. It no longer seemed all that certain that they were trying to join unconnected dots. "We need to look at the report of the assault on this Ryan Brown and interview him if necessary. In particular we need to know if he had any sort of connection with Mark Ripley. Did Bell mention if he had?"

"Not to me. They're both students at the same university, so it's possible that they might have known each other in some way, through their studies, or sporting activities, or clubs, for example." Less confidently, he added, "Kylie was a student too. It's possible that she knew Mark Ripley."

"I'm aware of that," Steph snapped. "Can you check the report on Ryan Brown's assault ASAP?"

"Yes, boss." Elias seemed hesitant. "Given that Kylie's killer could be the same man who harassed her in the restaurant, it's possible that he could have been stalking her for some time. In that case, he would probably have attacked her or killed her as soon as she rejected his advances. Jane Bell—"

Steph cut him off. "I know what you're trying to say, Detective Sergeant. But it still doesn't let Jane Bell off the hook. It doesn't matter whether this man already had Kylie in his sights. Bell was still potentially putting her in danger by agreeing to let her find out more about him. And before you say it, yes, I still intend to have her suspended."

Elias nodded. "You're the boss."

Yes, I am. Elias's manner towards her always remained in line with their respective ranks, but Steph had noticed that it was never deferential. She believed that professionally, he saw himself as her equal in all but name. There might come a time when he challenged her outright. She decided not to trust him too far. It was better that way. Trust, like pity, was a weakness.

Steph remained at the murder scene most of the rest of the night. By the time she got home, it was barely worth going to bed but she was bone weary, even if her mind was still racing. She sprayed her pillow liberally with lavender essence and inhaled deeply, hoping the aroma would induce a sense of calm and help ease her into sleep.

She awoke, hours later, feeling more rested than she had a right to be after so many disturbed nights, and after working a murder scene only a few hours earlier. Miraculously, Cal had left her alone.

In the shower, she let the hot water batter her aching neck and shoulders, easing some of the tension. She set off for work without breakfast, or even a cup of coffee. She was surprised to see that Elias was absent from his desk when she arrived. He'd flagged up the report on the assault of Ryan Brown for her to look at.

The report mentioned that PCS Bell had managed to find an approved translator at short notice. His name was familiar. He'd been present as a translator at previous interviews Steph had conducted with witnesses and suspects, she was sure. She'd had the odd conversation with him. Hadn't he once told her that his partner had cancer? She even remembered the woman's name — Yvonne. An image from the previous night popped into her head, the shiny silver balloons spelling out 'Happy birthday.' If it was the same Yvonne, that would explain how Bell had managed to magic up a translator in mere minutes. Jan Mazurek must be a friend.

Elias arrived, bearing coffee. It wasn't his usual custom.

"Guessed you might need one of these. Black, one sugar, right?"

"Yes, thanks. I don't suppose you grabbed anything to eat, did you?" Elias pulled open his desk drawer and tossed her a bar of chocolate. Dark chocolate with ginger. It was her favourite. How did he know? She eyed the chocolate, then her colleague with suspicion. Elias's gaze was fixed on his computer screen. Steph was distracted by a call from the duty desk.

"DI Warwick?"

"Speaking."

"I've just taken a call from a Charlotte Purdey. She's a student at Lincoln University, a friend of the young woman who was murdered last night. Kylie Bright? She wanted to report Kylie as a missing person. She knocked on Kylie's door at seven this morning. They were supposed to be going for a run together. There was no answer. Charlotte alerted the warden, who unlocked the door to Kylie's room. Her bed hadn't been slept in. Charlotte contacted the restaurant that Kylie said she was going to be working at the previous evening and was told she hadn't shown up. She was worried because Kylie had definitely set off for work and hadn't mentioned going anywhere afterwards."

"You didn't tell her what happened to Kylie?" Steph asked.

"Of course not. I have her contact details. I told her someone would be in touch soon."

Steph grabbed a pen. "Good. Thanks." She scribbled down the details. Elias looked at her expectantly when she came off the phone. "Kylie's been reported missing by a friend. I've got her details. I think we should see her right now."

Steph did some research on Charlotte Purdey on the way. "She's involved in quite a few groups and societies at the uni, and in town. Seems quite politically active. Into feminism, the environment. Probably opinionated." She noticed the look Elias gave her but merely told him to watch the road.

Charlotte lived on campus, in a residence consisting of five floors of long corridors of study bedrooms and shared kitchens. Her room was on the top floor. A voice from behind the door asked who was there. "Police." Steph held her police ID up to the spyhole. The door opened a crack. Eyes viewed them with suspicion. "How did you get in without a pass key?"

"We collected one from the accommodation office after showing our ID. Is it okay if we talk to you here, or would you rather go somewhere else?"

"Here's fine." Charlotte stood aside to let them enter. Her room was small, there was only one chair and a bean bag. Charlotte sat on the bed, leaving Steph to take the chair. Elias sank down onto the bean bag, stretching his long legs out in front of him.

"I can't believe you're actually taking me seriously. I thought I'd be told that Kylie's probably just staying with a boyfriend or something. I've read that a person has to be missing for days before the police sit up and take notice. So, thanks for coming, I guess."

Steph cleared her throat. "Charlotte—"

"Lottie. No one calls me Charlotte except my mum and dad. Oh, and both my grans."

"Lottie, then. I'm sorry but we have some bad news about your friend. Kylie was found dead late last night. We think she'd been murdered. I'm sorry. I know this must be a shock for you."

"Oh!" Then she added shakily, "Are you sure?"

"Yes. She had some ID with her, her driver's licence and her student card."

"I knew something had to be wrong. I knew it. She never misses a run. I only saw her last night. How can she be dead?" She caught her breath and held it for what seemed an alarmingly long time. "Excuse me a moment." Lottie got up and disappeared through a door into the en-suite bathroom.

Steph suppressed a sigh of impatience. It wasn't that she didn't feel for Lottie but time mattered. Five minutes passed before Lottie reappeared, face blotchy, eyes red-rimmed.

"If you feel up to it, I'd like to ask you some questions, Lottie. Is that okay?"

Lottie shrugged. Steph took that to mean that she was ready, and ploughed right in. "How did Kylie seem when you last saw her?"

"She was happy, pleased about getting the job at the café. The vegan one on Burton Road? Bit nervous because it was her first shift, and she didn't know what to expect. I told her to text me if she finished really late and didn't want to go for an early run. She didn't text."

"Okay. What about going back a bit. Has she been herself lately? Was she worrying about anything?"

Lottie picked at her sleeve. "No, not that she told me, and I think she would have. She tended to confide in me.

Kylie got off to a bit of a bad start at uni and I was there for her."

"How so?"

"In freshers' week. She met this guy."

"Go on."

"I met Kylie on our first day here. Her room's across the corridor from mine. She seemed so young, and a bit shy. She was just eighteen the August before she started here. She'd been the youngest in her class all the way through school. I'm twenty — I took a gap year after school. I felt protective of her. We went to Freshers' Fair together, got chatting to some second-year guys and they invited us to a party. We said no because we'd already arranged to go to another party that evening. They were a bit off about it. Borderline rude, to be honest. Then, a couple of days later, one of them approached Kylie in town and asked her back to his place for coffee." Steph's heart sank. "So, you can probably guess what happened next."

"I'd like you to tell me. I appreciate it must be difficult to talk about, but it might help us find out who hurt Kylie."

"*Killed*," Lottie corrected. "You don't need to use a euphemism." She gave a shiver and reached for a red hoodie on the cabinet next to her bed. Nerves, Steph knew, not cold, for the room was overheated.

"So," Lottie continued, "he kept offering Kylie alcohol, as if he wanted to get her drunk. She thinks she drank about three glasses of wine. He asked her to have sex with him. When she said she didn't want to, he started mocking her about still being a virgin. He told her she wasn't that pretty and that she shouldn't be so choosy, or she'd never get a boyfriend. He said she should be grateful to him for wanting to have sex with her because she probably wouldn't find anyone else willing to do it with her. That sort of thing. Eventually, she agreed."

Steph nodded. It was classic negging, a strategy coined and used by pick-up artists that involved paying a woman a backhanded compliment or insulting her in order to undermine her confidence and make her want to gain her abuser's approval. She thought of a case at another university where male students had made misogynistic and insulting comments about female students online. It depressed her to think that something similar might have taken place here.

"If anyone had said stuff like that to me, I'd have told them where to go, or reported them to the police, but as I said, Kylie was shy. She didn't have a lot of confidence. She took everything he said to heart. Plus, she wasn't used to drinking alcohol. I spent a long time afterwards getting her to see that he'd manipulated her, bullied her to get her to '*consent*' to having sex with him. I wanted her to tell someone about it, like student support or her personal tutor, but she wouldn't. She was too embarrassed. She refused even when I told her he'd keep on getting away with it with other women. I even suggested he might have raped her if she'd not consented."

"At least you tried," Steph said.

"He sent her a text the following day. It just said 'one out of ten,' like he was scoring her, you know?" Lottie's grief was forgotten in her anger. "Vile, misogynistic bastard. He probably had a good laugh about it with his mates."

She looked at Elias as though he represented all that was toxic about the male sex.

"What was the man's name?" Elias asked.

"Mark Ripley."

"Lottie, a young man, a student by that name, was murdered a couple of weeks ago," he said.

Lottie nodded. "I heard about that."

Elias held out his phone to show Lottie an image of Mark Ripley. "Is this the Mark Ripley you met during freshers' week?"

"Yes, that's him."

Steph tensed. "What about his friends? The other men he was with that day. Do you know their names?" Have you seen them around the campus since freshers' week?"

"Yes. Adam Eades and Phil Lavin. A pair of complete dickheads. The boyfriend of a mate of mine had some dealings with them."

"Go on," Steph said.

"My mate's called Ivy Cross. Her boyfriend's called Tristan Morley. They both live nearby. It'd probably be better if you heard Tristan's story from him. I have his mobile number if you want it."

"Yes, please, Lottie. That would be a big help." Sometimes all the buses come at once.

Steph thanked Lottie for her time, and she and Elias made their way back outside. "I wanted to say to her that not all men have so little respect for women," Elias said unexpectedly. "I saw her looking at me as though those morons represented my point of view also. I assure you that is not the case."

"I never thought it was." Steph meant what she said. She'd never witnessed Elias showing any signs of disrespect towards his female colleagues.

"I was brought up by women. My mother and my grandmother. I also have an older sister. They're all feminists."

"What about Daddy?" As soon as she asked, she knew she'd read the situation badly. Elias had opened up to her and she'd rebuffed him.

His voice stiff, he said, "He was never in the picture."

"Right." Steph didn't enquire further. She had other things on her mind. She called Tristan. As luck would have it, he was on campus. He gave them directions to his accommodation.

Tristan — average height, slightly pitted skin, pierced lip — greeted them with the words, "Lottie just called. She explained why you're here. I can't believe it. Poor Kylie." He paused, shaking his head. "Is it okay if my girlfriend Ivy joins us? She knew Kylie too." Steph agreed.

Tristan's fingers flitted over his phone. Within seconds, a door opened further down the corridor and a young woman peered out. Tristan broke the news to her, and they hugged.

"We can use the kitchen," Tristan suggested. "There won't be anyone else there at this time of day. Most of the other students who share our kitchen are scientists and mathematicians. They don't have as much free time as us."

Ivy — raven hair, black lipstick, gimlet eyes heavily lined with kohl — asked them if they'd like a cup of Japanese Sencha tea.

That's expensive stuff, Steph thought. For a moment she was tempted, but her gaze strayed to the sink, overflowing with dirty dishes, and she declined. As did Elias.

Tristan put the kettle on and took two mugs and two infusers out of a basin of murky water, gave them a shake and put them on the worktop.

Ivy spooned what looked like grass cuttings into two egg-shaped tea infusers. She placed them in the mugs and poured boiling water on top, then she handed one mug to Tristan, instructing him to let the tea infuse for five minutes.

Steph wondered what was wrong with plain old tea bags. She looked at Tristan. "Tell us how you got to know Mark Ripley and his friends, Adam Eades and Phil Lavin."

"I met them back in my first week here. Mark came up to me in the Swan. The Savvy Swan, a student bar and restaurant? Adam and Phil were with him. They're all second-years. They don't live on campus. Adam and Phil share a house in town. Somewhere off Monks Road, I think. Mark lived somewhere else. We chatted for a bit, then one of them, I think it was Adam, asked me if I had a girlfriend."

He glanced affectionately at Ivy, who gave him an encouraging smile. "I knew Ivy but we weren't in a relationship yet. I said I wasn't seeing anyone and admitted I'd never had a girlfriend at school. Too busy studying for my A levels, I guess. They were all like, *how can you still be a virgin at your age?* Actually, I wasn't. That was just an assumption they made and I didn't correct them. Mocking me, I suppose. Then Mark started telling me about this group he was starting up to coach 'people like me,'" — air apostrophes — "strategies to help them hit on girls. His words, not mine." Another glance at Ivy. "He said you could learn techniques to enhance your chances of success in persuading women to sleep with you."

Ivy butted in. "Manipulation, bullying, lies, deceit, coercion."

Tristan nodded. "Absolutely. I realised what their game was immediately, but I didn't let on. When Mark asked if I wanted to come along to one of their groups, I agreed. I told Ivy about what I thought they were up to and Ivy told Lottie. They agreed that it would be a good idea to have a spy in their camp, so to speak. When I got there, I realised it was exactly what I thought it was going to be. I was disgusted with their behaviour and all the pathetic misogynistic crap they came out with."

"Can you give an example of something you felt uncomfortable with?" Elias asked.

"Well, one of the strategies basically involved negging. That's—"

"I know what it means," Elias said. "Go on."

"First you go along to their group, and Adam and Phil do a presentation about the 'art of seduction.' Then they outline a couple of techniques. Afterwards, they take you out on the street to practise approaching women."

"Street harassment," Ivy said. Again, Tristan nodded. "Exactly."

"They gave us a lot of lines to use. Mark demonstrated what to say and do by going up to a couple of women and successfully getting their phone numbers. Then it was our turn. They advised starting by approaching a woman we liked the look of and maybe asking for directions, then complimenting her on some aspect of her appearance. Mark assured us it was okay, that you were making the woman feel good about herself. But when they did their talk ahead of taking us out, they focussed on the main goal, which was . . . well, obviously, getting a woman to have sex with you, even if she was initially reluctant. It was all about overcoming resistance, they said. I had to bite my tongue. I so wanted to ask if they really thought it fair that the man knew what the agenda was but the women didn't."

Ivy patted Tristan's hand. "Tell them what Mark said about young girls."

"He was pushing me to approach this girl who looked about fourteen, and I said, no, she's way too young. He told me it was up to me to decide the morality of it, but he made it quite clear that he didn't see anything wrong with approaching underage girls. That did it for me. I couldn't have taken any more without decking him. I walked away."

"You know about what happened to Kylie, right?" Ivy said.

She was referring to Kylie's experience with Mark. "Yes," Steph said.

"We should have put a stop to what they were doing," Ivy added.

"There's something else," Tristan said.

"Something else you were uncomfortable with?" Steph asked.

"Yes." They waited. Tristan took a breath. "I think Mark was secretly filming us approaching the women. Not Adam and Phil. Just Mark."

Steph frowned. "Did you confront him over it?"

"I asked him, and he denied it. He even showed me his phone. It didn't occur to me until afterwards that he might have had two."

"Did you mention it to Adam, or Phil?"

"Yes. They said no way was Mark doing that. I didn't have any proof, and after he showed me his phone, I thought I was just being paranoid."

Ivy interrupted. "If it was true, it kind of makes you wonder what else he might have been filming, right?"

Steph understood exactly what Ivy was insinuating. Still, she raised an enquiring eyebrow. Ivy elaborated. "Suppose Mark filmed himself having sex with the girls he picked up? You read about that sort of thing. I thought about it as soon as Kylie mentioned that nasty text Mark sent, marking her out of ten." Her face tightened.

Steph turned back to Tristan. "You said you walked away that day. What did you say to them?"

"I told them I didn't approve of what they were doing and pointed out that morons like them give all men a bad name. I said that I wouldn't be coming to any more sessions, even though I'd paid up front."

"Paid?" Elias said. They already knew from Jason Collins that Adam, Phil and Mark charged for their services.

"Yes. They charged me fifty quid. That covered the initial presentation plus a 'bootcamp,' as they called the walkabout, and a follow-up session. Then you could sign up for more if you found the sessions helpful."

"Did you get the impression they'd held a lot of these sessions?" Steph asked.

"They showed me a few testimonials — four, maybe five, from clients saying they felt more confident approaching women after attending the sessions. There was no way of telling whether the testimonials were genuine. I got the impression, though they never actually said it, that the bootcamp I attended was one of the first they'd organised. It was all pretty amateurish, to be honest, as well as morally suspect."

"Did you ever consider speaking to someone in authority at the university about what Mark and his cronies were up to?" Elias asked.

"No point. It's not against the law or university regulations to teach the so-called 'art of seduction,' as they called it. I couldn't prove that any bad stuff was going on. It all just seemed kind of . . . seedy. You know? Even though what they were all doing isn't against the law, that doesn't make it right. "

"Street harassment should be a crime," Elias said. Tristan and Ivy nodded.

Steph was mulling over what Tristan had said. There was no evidence that Mark Ripley's death was related to his being involved in Adam and Phil's group. But it was looking more and more likely that there was some connection between his murder and Kylie's. Her anger at Jane Bell rekindled. If Bell had alerted them to Kylie sooner, perhaps they could have made the link sooner, maybe even have prevented her death.

"You're here because you're investigating Kylie's murder, aren't you? Are you investigating Mark Ripley's murder too? Do you think their deaths had something to do with the pick-up group? With Adam and Phil?" Ivy's question echoed Steph's thoughts.

"We can't discuss our investigations with you, and I'd appreciate it if you'd avoid indulging in speculation. There's no evidence that Adam Eades and Phil Lavin are involved in any wrongdoing."

"I didn't feel sorry for Mark after what he did to poor Kylie." Ivy's eyes flashed with anger.

"Ivy!" Tristan looked shocked.

Ivy refused to back down. "Even if he didn't murder her, he humiliated and bullied her. He . . . He practically raped her. He could have caused her to become depressed, suicidal or . . . anything. Guys like him and Adam and Phil, they think they can get away with harassing and humiliating and harming women. Even if the university knew about it, they wouldn't do anything. You read about them persuading women to sign these non-disclosure agreements, so the university won't be dragged into a scandal."

Steph let Ivy rant. She was upset and angry, and what she was saying was, regrettably, all too true. Quite recently, she'd caught an item on the news about universities trying to hush up complaints from young female students who had been sexually assaulted or even raped. One young woman who had signed an NDA after her case was dismissed through lack of evidence had actually been thanked by the university for not messing up her rapist's life!

Steph wondered whether Ryan Brown had also been involved with the pick-up group in some way. If so, the theory that his assault was linked to the two murders would be much more plausible. It added a note of urgency to their need to interview Adam Eades and Phil Lavin.

Elias was already on it. "Have either of you heard of Ryan Brown? He's a student here. Was he one of the group's clients?"

Tristan and Ivy shook their heads.

"Kylie knew Ryan. You're sure she never mentioned him?" Elias said.

More head shaking. Not surprising really, Kylie and Ryan had probably not had much time to get to know each other. Steph rose to her feet. "Thanks for your time. Please don't discuss what's been said here with anyone."

"I take it we're going to be calling on Mark's buddies, Eades and Lavin?" Elias said when they were back outside.

"Yes, but first I need something to eat. I skipped breakfast and now I'm starving. Let's nip into Starbucks for a wrap or something."

Steph left Elias to contact the control room while she stood in the queue. She ordered a flat white for herself and a latte for Elias. When the barista asked their names, so that he could write them on their cups, Steph replied, "Holmes and Watson." His expression remained unaltered as he scribbled the names on the labels. It wasn't until they she placed Elias's cup in front of him that she noticed he'd written 'Holmes' on the latte.

"He got the names mixed up." She nodded at the cups. "I'm Holmes. Just so you know."

CHAPTER SIXTEEN

Adam Eades and Phil Lavin lived in a house share in a street off Monks Road, a busy thoroughfare east of the city centre.

Steph knew the area a little. She'd lived there herself, briefly. She liked the Victorian and Edwardian red-brick terraces with their bay windows and attractive period details. But many of them looked tired and in need of a facelift, and where nineteenth- and turn of-the-century houses had been lost, modern infills had been thrown up with little sympathy for the overall character of the area.

Originally built to accommodate workers in the factories alongside the nearby River Witham, and to give easy access to the railway for those working farther afield, the houses were now home to an eclectic group of people, from long-term residents to recent immigrants, students and young families looking for somewhere reasonably priced to rent.

Steph and Elias walked past the local FE college, dodging the busy traffic to cross the road and turn down by the side of an imposing red-brick church, one of many on Monks Road. Methodist, Anglican, Wesleyan, all had once vied for the souls of the local residents. Nowadays, some of the churches had been refurbished and served the local community in more practical ways as offices, residences, local shops.

"I used to live along here," Steph remarked to Elias. "Not this particular street, the one two blocks over. The landlady was putting the place on the market so she couldn't extend my contract beyond six months. I had to find somewhere else pretty fast."

"Nice and near the centre of town." Elias stopped suddenly. "This is it."

Steph noted that the downstairs curtains of the house were drawn. For privacy, no doubt. The landlord had probably turned the sitting-room into a bedroom so that he could fit in more tenants.

"Go on then," Steph said. "What are you waiting for?"

Elias pressed the doorbell, setting off a series of musical chimes that brought a response within seconds, no doubt because the sound was so annoying. Steph made a face. Get rid of the thing, put up a sign telling callers to knock loudly.

A bearded man in his early twenties gave them the once over. "Can I help you?"

"Good morning. I'm Detective Inspector Warwick and this is my colleague, Detective Sergeant Harper. Do you mind if we come in?"

The young man yawned. "I think you want number forty-two." He nodded at a house across the street with a boarded-up window. "They had a loud party last night and one of the neighbours put a brick through their window by way of a polite request to dial it down."

"Actually, that's not why we're here. We're here to speak with Adam Eades and Phil Lavin."

"I'm Adam. What's this about?" He took a step back, which Steph decided to interpret as an invitation for them to cross the threshold.

"Is there somewhere we can talk? It's a bit cramped out here."

"There's the kitchen, but some of my housemates might be in there having breakfast. My bedroom's tiny. There wouldn't be room for all three of us."

"Four," Steph said. "I'd be grateful if you'd ask your mate Phil to join us."

Adam took out his phone. "Sorry to wake you, bro', but there's a pair of detectives down here wanting to talk to us about something. No, no idea." He looked at Steph, raising his eyebrows in expectation.

Steph didn't respond. She disliked his tone. And why claim to be clueless about the likely reason for a police visit, when one of your friends had been murdered so recently? The question of why Adam and Phil had not been in touch with the police themselves also niggled.

"Do you want some tap water? I'm out of tea and coffee, and Phil only drinks beer."

"That's okay. We're fine."

"There's a café on Monks Road that does a decent cup of coffee."

"Just had one, thanks."

They were joined by another young man, Phil Lavin. He entered hesitantly, suggesting he was less self-assured than Adam. The first thing he did was catch Adam's eye.

"DC Harper and I are investigating the murder of Mark Ripley. I expect you've heard about it on the news. Maybe you knew him? He was a student at the university."

"There are a lot of students at the uni, but actually, Phil and I did know Mark, yes. He was a good mate. We were shocked at what happened to him."

"Terrible." Phil glanced at Adam. One hand strayed to his chin, then to the back of his head. He rolled his neck from side to side.

Steph directed her next question to Phil. Otherwise, she sensed, Adam would dominate. "When was the last time you saw him?"

"Last week. In a bar on the High Street. We were all watching the football."

"We've been speaking with a local lad, Jason Collins. He told us about your pick-up course."

"Who? What?"

Steph ignored Adam's interruption.

Phil gave Adam a nervous glance, as if to say there was no point in lying about it. Which, in Steph's estimation, made him smarter than his friend.

"I sort of remember him. He didn't sign up for the group."

"Was Mark involved with the group?"

"Er . . . yes."

"What was his role?"

"A bit of everything, but as the best looking out of all of us, he did the modelling. We got our clients to watch him in action, observe how he went about making successful connections with women."

"You mean harassing young women on the street. Hitting on them for sex?" Steph said.

"If you want to be crude about it," Adam said.

"So, he demonstrated the techniques you all taught on your course?" she asked.

"Must be rewarding work," Elias remarked.

Adam ignored the sarcasm. "Absolutely. I used to look around at all these sad young men who were really awkward and shy around women — you know, the undateables — and think, how can I help them?" He made it sound like a public service.

"That's very commendable of you," Steph said. "It might surprise you to learn that Jason Collins had been following Mark on the day of his murder."

Adam affected surprise. "Seriously? You think he killed Mark?"

Steph glanced at Elias who was studying Adam clinically. Adam appeared unperturbed. In fact, he seemed to be enjoying their interchange. Unlike Phil, who was jumpy as hell.

"Shit," he said. "He didn't seem like he'd have it in him to kill someone. Just shows you can't tell a book by its cover."

"We don't know who killed Mark," Elias said. "Yet."

Steph addressed Phil. "We're going to need more information on your group. A list of your former and current clients for starters."

"Sure. Whatever we can do to help. Mark was a good mate." Phil lowered his head. "But we don't have any clients now. We never had many in the first place. That's partly why we packed it in."

"Tell us about your group. When did you start it up? How many clients have you 'helped,' and how do you go about recruiting them?" Steph said.

"We talked about starting it up over the long break last summer. It seemed like a good idea to have our business up and running for freshers' week, so that we could take advantage of the fresh meat, so to speak."

He cleared his throat, as if realising how unfortunate that sounded. "It only ran for a couple of months, and we only ever had a handful of clients. As far as recruitment went, it was word of mouth mostly. To begin with we approached guys we thought might struggle connecting with women. You know, the less-confident ones who look awkward at mixed social gatherings."

"Right. I don't suppose it ever occurred to you that what you were doing when you went out on the streets with your 'clients' could be construed as harassment of the young women you approached?" Steph said.

"We didn't harass anyone," Adam said. "Where have you got that from? Some feminist types got the wrong idea and accused us of having an agenda that we really didn't have."

"Right. Feminists. Annoying lot, aren't they?" Steph said.

Adam didn't answer. His top lip curled. The notion of women having agency over their own lives was evidently distasteful to him. Steph scrutinised him and was startled to see his face transform, suddenly, into Cal's. She blinked and the illusion disappeared. But it left her with a sense of deep disquiet. Cal seldom showed his face in the daytime.

Elias must have noticed her momentary lapse. He took over. "The women you and your clients approach. Do they have any say in the matter? I mean, it's not like they get to decide who has the right to stop them from just going about their everyday business in the street without being pestered by people like you, do they?"

"They don't seem to mind. If I stop a woman in the street and pay her a compliment, nine times out of ten I'll end up with her phone number. They wouldn't do that if they didn't like being approached, would they?"

"What was your success rate with the men you coached in the 'art of seduction?'" Steph asked

"Well, admittedly, not all of them went on to get the girl of their dreams. To be honest with you, a lot of them needed a lot more help than we could offer." His unsympathetic tone spoke loudly about his real attitude towards these individuals. He didn't care about the outcomes for them, only about how he could exploit their insecurities for his own gain. In other company, Steph was sure, he would have referred to them as losers.

"Did any of them ever complain? Ask for their money back? We know you charged. Any of them get aggressive if they didn't seem to be getting any benefit out of your course? Or did any of them display unusual or disturbing behaviour towards the women?" Elias asked.

"There was that one bloke," Phil said, before Adam had a chance to reply. "Remember, Adam?"

Adam looked displeased. "Him?"

"Tell us about 'him,'" Steph said.

"There's nothing much to tell," Phil said. "He attended the initial presentation and went on a bootcamp with us. Unfortunately, he didn't have much success. He got a bit mouthy with one of the girls he'd approached, then he had a row with Mark. Adam had to step in."

"What did he row with Mark about?" she asked.

"Mark approached a couple of girls first," Adam said, "just to demonstrate how easy it was. Then this guy had a go and it was like three girls in a row just ignored him. He got a bit nasty with the final one, called her names, you know? Then, he turned on Mark, saying he wasn't teaching him properly."

"Do you remember the man's name?"

"Ronan Cox."

"Contact details?"

"No idea. We only asked for names. We got them all to pay up front, so we didn't have the hassle of chasing them for the money. Anyway, like Phil said, we only ran a couple of sessions before we packed it in through lack of interest." Adam looked at Steph. "Hey, you don't think this Ronan Cox killed Mark because he was pissed off about his lack of success after doing the course, do you?"

It was possible. The man might have harboured a grudge against Mark Ripley, especially after seeing how easily Mark was able to attract the attention of women and how, even when he copied Mark's technique, he was unable to achieve the same rate of success.

"So, Adam and I could be next on this psycho's target list? We always emphasised our own success rate to reassure our clients that we could help them. What if he harbours a grudge against us too?"

Adam glared at him. "Don't be stupid, Phil. Mark's murder has nothing to do with Ronan Cox, or any of our other clients. He was probably just in the wrong place at the wrong time. You ask me, Cox would be more likely to go after the women."

Steph changed direction. "One of you, I think it was you, Adam, said earlier that one of the reasons you packed the group in after a couple of sessions was through lack of clients. Was there another reason?"

Phil and Adam exchanged a glance. Phil looked uneasy. "Well?"

"No," Adam said.

Then, "Yes," Adam and Phil said simultaneously.

"Which?" Steph looked at Phil.

"I . . . We found out something about Mark."

"Come on! Do we have to drag it out of you?" Steph's patience was wearing out.

Phil gave Adam an apologetic look. "He was secretly filming the girls he and our clients approached."

Now we're getting somewhere. "Right. For what purpose?" she said.

"He said we could use the footage for training purposes. In the follow-up sessions, like, to show clients what they were doing well and badly. Adam and I didn't agree. We told him to stop."

"Did he? What else did he film, Phil?" Phil stared at the carpet. It was left to Adam to answer Steph's question.

"He filmed himself having sex with girls. Including some of the ones he approached on the bootcamps. He got a lot of phone numbers."

"Right. I take it he did this without their knowledge or consent," Steph said.

"Yes."

"How did you find out what he was doing?"

"He'd been boasting about how many women he'd had sex with. He must have thought we didn't believe him, so he showed us. He actually thought we'd approve. We rowed. I grabbed his phone off him and stamped on it," Adam said.

"Did you report what he was doing to anyone?" Steph asked.

"Phil wanted to. I talked him out of it. Mark said he wouldn't do it again. We ended up giving him the benefit of the doubt."

"Were either of you involved in filming women during sex?" she asked.

Phil appeared shocked at the suggestion. Adam was angry. "Come on, I just said, didn't I? Phil and I didn't want anything to do with that."

"You should have reported him." Elias's voice was raised. He was looking at Phil. Then, he turned to Adam. "You shouldn't have talked him out of it."

"Was that what got him killed?" Phil sounded feeble and afraid. "Maybe one of the girls found out and . . . and told her boyfriend or her dad, or her brother . . ." His eyes widened. "Or maybe one of them found out somehow and killed him herself."

Steph shook her head. "I suggest you leave the theorising to us."

"What happened to the phone, Adam? The one you stamped on," Elias said.

"I threw it in the river. I can show you where."

Great. "Did he have the footage stored elsewhere?" Steph asked.

"He told us he didn't, said it was too risky. He didn't use his regular phone either. He had another one that he kept exclusively for filming."

Which would explain why they had found nothing on his laptop.

"What can you tell us about Mark Ripley's relationship with a woman named Kylie Bright?" she asked.

Adam scowled. "There was no relationship between them. Who've you been talking to? Lottie Purdey and her mates? I bet that's who's told you this crap. There's not a chance Mark assaulted that girl. Filmed her maybe, but he wouldn't have forced himself on her. He didn't have to. Women lined up begging him for it and Kylie was no different. I should also point out that when we ran the group, we were really big on consent. And respect. We drummed that into our clients from day one."

Steph was speechless. Elias asked, "Which mates of Lottie's were you referring to just then?"

"Ivy Cross and her loser boyfriend, Tristan Morley."

"Tristan was one of your clients. He disapproved of your methods. He told us Mark encouraged him to approach underage girls. And he suspected Mark was filming the girls, though he didn't have any proof."

Steph noticed the muscles in Adam's jaw tauten. "Yeah, and look who he ended up with. That little . . ."

"You were saying? Do I take it you don't approve of Ivy?" Steph said.

"All three of them are morons. They tried to sabotage one of our bootcamps by turning up and protesting, and Lottie Purdey posted stuff online about us. Fake information, I might add."

"Like what?" Steph asked.

"She writes a feminist blog. She did a post about staying safe on campus and all but called me, Mark and Phil out as sexual predators and perverts. She didn't exactly name us but she dropped plenty of hints."

Steph thought it interesting that Lottie, Ivy and Tristan hadn't mentioned the blog. Then again, they had just heard the news of their friend's murder.

"Talking of perverts," she said, "what's your response to what DS Harper just said? That, according to Tristan, Mark encouraged him to approach a young woman who was obviously underage?"

"No way that's true," Adam said. "Tell them, Phil." Phil dutifully shook his head. "He's talking out of his arse."

"Right." There was no point in pushing the matter with Phil acting as Adam's puppet.

"You know what, maybe it's those three you should be investigating for Mark's murder. They've got extremist views. Maybe they went after Mark because of the lies Kylie Bright told them about him." Adam looked supremely pleased with himself for coming up with this theory. "You could start with speaking to Kylie."

"Kylie's dead." Steph looked Adam in the eye. "She was murdered."

"What the fuck?" Phil exclaimed, hands to his head.

"So, what are you doing here?" Adam's *sang-froid* was slightly unnerving. "When you could be out looking for real suspects."

"Oh, believe me, we are looking for 'real' suspects," Steph said. "Can the pair of you confirm your whereabouts last night?"

"We were both here. Our flatmate can vouch for us. We were gaming into the early hours."

"Is your flatmate in?" He was. They called him down and he backed them up.

"I think that's all for now. Just one more thing, have either of you heard of Ryan Brown?" They shook their heads. Steph looked at Elias. He had no other questions. "Right. That's all then. We'll be in touch."

They saw themselves out and walked back to Monks Road.

"Adam's arrogance got me riled," Steph admitted "They got to you, too, I think."

"I told you, I was brought up by women," Elias said. "If there's one thing I've learned, it's to be able to view men from a woman's perspective. And that there's more than one way of being a man."

"That's two things."

Elias smiled. "Actually, they taught me almost everything I know. Look, I just don't want you thinking I'm like that pair back there."

"Okay. I haven't known you very long, but I picked up straightaway that you weren't like a lot of men I've met. You have respect for women."

"It's what I'm used to," Elias said. "The women who brought me up taught me respect, and that I didn't need to conform to traditional male stereotypes in order to be a 'real' man."

"You're so woke."

"I do my best." They exchanged a smile.

Fearing they might actually start bonding, Steph reverted to the case. "Sounds like Adam and co. had some pretty dissatisfied customers, doesn't it? Doesn't say much for their skill as trainers."

"Hmm. They probably watched a few videos on YouTube and fancied themselves ideally suited to the job. Hashed together a pep talk and assumed the bootcamp would be a piece of cake. Coaching pick-up skills probably seemed a more attractive proposition than getting a proper job to supplement their student finances. Mind you, I got the impression that Phil's heart wasn't really in it. Adam, not so much. He's a cool customer."

"I agree. So, what did you think of Adam's insinuation that Lottie and friends could have murdered Mark?"

"Somewhat far-fetched. I think it was a feeble attempt to bounce the blame elsewhere, but I also think we need to seriously consider that these murders are linked in some way. There's the number of connections between Lottie and her friends, and the fact that Mark Ripley was a member of Adam's little gang. Then there's Ryan Brown, although none of them claims to have heard of him."

He didn't mention Jane Bell, Steph noted, but she was another link in the chain, it seemed. "Maybe we need to find out if there's anything else Jane Bell knows that she's not telling us about. If she'd told us about Kylie sooner, we'd have connected her to Mark sooner."

"Do you really think so?" Elias's tone was borderline insubordinate. And he'd omitted to say 'boss.'

Steph didn't comment. She wasn't confident she could justify her claim. Whatever bonding may have taken place between them earlier had gone.

CHAPTER SEVENTEEN

A trawl of the usual databases had failed to find a suitable match for Ronan Cox. Which led Elias to state the obvious at the team briefing. "He must have given a false name to Ripley and his friends."

A murmur of amusement rippled around the room, a "You don't say?" and the predictable, "Nice work, Sherlock," until Steph brought them to order.

"All right, that's enough, you lot. Get back to work."

They needed to interview Ronan Cox. An interview with Ryan Brown had yielded no new information. Ryan hadn't known Mark, Adam or any of their crowd. He'd never heard of Ronan Cox, and he had a solid alibi for the time of both murders.

PC Fairbairn had been in touch with the restaurant Kylie and Ryan had visited on the night of Ryan's attack. Frustratingly, they'd deleted their CCTV footage of that evening before the recommended thirty days.

Adam Eades had given the police a list of the pick-up group's clients. The pair claimed only to have organised three bootcamps in all. There had been three or four clients per bootcamp. They had already interviewed Tristan Morley, but there were a number of others to track down. Steph was most interested in the ones who had been in the same group as Cox. She elected to interview these, accompanied by Elias. The rest she assigned to other members of the team.

The first man they interviewed was another student, Scott Brocklehurst, shortish, overweight, diffident. In a roomful of people, he would be the one no one remembered. He remembered Ronan Cox.

"He started to get agitated after he'd approached two women in a row and they basically ignored him. That was when he got sort of jittery, like he couldn't keep still. Maybe he was on drugs or something. I thought afterwards that maybe he was just bursting with frustration and had to keep moving to contain it." He added an unfortunate after-thought. "Couldn't really blame him though. Those women were disrespectful."

"How so?" Steph asked.

Brocklehurst shrugged. "They just thought they were too good to talk to us. I'd have thought they'd be all over Ronan, mind. He was the type women usually go for. You know, big, muscly, but I guess he did come across as a bit aggressive. Maybe they sensed that about him."

"How do you know what their thoughts were? Maybe they were on an errand from work and didn't have time to stop. Maybe they just wanted to get on with their daily lives without being harassed." Steph wondered if it had ever occurred to Scott that a woman had a right to go about her everyday business without being pestered by predatory men.

"He only asked them for directions."

Oh Please. "Do you know how many times men have stopped me in the street to ask for directions and then pressed me for my phone number?"

"That's a compliment, isn't it?" Scott said. He'd missed her point entirely.

Elias said, "What happened on his third attempt?"

"Well, he went up to this woman and politely asked if she could give him directions to the train station. It was obvious she didn't want to stop, but at the last moment, she did. She told him how to get there, then he said something else to her and she shook her head and just started to walk away."

How dare she? Steph felt a surge of anger towards these men and their sense of entitlement. What on earth was disrespectful in not wanting to hang around talking to a complete stranger who'd accosted you on the street? Only her training and her sense of professionalism prevented her from showing Scott the true meaning of disrespect.

"What did he say to her? Was he using a script he'd rehearsed beforehand?" Elias asked.

"Yes. He was supposed to tell her she had pretty hair, I think, but I didn't hear what he actually said."

"What happened next?"

"Ronan called after her. Again, I didn't catch what he said, but she looked angry. She turned around, and I think she said something back. That's when Ronan grabbed her by the arm."

Eades and Adam had made no mention of this. "Roughly?" Steph said.

"Maybe a bit. Yeah, probably. I would say so, yes."

"Then what happened?" Elias asked.

"That's when it turned a bit nastier. She tried to shake him off. I think she told him he was hurting her, but he wouldn't let go. He started calling her names."

"What names?"

"You know, like 'Stuck-up bitch.' I don't know, whore, maybe. Other things." He looked uncomfortable. "I didn't approve of that, just so's you know."

"Right. Was that when Mark intervened?"

"Yes. Ronan had gone way off script. You're not supposed to do that, even if the woman disrespects you."

At least some standards had been set. Steph almost laughed. "And Ronan was aggressive to Mark?"

"A bit. He didn't get much chance though. Mark grappled with him. I guess he thought Ronan might go for the girl. Adam and Phil helped. They held Ronan until he got himself under control. It took a while. Then they told him they were chucking him off the course."

"So, Ronan didn't return to the group for the follow-up session?"

"No. I never saw him after that."

"Never? You haven't seen him around town any time?"

"No." He looked suddenly appalled. "You think he was the one who killed Mark? Is that why you're asking me all these questions?" Scott was a slow processor.

"We're interested in speaking with people who knew Mark, that's all. Ronan wasn't his real name. Did you know that? Did you ever hear him refer to himself by any other name?"

"No. I didn't talk to him much. We were at the presentation, then we went out in the field. There wasn't a lot of opportunity to get to know one another. And, like I said, he wasn't at the debriefing."

"Is there anything you remember about him that stands out? About his physical appearance or his personality?"

"Not really. He was just ordinary. Good physique, like I said. I'm not good with faces." Scott was silent for a moment, before adding, "Not sure what he was doing on the course, really. He seemed more confident than me and the other guy. And he was okay looking. Just had an aggressive nature, I suppose. Way he went after that woman, I wouldn't be surprised if he was the type to beat a woman up in a relationship. He really took it badly being talked back to."

Steph nodded. "What was your impression of Adam, Phil and Mark, and their course?"

"I thought it was all kind of lame. Their advice was pretty obvious, the sort of thing I could have worked out for myself. I'm basically a shy person. No amount of coaching is going to change that." He didn't quite meet Steph's eyes. "What you said about women having a right to go about their daily lives without being pestered by men trying to hit on them, I never thought about it that way before."

There was hope for him then, Steph thought. "Good. I hope you'll remember it in future. Besides you and Ronan, there was a third client on the course that day. What do you remember about him?"

"His name was Jake Flood, I think. He wasn't a student. That's all, really. Like I said, we didn't talk that much. I thought the same about him as I did about Ronan Cox, or whatever his name is. He wasn't bad looking, and he seemed confident enough. I wouldn't have thought he'd have that much trouble approaching women."

Steph wondered if she should tell Scott he wasn't bad looking either, but the moment passed. Instead, she thanked him for his time.

"Easy to see why Adam and his cronies saw poor Scott as perfect recruitment fodder," Elias remarked when they were out of earshot. "Low self-esteem, shy and unconfident. He was ripe for exploiting. Interesting that he didn't see things from the woman's point of view until you pointed it out to him. That's the thing with these pick-up gurus. They teach men that women enjoy being hit on, that it makes them feel good about themselves, therefore men shouldn't feel bad about it. More than that, they preach that it's men's right to do it. They don't stop to consider it from the woman's perspective."

Steph nodded. "All about perspective, isn't it? What some men see as harmless chatting up, women may consider harassment. The worst thing is, it makes men think of it as their entitlement. You know it's the women who end up feeling bad when a man makes an unwelcome comment or approach? They have to invent an excuse like, 'Sorry, I've already got a boyfriend.' Or 'Sorry, I'm in a hurry,' as though they owe these men an excuse, or even an apology for not wanting to engage with them. How stupid is that?"

"Hmm. You're right. My sister has experienced that kind of thing many times. I read *The Game* when I was a teenager," Elias said. "It was my sister who gave it to me. She told me to read it so I'd learn how not to treat women. Forget about learning tricks to impress women, she said. The only strategy you need when it comes to succeeding with them is to be respectful."

"Your sister is a wise woman."

Elias had been referring to the internationally bestselling book by the American author, Neil Strauss. Published in 2005, it had introduced a generation of young men to the world of pick-up artistry. The problem was that the Internet had enabled a darker variety of pick-up ideology to evolve and proliferate.

Steph pondered a moment. "Are you familiar with the word Incel?"

"A very nasty lot," Elias said.

"Yes." Beginning in the early nineties Incels, or involuntary celibates as they styled themselves, had been expressing their frustrations over their lack of access to sex in dark regions of the Internet. Mostly men, they blamed women for their predicament, complaining that the vast majority of women were attracted to a very small percentage of the most attractive men. The Incel community was associated with misogyny and at its most extreme, violence towards women, and towards the 'alpha' males who could have any woman they desired.

"Nasty doesn't begin to describe them," Steph said. "You touched on this sort of thing before, didn't you, when you suggested our killer might be an unconfident male who targets both the women who reject him, and the alphas, men like Mark, who get to have their pick of women. If our perp spent a lot of time in forums where Incel-like beliefs were circulating, his own beliefs would have been affirmed and reinforced. These forums are basically echo chambers. He would come to believe all the bullshit they espouse. He would be likely to believe that he wasn't to blame for his lack of success with women, but that it was the fault of modern, liberated women who have agency over their sex lives and who can make choices about who they want to date. If our killer fits this type of profile it would explain why he killed both Mark and Kylie. And committing murder would be a sure way of attracting attention to his cause."

Elias frowned. "I hope you're not suggesting we might be looking at an Elliot Rodger scenario here."

In 2014, Elliot Rodger had become a hero of the Incel community after he killed six people and injured fourteen others in California. Tragically, he had inspired others to follow his example.

Grim-faced, Steph said, "Jesus, Elias. Let's hope not."

CHAPTER EIGHTEEN

The news of her suspension sent Jane into a spiral of guilt. She'd exceeded her authority as a special by involving herself in a murder investigation, and her actions might well have contributed to the death of a young woman. DI Warwick was right to have her suspended before she could do any more harm.

She'd had a call from Allie the morning after Yvonne's party, asking if everything was okay. Jane knew she was desperate to hear why the police had wanted to talk with her, so she'd told her friend about Kylie's murder.

She didn't tell Allie about her suspension. Thankfully, Allie hadn't asked too many questions.

Jane couldn't help wondering whether DI Warwick and DS Harper had spoken with Ryan Brown yet. Had Ryan and Kylie gone on a date? She felt a stab of sadness for Ryan's loss. Another person whose life she had potentially ruined. To add to his trials, poor Ryan would probably be counted as a suspect.

Still, there was a small part of her that harboured some hope that she wasn't responsible for what had happened to Kylie. It was possible that Kylie had never tracked down the man who harassed her in the restaurant, that even if she had, he had nothing to do with her murder.

There was also another possibility. Perhaps it wasn't merely coincidence that the man had been in the restaurant at the same time as Kylie that day. He could have been stalking her and it might well have enraged him to see Ryan succeed in connecting with her. He'd gone after Ryan, and then Kylie. In that scenario, Jane couldn't be blamed for Kylie's death. She sighed. She was clutching at straws. Anything but face the fact that she'd made a serious error of judgement.

With Kylie dead, Jane could see no way of discovering the identity of the man in the Chinese buffet. She assumed that the police would have looked at CCTV footage of the time Kylie spent there. She wondered how else DI Warwick might proceed. By questioning Kylie's friends, putting together a picture of her movements, her behaviour, her contacts over the past few weeks. Looking for patterns. Making connections. She envied Warwick's freedom of access to people and resources.

Becoming a special had awakened unexpected feelings of frustration about the choices she had made. She'd been born in the seventies to working-class parents who had grown up in the forties. Their attitude to the value of education for girls mirrored that of their parents' generation — it was a waste of time. When Jane had broached the possibility of going to university with them, she'd met with resistance. Her choice of teaching as a career was just about acceptable. At least it was a respectable enough job for a woman.

Bloody hell! She really must be feeling sorry for herself if she'd started blaming her parents. She'd got a lot out of her career as a teacher, and it wasn't as if she couldn't have switched jobs at some point in her life. It was just . . . sometimes she worried that she'd let her mum and dad emotionally blackmail her into choosing a career they approved of. She wished she'd taken more time to think about what else she might have done. At least she hadn't perpetuated this brand of sexism in the family. Norah had been given free rein to do whatever she wanted in life.

But she had to put all that aside for now. She was due at Thea's for a lesson.

By the time she arrived at Thea's house, Jane's mood was a little more upbeat. "Parents still away?" she asked when she saw that Thea was alone.

"Yes. No idea when they're coming back. It doesn't matter though. Imagine how many teenagers would love to have a house this size to themselves. Stacey keeps saying I should have a party." She grinned.

But Thea's cheeriness seemed feigned. She looked tired. She was still wearing her pyjamas under a jumper that looked much too big.

"Have you had any breakfast?" Jane asked.

"Not yet. I'll just get dressed, and then I'll make us some coffee."

"I'll make the coffee. You go and get dressed."

Thea returned wearing black leggings and a pink fleecy hoodie. She went straight to the fridge, took out a carton of milk and placed it on the island. "I'll just have a quick bowl of cereal if you don't mind. I'm up to date with the work you left last time and I've already gone through a couple of practice papers, so it doesn't matter if we don't start right on time."

"Did you sleep in?" Surely Pearl and Buddy must have demanded their early morning walk?

"I went back to bed after taking the mutts for a walk. I stayed up late last night binge-watching *The Walking Dead*. Have you seen it?"

Jane smiled. "I don't share your obsession with zombies, remember?"

"Come on, Jane. Everybody loves a zombie." Thea had given Jane a copy of *Pride and Prejudice and Zombies* for Christmas. She'd rather enjoyed it. Jane thought Thea herself looked a bit zombie-like this morning. She hoped she was just tired and not coming down with something.

"So, have you been to see Adam Eades and Phil Lavin yet?"

It was inevitable that she would ask. Jane considered telling Thea about her suspension, then changed her mind. It would involve revealing more details about the case, and about Kylie's murder. Thea would probably have heard about Kylie by now, but Jane didn't want her to make any connections between Kylie's murder and Mark's.

"No. It's not my job. I'm only a volunteer. It's up to the detectives on the investigation to do that."

"But you've told them about Adam and Phil being friends of Mark's? Did you tell them I put you on to them?"

"They know about Adam and Phil." Jane was certain that by now they must have checked out Mark's friends. "They didn't need me to tell them."

Thea studied her spoonful of muesli before conveying it to her mouth. "Don't go berserk when I tell you this, right?"

"Tell me what?"

"So, Stacey and I have been doing a bit of research on those two."

"Thea!" Jane's heart sank. Was she guilty of putting Thea in danger too?

"Don't worry. We haven't put ourselves at any risk. Stacey's big sister, Karina, is in her second year at the uni. Stacey asked her if she could find out more about them from her friends."

Was it wrong that she was eager to hear what Thea had to report? She hadn't encouraged her to do this and would have forbidden it if she'd known.

Thea took a few more mouthfuls of her cereal, as if giving Jane time to assimilate what she'd just told her. Then she said, "Karina had heard of them through a friend she'd met at one of the societies she joined. Her name is Ivy Cross."

She set her bowl aside and leaned across the granite-topped island, lowering her voice, though only Buddy and Pearl were around to hear. Judging by their snores, they weren't in the least interested.

"It turns out that Adam, Phil and the late Mark Ripley ran a sort of group for men, coaching them on how to go about hitting on girls."

"Okaaay."

"Ivy's boyfriend, Tristan, was one of their ex-clients. He told Ivy about it. Apparently, when they took their students on a walkabout to practice hitting on women, Mark would demonstrate how to approach girls and get their phone numbers. Then the clients would have a go. According to Tristan, Mark encouraged him to stop a girl who was obviously underage, so Tristan walked off in disgust."

Thea leaned back again. "Remember what I told you about that time Stacey and I were in the café at the sport's club, and we saw Mark with his friends?"

"Yes."

"I didn't tell you that we were goofing around, being silly and trying to attract their attention. Mark was the only one who took any notice. The other two ignored us. Probably thought we were just a pair of silly schoolgirls."

"I remember you saying that he winked at you."

"Yeah, well, he did more than that. I didn't tell you at the time because you went all protective on me."

"What did he do?"

"He came over and spoke to us while his mates were talking to one of the staff. He asked us if we'd like to meet him later, go round to his place for drinks. Of course, we didn't take him up on it. Mind you, Stacey might have been game if I hadn't been there."

Jane was silent. "Anyway," Thea said, "back to what Karina found out. Apparently, Tristan was uncomfortable with a lot of other stuff Mark and his friends recommended. He'd joined the group because he wanted to boost his confidence but he wasn't at all impressed with what was actually going on. He realised pretty fast that Mark and his mates were all about tricking girls into having sex with them."

Thea pulled her bowl back towards her. She held it in one hand while spooning cereal into her mouth with the other. She ate quickly, ravenously almost. It made Jane wonder how long it had been since she'd eaten a proper meal. Thea looked at her over the rim of the bowl.

"Your friend Stacey is certainly a useful person to know," Jane said.

"There's more," Thea said, swapping bowl for coffee cup. "You know that student who was murdered the other day?"

"Kylie Bright." Jane couldn't keep the sadness from her voice.

"Yes, Kylie. Karina told Stacey that Ivy's friend, Lottie, told Ivy that Mark Ripley bullied Kylie into having sex with him!"

Jane tracked the confusing chain of people in her head. Was there any hint of truth here, or was it all just rumour, Chinese whispers?

"So, what do you make of that, Special Constable Jane Bell?"

To Jane it suggested that there was some sort of connection between the murders of Mark Ripley and Kylie Bright. But how to make sense of that knowledge? It seemed an impossible task.

Not for Thea. "So, here's what I think. Kylie either killed Mark or had him killed in revenge. Maybe she just meant to teach him a lesson, you know, get him roughed up a bit, but it went too far. Then Mark's friends found out what Kylie had done and murdered her in revenge." Her eyes gleamed. "What do you think?"

"Neat," Jane said.

Thea looked disappointed. "You're not convinced, are you?"

"I don't know what to think," Jane said. "Presumably you need to go at a thing like this from all possible angles to avoid pursuing a single theory down an ever-narrowing tunnel."

"Maybe. Anyway, that's my theory, for what it's worth."

After the lesson, Jane again asked Thea if she minded her parents being absent for so long. Thea's answer was the same.

"Of course not. I'm not a little kid. They shouldn't feel they have to stay home and look after me all the time. Besides, it's cool having the house to myself."

Again, despite her upbeat tone, Jane couldn't help thinking that Thea wasn't being quite honest. She'd all but said previously that her parents had been neglectful when she was younger.

But she needn't poke her nose in. She was a private tutor now. It was no longer in her job description to double up as a social worker. Except, old habits die hard. Moreover, people always said she was a caring soul. That's why she reminded Thea to contact her if she needed her — any time, for any reason.

Later, Jane mulled over what she'd learned from Thea over a glass of wine. She dismissed Thea's theory that Kylie had killed Mark. She wondered how the attack on Ryan Brown fitted in with the two murders, if at all. She wished she'd asked Ryan if he'd known Mark and his friends.

She was aware that she had to be wary of making the facts fit the theory. Starting with a hypothesis was fair enough, so long as you subjected it to rigorous testing. She had no reason to connect Ryan Brown with Mark Ripley. She sighed. *I'm such an amateur at all of this. Maybe I need to leave it to the professionals.*

Her thoughts were interrupted by a knock at the door. DI Warwick was the last person she expected to see standing on her doorstep. For a few moments, the two women stared at each other, eyes reflecting their mutual distrust.

"Would you like to come in?" Jane asked at last. She looked over Warwick's shoulder for her sidekick, DS Harper, but Warwick was alone.

"If it's convenient."

"I was supposed to be on duty later but seeing as how you've put paid to that . . ." Jane trailed off, aware that she needed to swallow her pride and apologise.

"Look," she went on, "I know I shouldn't have agreed to Kylie trying to find out about the man who harassed her." *I did caution her not to approach him.* It was tempting to say the words aloud, but Jane sensed it was better not to try and justify her behaviour. Warwick didn't seem the type to accept half measures, nothing less than a full admission of guilt would suffice. Maybe she should prostrate herself before her and beg forgiveness?

"Damn right you shouldn't. You put a member of the public at risk. That's unforgiveable. No doubt they'll put it down to a rookie mistake. Better incompetents on the streets than no one at all seems to be the policy these days." Warwick cleared her throat. "Anyway, that's not what I'm here about."

Jane led the way into the kitchen. Warwick went straight to the window and looked out at the garden. "That where you were attacked?" She nodded at the wheelie bins.

"Yes."

"Lucky your neighbour was around."

"Oh, it was Dudgeon really. He was the actual hero. Dudge is Allie's Staffie," Jane said.

"Right. I've read the report. And nothing was stolen from your home."

"No. I think that was because Dudge scared my attacker off with his barking."

"Perhaps."

"You aren't still thinking my attack had something to do with my special constable duties, are you?" Jane asked.

"What do you think?"

"I think it unlikely."

"That's what I thought at first. Before I found out that you were playing amateur detective. Who knows what other damage you've done. How many other boats you've rocked."

Jane took it on the chin and kept her mouth shut. It wasn't easy.

"So, is there anything else you haven't told me? Anything else you've discovered through your amateur sleuthing?"

The silence went on too long for Jane to claim she knew nothing more.

Warwick sat down, uninvited, on one of Jane's kitchen chairs. "Well, are you going to tell me?"

"I've discovered that Kylie Bright was bullied by Mark Ripley. He coerced her into having sex with him." She had the satisfaction of seeing Warwick raise an eyebrow, the closest she'd come so far to betraying any feeling besides annoyance.

"Yes, we know about that. How did you find out?"

"I . . . through a friend." Too late, Jane realised Warwick would understand that she had again withheld information. "I should have mentioned that a friend of mine recognised Mark Ripley from his photograph in the local paper. She'd seen him with two of his friends at the fitness club on Outer Circle Road, Hi! To Fitness. She and her friend were in the café at the club and they flirted with Mark and his friends. Mark was the only one who responded. He didn't seem to mind that they were a bit young. She also found out that Mark Ripley and these friends — Adam Eades and Phil Lavin — ran a group coaching unconfident men on how to hit on girls. I only found that bit out this morning."

Jane expected another rebuke. Warwick's silence was unsettling.

"Well well," she said at last. "You have been busy. Go on."

"That's it, really."

"What about theories? Do you have any?"

Jane was taken aback. She hadn't expected to be asked her opinion. She was immediately suspicious. "I'm reluctant to draw any conclusions, but I can't help feeling that it must be more than coincidence that Kylie and Mark knew each other, and now they're both dead."

Warwick mumbled something that Jane couldn't make out. Something sarcastic, no doubt.

"I thought that the attack on Ryan Brown might have been perpetrated by the man who harassed Kylie in the restaurant, and that he might also have killed Mark, but I realise that's probably just me making connections where none exist. Just because both of them knew Kylie didn't mean it was significant. Kylie and Ryan had only just connected, after all."

She felt that she was rambling. She expected to see a gloating look on Warwick's face, but instead she was surprised to see the DI looking at her with something resembling respect. A momentary illusion, obviously.

"How exactly did your friend learn about the pick-up group?" Warwick asked, stone-faced again.

"From her friend's sister who's at Lincoln University. My friend's name is Thea Martin. She's actually one of my students. I'm an English tutor."

"Yes, I know."

She's been checking up on me. "Thea's friend, Stacey, asked her sister to see what she could find out about Adam and Phil." Jane paused, adding, "I didn't ask Thea do to that."

Warwick ignored Jane's claim. "You seem to have recruited a legion of young women to do your snooping for you." She let her remark sink in before saying, "What else?"

"Nothing. That's all I know.

"Are you sure?"

Warwick got up and stepped forward, trespassing on Jane's personal space. "No more private investigating. Our job is difficult enough without bloody amateurs putting good, solid police work at risk. Understood?"

At least she didn't point her finger, but Jane imagined it stabbing at her chest. One stab for each word. "Yes."

"Good."

Jane was sure she would go then, but Warwick lingered. *What does she want? A cup of bloody tea? A glass of wine? Well, she can sing for it.*

Warwick looked around the pleasant kitchen. "Nice place you have here." She leaned closer, suddenly fierce. "You have all this, a successful career, a family. Why do you still want more? Your meddling probably cost that young woman her life. If you'd told me about Kylie sooner, mentioned Eades and Lavin . . ."

Once more, Jane was taken aback. She stared at Warwick, speechless. Their eyes locked. Warwick's glinted with anger. Jane wondered what Warwick saw in hers. Anger, undoubtedly. But also puzzlement.

Their stare lengthened. For the first time, Jane saw what Frieda had meant when she described Warwick as 'vulnerable.' Frieda was right about her brittleness too. Warwick maintained the stare, but she was edgy as hell. What was she afraid of Jane seeing in those striking green eyes?

Suddenly, Jane thought she understood. Warwick's arrogance, her aloofness, everything that made up her hard-as-nails persona came from a place of deep pain. As soon as she intuited this, she looked away. Out of pity.

Warwick probably misinterpreted her surrender as weakness. Much as she knew she should hold her tongue, Jane let the words slip out.

"I feel sorry for you."

The atmosphere, already charged, became incendiary. For a moment, Jane thought that Warwick was going to slap her across the face. She took a step away.

But Warwick brought herself under control. She turned, stormed off down the hallway, slammed the door behind her. Jane waited until she saw the DI's legs pass her kitchen window before heaving a sigh of relief.

CHAPTER NINETEEN

Jake Flood lived with his parents. Their house, a mile from the nearest village, was set back from a quiet country road, concealed from view behind a tall yew hedge.

His mother directed Steph and Elias to the garage. "He's converted it into a sort of den for himself."

The garage was at the end of a path running alongside the house. Steph looked through a window and saw a bare-foot, bare-chested young man in silky red shorts and red boxing gloves laying into a free-standing yellow punch bag.

"See anything?" Elias asked.

"Skinny kid beating up a big yellow penis."

Jake started when they stepped into his view. For a couple of moments, the punch bag swayed between them like a silent, accusing metronome, before Jake stilled it with a gloved hand.

"Jake Flood?" Steph asked.

"That's me." He eyed them with distrust.

"I'm Detective Inspector Warwick and this is my colleague, Detective Sergeant Harper. Okay if we have a word?"

"What about?"

"It's concerning a murder we're investigating."

Jake's jaw dropped. "A murder?" He began untying his boxing gloves. Once his hands were free, he grabbed a T-shirt and pulled it over his head. The thin material clung to his sweat-soaked torso. Steph wondered why he hadn't dried himself off a bit first.

"You recently paid some students at the university for coaching on techniques to help you become successful with women. Is that right, Jake?" she said.

Jake reddened. Like Scott Brocklehurst, he seemed shy and unconfident.

"Yeah. Oh, I get what you're here about. That student who was murdered on Greestone Stairs, right?"

"Yes. Mark Ripley. Did you realise you'd met him when you heard the story?"

"I knew him as one of the blokes who ran the course I went on, yeah. I don't know anything about his murder. I was at home the night it happened. In my bedroom playing a new game. Ask my mum and dad."

Steph nodded. "We will. I need to ask you some questions about the 'bootcamp' you went on. What do you remember about the other two lads who were with you?"

"Adam and Phil?"

"No, I'm talking about the other clients, Scott Brocklehurst and Ronan Cox."

"I didn't speak much to either of them really. Scott seemed okay. Ronan was a bit of a psycho."

"How so?"

"He went for a girl. She ignored him, and he got really mad. Mark, Adam and Phil had to stop him before he did her some harm. He went for Mark too. He got chucked off the course, and rightly so."

Steph couldn't help noticing the difference between Jake and Scott's attitude to how the young woman had been treated. Jake made no attempt to blame the woman or condone Cox's behaviour.

"Ronan Cox was an invented name. Did you hear him refer to himself any other way? What do you remember about him, Jake? We're trying to trace him," she said.

Sweat trickled down Jake's forehead. He reached for a towel, wiped his brow, then draped it around his neck. "What, apart from the fact that he was a complete dickhead?" He thought for a moment. "He was about five ten or eleven. Muscly. Brownish hair. I think the girls he approached could tell there was something off about him."

"What makes you say that?"

"Just a hunch, really. Mark stopped a couple of girls first, just to show us how to go about it, then the other lad, Scott, and I had a go. We didn't get any phone numbers but at least the girls stopped to answer our initial question. With Ronan, they sort of shied away. If you ask me, I think he was overconfident and put them off." Jake shrugged. He said, rather generously to Steph's mind, "Maybe he was nervous. He did seem edgy. Scott thought he was on drugs. Maybe he was stressed out about it all and that's why he kicked off the way he did."

No, you were right the first time. He was a dickhead. Steph signalled to Elias to take over.

"There was another murder last week, Jake. A young woman by the name of Kylie Bright," Elias said.

"I know. I read about it. She was a student too, wasn't she?"

"Yes. Did you know her?"

"No, and I was here the night she was murdered as well. I play most nights, usually online. I don't know many other students, not female ones anyway." His expression saddened. "Don't know many girls full stop."

"You'll meet the right one, one of these days," Elias said, gently.

Jake brightened. "I hope so. My mum and dad didn't get together until they were in their thirties. Neither of them had had partners beforehand, they were both too shy. They got engaged a week after they met. Been married twenty-four years now. Tell you something, mind. I'm not going to pester any more women in the street. I never felt right about doing that."

"Good man," Elias said. They left him to his punch bag.

"Interesting what he said about women seeming to sense that Cox was bad news, wasn't it? Pity I . . ." Steph checked herself. *Pity I never had that gift. I might have seen Cal coming.*

"Pity you, what?" Elias said. His eyes were on the road, but Steph sensed his curiosity.

"Pity he hasn't got a girlfriend," she said. "He seemed like a nice lad, under all the shyness."

"People aren't always how they appear," Elias said. His head turned fractionally in her direction. Steph looked ahead.

* * *

It was late in the evening. Steph was thinking back to her first encounter with Cal. She'd been lying on the beach wearing a skimpy red bikini that her friend Marketa had encouraged her to buy the day before they jetted off for their week in the sun.

"Two hunks at twelve o'clock," Marketa whispered. Reluctantly, Steph raised her head. She'd come to Corfu to recharge her batteries, not for a holiday romance. She propped herself up on her elbows, dipped her head to look over her sunglasses and saw . . . two Greek gods emerging from the waves, tanned and golden.

"OMG," she said under her breath. Marketa giggled.

Their names were Cal and Jay. Close up, out of the sun's radiance, they weren't god-like at all, just two moderately good-looking Mancunian blokes with fair hair and lean, tanned bodies.

Cal and Jay had stopped to say 'Hi,' and they'd all ended up having drinks in the bar at the hotel where Steph and Marketa were staying. Afternoon blended into evening, and it was midnight before they parted company.

Right from the start, there was a mutual attraction between Steph and Cal. Jay and Marketa, not so much. They played along for a couple of days, but soon the foursome fizzled out. Steph wanted to spend time alone with Cal, but she didn't want to abandon Marketa. It was Marketa who assured her that, though she and Jay weren't attracted to each other, they were happy to keep each other company and give their friends space for their romance to blossom.

Steph and Cal were inseparable for the last three days of the holiday. The boys were staying on in Corfu for another week. All the following week, Steph worried that Cal would take up with someone else as soon as she boarded her flight home. She reminded herself that she hadn't gone on holiday to fall in love. Better to enjoy the memory of the fun days she'd spent with Cal, even as she forgot all about him. Later, she wished she'd followed her own advice.

Cal had turned up at her door with a huge bunch of red roses and a bottle of champagne the day after he arrived back in England. She'd been so delighted to see him that she hadn't stopped to wonder how he'd found out her address. She'd only given him her mobile number. She never overlooked something so basic again. At the time, she was twenty years old and worked in a bank. She hadn't started thinking like a detective yet.

Almost from the start, Cal began to spend most nights at the flat she shared with Marketa in Manchester. When Marketa pointed out that maybe their relationship was moving a bit too fast, Steph accused her of being jealous. Cal agreed. In fact, Cal had put the idea in Steph's head, something Steph didn't appreciate until after Marketa moved out and she was alone with Cal, who gradually began to reveal his true nature.

Again with hindsight, she could see how she'd overlooked the subtle ways in which Cal set about subverting her relationship with Marketa. Marketa was too possessive of her, she was a bad flatmate. She never did her fair share of the chores, she was pinching food from Steph's shelf in the fridge, borrowing her make-up and trying on her clothes when she was out. He claimed he'd heard Marketa on her phone, talking about Steph behind her back. Saying spiteful things about her to her other friends.

All these accusations and insinuations built up to a terrible day of reckoning. Steph returned home from work to find Cal with angry scratch marks on his cheek, which he claimed Marketa had made when he rejected her blatantly sexual advances.

"You should have seen her, Steph. She was like a wildcat. She wants me, Steph. Always has. Jay said she told him she fancied me right from the start, but you bulldozed her chances of getting off with me. She hates you, Steph."

Marketa denied scratching Cal, or that she'd ever fancied him. "Can't you see what he's doing, Steph? He can't stand you being friends with me. He wants you all to himself. Can't you see he's one of those men who needs to have total control over the people around him, and especially his partner?"

Steph didn't see. She covered her ears, closed her mind. She was infatuated with Cal. He was the love of her life. He would never harm her.

"Shut up. You're just jealous because Cal chose me instead of you."

"Is that what he told you? It's a lie, Steph. Come on, we've been friends for years, you've known him for six weeks. Think hard about who's more likely to be lying to you."

They'd argued late into the evening. Steph said things to her friend that could never be unsaid. Hateful things, fuelled by the lies that Cal had told her.

Marketa moved out the following day, leaving her share of the rent for the rest of the month in an envelope on the kitchen table. When Steph came down for breakfast, Cal was busy counting the notes to make sure it was all there. Steph, emotionally drained by the events of the night before, went off to take a shower. When she came back, the envelope was gone, the rent money with it. She never questioned Cal about its disappearance. The following day he moved in.

CHAPTER TWENTY

"I think I've found Ronan Cox."

Steph had just sat down at her desk. She stared at Elias. "What?"

"I might have—"

"I heard you. How?"

"A man by the name of Dominic Tickle was arrested on a domestic abuse charge a few of weeks ago. His victim, Holly Carpenter, recently gave her victim support officer some information she hadn't mentioned previously. Apparently, she hadn't considered it important, and in any case she'd forgotten about it."

"Yes, yes. Get to the point."

"When Holly first met Dominic Tickle, he told her his name was Ronan Cox."

"What? Seriously?"

"Yes. She found him out when she was in the pub with him one evening. A mate came up to him, greeted him as Dominic and started tickling him. He had to own up to Holly that his real name was Dominic Tickle. He told her he was thinking of changing it because he hated his surname.

"Who was Holly Carpenter's victim support officer?"

"DS Alby."

"Clair Alby?"

"Yes. Do you know her?"

"I worked with her on a couple of occasions when I was a DS over Boston way. She was a DC then. She's sharp. Did she contact you?"

"Yes. When she discovered we were trying to find out Cox's real identity."

"Right." Steph felt slightly irritated that Elias had been the one to receive this information first. But it was exciting news. "Good."

"You'll never believe who was one of the officers in attendance when Tickle was arrested."

"Jane Bell?"

"Yes."

Steph's irritation flared anew. "That bloody woman again. She seems to be everywhere."

"Tickle was charged and bailed to appear at court. I've got an address and place of work. I checked, and he's at work now."

"Well done," Steph said. "Let's go."

Tickle worked as a maintenance fitter for an engineering firm located just south of the city centre. His manager showed them into his office when they arrived. He was aware that Tickle had been charged with domestic abuse and was on bail, but he'd kept him on. He wanted to know if Tickle was in more trouble.

Steph advised him that they wished to question Tickle on a different matter but gave no details. The manager's expression suggested that his patience with his employee was running out.

Tickle hovered outside the door. The manager beckoned him in. The room had windows overlooking the shop floor and, before leaving them to it, he pulled the blind down.

"So, who are we talking to today?" Steph began. "Dominic Tickle, or Ronan Cox?" She waited. Tickle looked sullen. "Why the alias?"

Tickle shrugged.

"Mr Tickle it is then."

"I've already been questioned about the domestic," Tickle said. "What do you lot want now?"

"We're not here about your domestic abuse charge." Steph showed him a picture of Mark Ripley. "Recognise him?"

Tickle stared at the picture for a few moments. "Yeah. He's the dead guy."

"You knew him before he died, though, didn't you, Mr Tickle? We know that you attended a so-called 'bootcamp,' organised by Mark and two of his friends, Adam Eades and Phil Lavin."

"Waste of bloody time. And money."

"We've spoken to witnesses who've told us that you had to be restrained from assaulting a young woman who ignored you when you stopped her in the street."

"I never touched her."

"We have witnesses who've told us otherwise. You grabbed her arm and had to be restrained from harming her. Then you turned on Ripley."

"I never touched him either."

"Prefer hurting women, do you?" Elias said. Tickle glared at him.

Steph showed Tickle a picture of Kylie Bright. "Do you recognise this woman?"

"No. Never seen her before in my life. What am I supposed to have done to her then?"

"She was murdered too. A friend of hers, Ryan Brown, was assaulted. Ever heard of him?"

Tickle shook his head. "You're having a laugh, aren't you?"

"Do I look amused?" Steph asked dryly.

"Look, I work twelve-hour shifts at this place. How the hell am I supposed to find the time and energy to run around murdering everybody and their auntie?"

"We're going to need you to tell us what you were doing when Mark Ripley and Kylie Bright were murdered. And when Ryan Brown was assaulted."

"No problem."

Steph read out the dates. Tickle made a good show of thinking about it, before counting off his alibis on his fingers. "Pub quiz, worked a double shift, hospital procedure — I was kept in overnight." He named the pub and a couple of bar staff who could confirm that he'd been at the quiz.

"You can check with the guvnor what time my shift covered that night, and the hospital can confirm that I was admitted overnight after having my procedure."

Damn. If his alibis checked out, he'd be in the clear, and they'd be back to square one.

"I'm curious, Mr Tickle. Why did you enrol on the pick-up course? Do you have a problem attracting women?" Steph knew her question was provocative. She met Tickle's gaze and held it, though it made her feel deeply uncomfortable.

"No. Not in the slightest." Tickle flexed his arms. Beneath his overalls, his biceps bulged. "I thought it might be a good business venture for me, that's why. Thought I might pick up some tips on how to set myself up, but they were a bunch of idiots. Couldn't have organised a piss-up in a brewery."

"How did you find out about Mark and his friends' 'business' venture?"

"I overheard them talking about it in the changing room at the gym. Boasting about how many women they could pick up, and how they could put their skills and knowledge to use teaching saddos some of their secrets. I thought I could do that. Like I said, I have no problem attracting women."

Liar. They're afraid of you. Steph thought of what Jake Flood had said about women instinctively shying away from Tickle. Up close to him, she could appreciate why. Not that Tickle himself was aware of it. An ego as big as his wouldn't allow him to doubt himself.

"Perhaps," Elias said, "your money would have been better spent on a course in anger management, or a few sessions with a therapist specialising in treating abusive behaviours." That earned him another glare.

Steph noticed Tickle's fists curl. "Why did you get violent when that girl ignored you then, if you were only there to watch and learn?"

"Dunno. Maybe I just don't like being ignored."

"Hmm. Some other members of the group that day said that you seemed jittery. Had you taken something, Dominic?"

"No."

Steph shrugged, unconvinced. "I've read the statement given by the young woman you beat up at your house, Holly Carpenter. She says that you roughed her up because you thought she was cheating on you with her work colleague."

Tickle's eyes darkened. "She was, the little whore." Then, "We finished?"

Steph stood up and looked down on him. "Yes. For now."

* * *

Jane arrived at Thea's house and found her already waiting at the end of the long tree-lined drive. She was taking Thea to see a production of *The Winter's Tale* by a local amateur Shakespearean theatre group in a school hall not far from Veganbites. Jane had seen productions by this group before, most memorably an outdoor production of *A Midsummer Night's Dream* performed on a warm August evening in the grounds of Lincoln Castle.

On the way, she gave Thea a quick summary of the plot. When she'd finished, Thea commented, "So, basically it's about a misogynistic, jealous, prick who causes his own wife's death after falsely accusing her of getting pregnant with his best mate."

"In a nutshell." Jane smiled. She hadn't told Thea anything about the ending of the play.

"Can't wait." Thea's tone was mocking, but Jane knew she was looking forward to the outing. They'd watched Baz Luhrmann's *Romeo + Juliet* together and Thea had loved it.

She'd talked about going to London in the summer to see a play at the Globe. So, when this production was advertised, Jane had bought the tickets, thinking that she could go with Allie if Thea didn't fancy it. "Sorry it's not the Globe," she said, "but it's not a bad little venue."

They had good seats, giving an excellent view of the stage. Thea was obviously engrossed in the play right from the start.

Out of nowhere, the thought popped into Jane's head that it would have been nice to have been sitting here with Ed. She wondered if he liked Shakespeare. He liked books and reading. Perhaps she could invite him next time there was a production in town.

When a scene change interrupted the drama, Jane looked around the theatre, wondering if she'd see anyone she recognised. As her eyes scanned the rows near the back, they came to rest on a familiar, if not friendly, face. Jane scowled. What the hell was DI Warwick doing here? She hadn't struck Jane as a thespian. Was she stalking her now? Or spying on her, looking for evidence that she was still 'sticking her nose' into her investigation, despite having been suspended.

Jane turned away quickly. Had Warwick seen her? She hadn't seemed to, but Warwick wasn't the sort to miss anything — or anyone. She'd probably spotted Jane first, when she arrived with Thea, whom she'd probably assumed was one of the 'legions of young women' Jane had recruited to help run her own inquiry into the murders.

The setting for the next scene was in place. A prison. Paulina was asking for the queen's permission to take the newly born Perdita to King Leontes — *the misogynistic, jealous prick*, as Thea had rather aptly labelled him. It was hard to concentrate after seeing Warwick. Jane could feel the DI's hostile gaze burning her neck. She rubbed it furiously, prompting Thea to whisper, "Are you okay?"

At the interval, Jane worried that Thea would want a drink or an ice cream, which would necessitate getting out of their seats, thereby increasing her chance of encountering

Warwick. Thankfully, Thea seemed content to peruse the programme. Jane needed to pee but decided to cross her legs.

At the end of the play, they filed out of the hall. To Jane's great relief, Warwick had already vacated her seat. Thea asked one of the attendants if she could wait for the cast to come out. She wanted to have her programme signed. They were directed outside to the stage door, which was just an exit at the back of the school.

Jane hurried off to the toilet, saying she'd meet Thea outside. Thea was still waiting at the 'stage door' when she eventually joined her. She was talking to the only other person in the queue. Jane's heart sank when she saw who it was. She gave DI Warwick a brief, forced smile. It wasn't reciprocated.

"Hi, Jane, we were just talking about the ending of the play. I don't think Leontes deserved to have a happy ending," Thea said.

"I'd have locked him up and thrown away the key. Jealous, controlling men don't change," Warwick said. She turned to Jane. "What do you think?" It sounded like a challenge.

"Well, he did suffer years of guilt . . ." Jane began uncertainly, muttering words about atonement and redemption, feeling obliged to offer a different perspective. But she didn't want to go into a lengthy explanation of the complexities of Shakespeare's late romances in front of Warwick. Besides, she'd never felt much sympathy for Leontes either, so she agreed, "He was a bit of a dick."

Fortunately, at that moment the stage door opened, and two members of the cast stepped outside. They pretended to be overwhelmed by the crowd of three. One by one the cast came out and signed Thea's programme. Warwick stood to the side. Jane wondered why she was there, if it wasn't to congratulate the actors.

A young man appeared in the doorway. Jane didn't recognise him at first.

"Thanks for coming, boss," he said, addressing Warwick. It was her colleague DS Harper.

"No problem," Warwick said. "You're clearly wasted as a police officer."

Thea thrust her programme in front of him, and he signed, clearly delighted to be asked. Jane couldn't remember what part he'd played. It must have been very small.

On the way home, Thea talked non-stop about the play. "I thought it was going to be rubbish. I was sort of looking forward to it, but my expectations weren't very high. They're only a local amateur group, but they were really good, weren't they? Especially Florizel."

So, DS Harper had played Florizel? Jane wouldn't have known. His dark hair had been hidden under a curly blond wig.

"I might audition for a part in their next production. What do you think, Jane?" Thea had never expressed any interest in acting before she'd set eyes on DS Harper.

"I think that's a very good idea." She meant it. Thea was good at most things. Why not acting too?

Thea's house was in darkness when Jane dropped her off. "Will you be okay?" It seemed rather sad for a sixteen-year-old to be returning alone to a big, empty house this late in the evening.

"Why wouldn't I be? I've got Buddy and Pearl for company. They'll be dying for a walk."

"Any news about when your parents are coming back, Thea? Have you heard from them this week?"

Thea shrugged. "They'll be gone for at least another two weeks."

Jane noticed that Thea avoided looking at her when she said this. Did she always do that? She was always a bit flippant whenever Jane asked about her parents. Could her flippancy be a cover for evasion?

The Martins paid Jane monthly by bank transfer. Jane had had no direct dealings with them since before they'd departed, which was a bit unusual. Most parents wanted regular updates on their child's progress.

"I'd like to speak with your mum or dad, let them know how you're coming along. Do you think you could give me a mobile number for them?" Jane had tried the landline number she'd been given by Thea's mother, but no one answered or bothered to call back.

Thea hesitated, but only a beat. "Sure. Next time you come round. I need to let the dogs out now. Goodnight, Jane." And she was off.

On the drive home, thoughts about the play intermingled with thoughts about the events of the past few weeks. It seemed apt that she'd just watched a play about a jealous, controlling man.

These days she couldn't seem to get away from misogynistic men who sought to deny women agency over their own lives. She thought of Holly, beaten by Dominic Tickle because she'd dared to talk to another man. Then there was Kylie, coerced and manipulated by Mark Ripley, murdered by an unknown man. Was it a man? She couldn't be sure of that. And the fact that Mark and his friends had run a group that was essentially about harassing women in the street and tricking them into having sex. Or was she being unfair? *Nope.*

Jane pondered over whether she agreed with Thea and Warwick's view that Leontes didn't deserve a happy ending. People in the grip of strong passions often behave outrageously. Many live to repent. Should they be condemned for ever for their actions resulting from such passions?

Leontes regretted his foolish behaviour. He'd suffered for the loss of his wife and child for many years. Even after his 'happy' ending, he would continue to suffer whenever he reflected on the harm he'd done to others, to himself, through his actions. Nothing in life was black and white, as Shakespeare knew only too well.

CHAPTER TWENTY-ONE

"Can you believe that woman being at the play last night? It's starting to feel creepy the way she keeps turning up everywhere."

Elias didn't comment. He was probably bored with her rants about Jane Bell. Steph bit back the further comments she'd been about to make. But it was Elias who mentioned Bell next.

"She was with that young girl who asked me to sign her programme, wasn't she? Was she her daughter, do you think?"

"No. Too young. She's got two kids, a boy and a girl, both in their twenties. Bell used to teach English. She still does tutoring. Maybe the girl was one of her students." Steph thought for a moment. "Damn it."

"What?"

"I wonder if she's the student who met Mark, Adam and Phil at the leisure club?"

"And told Bell about their group?"

"Yes."

"Does it matter? You could interview her any time you like."

"It might be worth speaking with her, if only to tell her to stop snooping around on Bell's behalf. I doubt there's any more she can tell us. Bell's already told me everything the girl told her. I'm not sure I believe her, mind you."

"Given that we've now interviewed and eliminated almost all of the men who signed up for the pick-up course, where does that leave us?" Elias sounded tired and slightly hoarse. He hadn't made it to work until nine this morning, late for him.

He'd invited Steph along to the pub for drinks with the rest of the cast and crew the previous evening. She'd stayed for one drink, then made her excuses. She'd seen another side of her young sergeant at the pub. He was clearly in his element with all his acting friends. It was slightly concerning that she'd failed to guess at this side of his personality. Maybe she wasn't such a good judge of people as she'd thought.

Immediately, Cal spoke up, reminding her that she'd misjudged him too. She cupped a hand over her ear as if to block the sound, but his voice was in her head.

"You okay, boss?"

Steph realised she'd screwed her eyes tightly shut, forgetting Elias was there. "I'm fine." She hadn't meant to snap, but Cal was an irritant. "Bit of a headache." She looked at him. "Could be worse. Could be a hangover."

Elias gave her a sympathetic smile. He took a packet of paracetamol out of his drawer and held it out to her. "Want a couple of these?" She almost laughed aloud. She'd swallow any number of pills if she thought they would get Cal out of her head.

With reluctance, she picked up her phone and called Jane Bell, but the call diverted to voicemail. She checked whether Bell had a landline and quickly obtained the number. Bell answered on the third ring. "Why didn't you answer when I called your mobile?" Steph said.

"Sorry? Who is this? Oh, it's you, DI Warwick. I turn the sound down on my mobile when I'm at home. It makes too many noises."

"Like the ringtone?"

"I was thinking more of all the irritating sounds it makes to let you know you've received some kind of message."

"That's kind of the point," Steph commented, exasperated. They hadn't even greeted one another yet and already Bell was getting her back up.

"Look, can I help you? I'm due at a student's house soon."

"That girl you were with at the theatre last night. Was she the one who told you about Adam and Phil's pick-up group?"

There was a prolonged silence, then a quiet, "Thea? Yes."

"I'd like to talk to her. Do you have her contact details?"

"What do you want to talk to Thea about?"

"Excuse me?" Bell didn't repeat her question, forcing Steph to speak again. "I would have thought you could guess without too much difficulty, not that it's any of your concern."

"Thea is my concern."

Steph snorted. "Hardly. What is she, fifteen? She's her parents' concern, not yours. Obviously, as she's a minor, I'll ask their permission to question her."

"She's sixteen and her parents aren't available. They're in London. I'd be happy to represent them if Thea's okay with that. I'll give you her phone number and you can ask her."

Damn, damn, damn. Steph took down the details and ended the call with an abrupt thank you. Then she contacted Thea.

Elias was extracting a couple of pills from his packet. He swallowed them the way they do in the movies, without water.

"We're visiting your fangirl this afternoon. She gets home from school around four."

Steph spent the day reviewing her cases, obtaining updates from other members of the team and chasing forensics. At four fifteen, she and Elias arrived in Thea's village and located her home, set at the end of a tree-lined drive. A scruffy little Skoda was parked outside, a meerkat grinning at them from its back window.

"Looks like Bell's beaten us to it," Steph remarked.

Elias rang the doorbell. It was answered by a lot of loud barking, prompting Elias to quote, "Cry havoc and let slip the dogs of war."

Steph rolled her eyes. She hoped he wasn't going to start spouting the bard at every opportunity now that he'd come out as an actor.

The door was answered by the young woman who had been at the stage door the previous evening. She held the collars of two excited labradoodles.

"Thea Martin?"

"Yes, come in. These two brutes aren't as fierce as they look or sound. They might lick you to death though."

"You shouldn't invite strangers into your home without asking to see some ID, you know."

Thea looked puzzled. "You aren't strangers. He's Florizel and you're his boss."

Steph raised an eyebrow. She and Elias followed Thea inside. They were in a wide hall with a central staircase and rooms leading off either side.

"I'll just put these two in the orangery. They'll soon settle down. They like it in there. You can wait in the sitting-room if you like." She nodded at one of the rooms to the left of the staircase. "Back in a sec."

Steph led the way. As soon as she walked into the room, she came face to face with Jane Bell. She was sitting on a brown leather sofa, a laptop balanced on her knees. They nodded at each other. Jane again congratulated Elias on his performance. As if his head wasn't big enough.

Thea returned and sat next to Jane on the sofa. Steph and Elias took an armchair each.

"You were brilliant in the play last night." Thea beamed at Elias. To Steph's dismay, he gave a little bow.

"It's one of my favourite Shakespeare plays," Bell said.

"I didn't know it at all before I was offered the part of Florizel. I—"

Steph gave a cough. All eyes turned on her as if she too were about to give a performance. She looked at Thea.

"We're here to ask you some questions about your dealings with Mark Ripley, Adam Eades and Phil Lavin, Thea."

"Sure, but I thought Jane already filled you in on what I told her."

"Yes, but we need to hear it from you. Jane isn't currently a police officer."

Thea frowned. She gave Bell a puzzled look.

"Hasn't Ms Bell told you about her suspension?" The young woman's dismayed expression answered her question.

"Ms Bell was suspended for endangering the life of a young woman."

"I was never in any danger!"

"I'm not talking about you. I'm talking about a young woman who was murdered."

There was a prolonged silence. Steph was unsurprised to sense the hostility directed towards her. She looked at Elias. He avoided her gaze. Had she gone too far? Was spite her main motivation for sharing this with Thea?

"You came across Mark and his friends at the leisure club, didn't you? The one on Outer Circle Road."

"Hi! To Fitness, yes. I'd been swimming there with my friend, Stacey. Afterwards, we went up to the café for a hot chocolate."

"Mark and his friends were already in the café when you arrived?"

"Yes. We sat at a table near theirs. Stacey whispered that they were hot. She started sort of trying to attract their attention."

"How so?"

"You know. Giggling and taking selfies. Posing a bit, I suppose."

Steph thought Thea looked embarrassed. She pictured Thea and her friend pouting and striking poses for the camera. Given that Thea looked about fourteen, she couldn't imagine grown men taking an interest, but she already knew that Mark Ripley had no scruples about pursuing underage girls.

At a nod from Steph, Thea carried on. "Stacey dared me to go over and talk to them, but I told her that was a silly idea. They were a quite a bit older than us and I could tell they thought we were being stupid."

"What did Stacey say?"

"She thought one of them was interested in us."

"Mark Ripley?"

"Yes. He hung back when his mates left and came over to speak to us. He asked if we'd like to join him for drinks later. I said no. I had a feeling Stacey was thinking about it, but she said no eventually too."

"Did he try to persuade you?"

"He said we could all go back to his place. He probably thought we looked too young to go to a pub. Stace looks older than me, but she got asked her age when she tried to get us a bottle of wine in the supermarket last week." Thea's eyes slid to Bell's as though expecting a frown of disapproval. Bell obliged.

"Your friend Stacey is lucky you had the sense you were born with," Steph remarked dryly. "What happened then?"

Thea shrugged. "He just said something like, 'Have a good day, girls,' and left."

"Were there many other customers in the café at the time? Anyone who might have noticed Mark talking to you?" She noticed Jane Bell look up at the question. One she'd probably never thought to ask.

Thea took a few moments to think about it, raising her eyes to the ceiling and frowning deeply. "Nope. There weren't any other customers, just a couple of members of staff hanging around, but they were chatting to each another. I don't think they were paying us much attention."

"Right," Steph said. "I also wanted to talk to you about the information you shared with Ms Bell about Kylie Bright. I understand you obtained this from your friend Stacey, whose sister is at the university?"

"Yes. I told Jane everything Stace told me. About Tristan being disgusted with Mark for encouraging him to hit on an

obviously underage girl, and about Mark bullying Kylie into
. . ." Thea looked at Elias and blushed. "Doing it with him."

"Yes. We know about all of that. What else did your
friend's sister discover?"

"That's it. Except . . ." Thea looked at Jane uncertainly.

"Out with it," Steph barked.

"It's probably not relevant, but last time I spoke to
Stacey, she said that her sister told her that Ivy, Tristan and
Lottie have been bad-mouthing Adam and Phil on Lottie's
blog. All sorts of rumours are flying around that they had
something to do with the murders. Not mentioning them by
name, but sort of making it obvious that it's them."

Great. Steph hoped she'd warned them off this sort of
thing, but it seemed they'd ignored her. She'd need to have
another word. Not least because they might be antagonising
the killer.

"Thanks, Thea. You let me know if you learn anything
else from your friend Stacey, or if anything else comes to mind,
okay?" She looked pointedly at Thea as she said this and put a
slight emphasis on the word 'me.' *Me. Not Jane Bell.* She hoped
the message got through. "Or you could contact Detective
Sergeant Harper here." Thea's wide smile suggested that she'd
be more than happy for an excuse to speak with Elias again.

* * *

When the detectives had gone, Thea turned to Jane and said,
"I'm sorry I didn't tell you about the blog thing. Stacey only told
me about it this morning and it didn't seem all that important."

"That's okay." Jane smiled. "If Stacey tells you anything
else, you should get in touch with DI Warwick or DS Harper
in future."

"Okay. Is it true what she said? That you've been
suspended?"

Jane gave a heavy sigh. "Yes."

"Was it her that got you suspended? I could tell she
doesn't like you."

It was good to hear that. It meant she wasn't alone in sensing hostility bouncing her way every time she encountered Warwick.

"Sort of. She reported me, but I was the one who did a stupid thing."

"What did you do?"

"I didn't put Kylie Bright off when she told me she'd try to identify a suspect for me. It might have put her in danger, even got her killed."

"I bet that Warwick woman's just trying to make you feel bad."

Jane appreciated Thea's loyalty.

"Why do you think she hates you?" Thea said.

"I'm not sure." Jane had been giving the matter some thought. "Maybe she just doesn't like specials. And she seems to think I'm compromising her investigation with what she calls my 'meddling.' I can't help wanting to be more involved. I'm a curious person."

Thea laughed. "I'm not going to argue with that. Hmm. Maybe you just upset her in a past life."

"Maybe." Thea was joking, but Jane had a feeling that Warwick's dislike of her went beyond her voluntary status. It seemed deeply irrational. The way Warwick had flown off the handle when she came to her house. It was like she brought out the worst in the DI, and she had no real idea why.

After looking into Warwick's eyes and seeing so much pain behind them, Jane couldn't bring herself to hate her. Still, that didn't mean she had to like her.

Did Warwick have any friends? Anyone she could confide in? Jane knew nothing at all about her. She didn't wear a wedding ring. Was she divorced, single, in a relationship? Jane couldn't imagine anyone wanting to live with someone with such a volatile, prickly personality.

She didn't seem particularly close to her colleague. Yet she had suffered through a play that she clearly didn't enjoy for his sake. Suggesting she wasn't all bad.

The lesson over, Jane began packing away her materials. Thea's phone rang. She covered her mouth and whispered, "Stacey." Jane excused herself and went off to the kitchen. Often, before, or after a lesson, they would have a drink together. Thea seemed to like Jane's company — odd considering the age difference. Of course, it had occurred to her that Thea possibly saw her as a surrogate mother. She didn't mind. She didn't see much of her own daughter these days. Maybe it was a two-way thing.

She made two cups of hot chocolate and popped them on a tray, along with some biscuits from the biscuit barrel, a forlorn looking ceramic dog. *I'd look forlorn too*, Jane thought, *if people kept yanking off my head and stealing my chocolate digestives.*

As she crossed the hallway, she heard Thea still talking with Stacey. She paused at the foot of the staircase.

". . . So, the cops have been round asking me about what your sister told you, and some other stuff . . . I know. Mad, isn't it?" At that moment, Thea looked up and saw Jane waiting in the hall. Jane held up the tray and Thea nodded vigorously. "Listen, Stace, I've got to go. My tutor's here. Speak to you later."

Jane put the tray down on the coffee table and they sat side by side on the sofa.

"Did DI Warwick ask where your parents were?" Jane said.

"Yes. I told her they were at our home in London."

"She asked me too. When are they coming back, Thea? You keep changing the subject when I ask you."

"They're not," Thea said. "Not for a while anyway. They met a 'wonderful couple' who own a yacht, and they've been invited to sail around the world with them and their friends for at least six months. I don't suppose Mum meant literally around the world, maybe just half of it." She gave Jane a weak smile.

"How do you feel about that?"

"Don't care really. It's not as if they're ever there for me, even when they're home. And I'm not close to my brother,

Hugo. Because of the age difference, I suppose. He's actually my half-brother. Dad was married before. I don't think he really wanted any more children, but Mum wanted to experience being a mother. Don't think she realised a kid was for life, not just for Christmas."

Jane squeezed her arm. "You can talk to me any time you like, Thea. About anything."

"Sure. Thanks, Jane. That means a lot." She let out a sigh. "My brother's coming for the dogs at the end of the month. Pearl and Buddy are his. He's moving in with his girlfriend, so there'll be room for them now."

"I'm sorry, Thea. You'll miss them, won't you?"

"Yep. They're crazy, but I love them to bits. Still, it means I can have a sleepover at Stacey's whenever I like."

"Is there anything I can do for you right now?"

"A hug would be nice."

Jane smiled. "Come here," She hugged Thea, thinking not just of her, but of Norah.

Jane hugged Buddy and Pearl too, before she left. She wouldn't see them again. She had grown fond of them, but she wouldn't miss the itchy eyes and runny nose whenever she came to visit Thea. Dog and cat fur always triggered an allergic reaction. Even hypoallergenic ones, it seemed.

As soon as she got home, Jane texted Norah and asked if she was free for a chat. Her reply came back immediately. *Not now, Mum. I'm busy!* The words were accompanied by an emoji with rolling eyes. Jane didn't mind. Norah knew Jane would always be there for her. That's why she could afford to be dismissive. Jane's heart went out to Thea, alone in that big house, her parents cruising around the world. She texted to remind her to contact her for whatever reason. A moment later, her phone pinged. It was Thea, thanking her for her kindness. At the end of the message was a big red heart and three kisses.

CHAPTER TWENTY-TWO

Elias had been reading Lottie Purdey's blog. Steph asked him for a summary of the contents.

"There's plenty to summarise," Elias said. "Lottie Purdey is an angry young woman and she has a lot to say."

"Yeah, well, I'm mostly interested in what she has to say about Adam and his mates."

"She started her blog a couple of weeks into her first term at the uni," Elias said.

"So, after Kylie had told her about her experience with Mark Ripley."

"Yes. And some posts are obviously a response to what Tristan told her about Adam and co.'s group and the strategies employed by so-called seduction experts. She dedicates one blog to Kylie's experience without actually naming Kylie or any of the others. There are references to the sort of lad culture that she believes is prevalent in young men at universities. Mostly she's trying to raise awareness among young women of the sort of behaviours to look out for when they're out socialising, or in a relationship. For example, she describes negging and gaslighting, and gives some classic examples. Talks a lot about consent. Responses from her readers range from positive to obscene, as you'd imagine. She has been speculating about the murders and making thinly veiled accusations."

"I think we need to have another talk with Lottie."

This time Steph called ahead to arrange a meeting. Recalling the lack of space and seating in Lottie's room, she suggested that they meet in a café near the campus.

Lottie was already seated when they arrived. "I'd get you both a drink, but I'm broke. I don't get paid till Friday."

Steph sent Elias off to queue for three coffees. "So, where do you work?" she asked.

Lottie named a popular bar and restaurant on the Brayford. "I do two shifts a week, Friday and Saturday, so it's not so bad. I get Sundays off."

Steph nodded. "What are you studying here?"

"Politics and gender studies."

Elias returned with the coffees. Steph was relieved. Small talk wasn't her thing. She got down to business. "Lottie, why didn't you tell us about your blog last time we spoke?"

"Isn't it obvious? I thought you'd think I killed Mark."

"Why would we think that?"

"Because of what I wrote, and because—"

"Because you felt protective of Kylie," Elias said.

"Yes. I told you how I kind of took her under my wing. I thought of her a bit as my little sister."

"Didn't you think not telling us about your blog would make us more inclined to suspect you? It makes us wonder why you kept quiet about it, and whether there's anything else you're keeping quiet about," Steph said.

"I told you why I kept quiet about it. But of course, I knew you'd find out about it eventually. Give me a break. Last time we spoke I'd just heard that Kylie had been murdered."

She turned fiery eyes on Steph. "Have you interviewed Adam Eades and Phil Lavin? What did they have to say for themselves? Let me guess — their mate Mark was absolutely respectful of women. He would never have belittled Kylie for being reluctant to have sex with him. Adam claimed that respect for women underpinned everything that their pathetic pick-up group taught."

She practically growled as she strove to articulate her anger. "But everything he and the others practised and preached proved just the opposite. I wish I'd named and shamed them in my blog, even if it did get me into trouble."

"It's as well you didn't. But I think most people would have a good guess about who you meant from what you wrote," Elias said. "You stopped just short of revealing their identities."

Lottie glared at him. Just for being a man, perhaps.

"Tristan told me how rubbish their course was. I bet you didn't know that they paid some women to respond favourably to their stupid chat-up lines during their street harassment exercises. No wonder their success rate looked impressive to their clients."

"We guessed that might be the case," Steph said.

"So? Have you? Interviewed them?" She looked at Steph.

Steph raised an eyebrow. Just who was running the interview?

"Yes, we've interviewed them. They mentioned your blog. And that you tried to sabotage one of their bootcamps."

Lottie smiled. "Ivy and I staged a protest. We handed out leaflets to some of the women that they and their so-called clients approached in the High Street. Even the paid ones. I used my blog to warn other female students about their tactics. I even challenged Adam Eades to a debate. He declined, of course." For some reason she shot Elias a sneering look when she said this.

"Your blog attracted a lot of unpleasant comments," Steph prompted.

Lottie was silent for a moment. "Unpleasant. That's one way of putting it. Hateful, misogynistic, virulent, toxic—"

Fearing Lottie might never run out of adjectives, Steph held up a hand to show she understood.

"None of them had the balls to own their comments, of course. All anonymous." Lottie took a sip of her coffee, wiped froth from her top lip. "I'm surprised Adam didn't suggest to you that I murdered Mark Ripley."

"Actually, he did."

Lottie shook her head. "So, are you going to arrest me?"

"Not today. And if I ever do, it won't be on the back of anything Adam Eades recommends. Lottie, did Adam, or Phil, or Mark, ever threaten you outright over the protest or over the content of your blog?"

"Depends what you call a threat. Does, 'I hope you die of cancer of the cunt' count?"

It was one of the viler comments that Elias had earlier quoted from Lottie's blog.

"Lottie. When I last spoke with you, I mentioned that a young man called Ryan Brown had been attacked after leaving a café where he'd been chatting with Kylie. I also mentioned that another man had harassed Kylie before Ryan arrived. Have you had any thoughts yet about who that might have been?"

"It could have been anyone. Like I said before, she never mentioned it. Never mentioned Ryan Brown either." Lottie sounded bitter.

"She didn't say that someone was bothering her? Paying her too much attention?"

"What, like a stalker? No. She would have told me about that." After a moment, she added, "I think."

"Thanks for your time, Lottie," Steph said. "I admire what you're trying to achieve through your blog and direct action, but please be careful that you don't leave yourself open to charges of libel or slander." She signalled to Elias that it was time to go.

"Okay. Thanks for the coffee."

"Intense, isn't she?" Elias said to Steph when they were out of earshot.

"Very," Steph said. "And, like you said, angry."

"Could she have done it?"

Steph frowned. "She had motive, opportunity. She works on Friday evenings, but she would have been finished in time to follow Mark. She cared about Kylie. It must have pissed her off no end that a dickhead like Mark — I know I'm speaking ill of the dead, but he wasn't exactly Mr Nice Guy — could get her to go on a date with him and then treat her so badly."

"I'm not sure how she could have worked out where he'd be that evening," Elias said. "Mark didn't plan to go out with Elle Darrow. Unless it all happened by chance. She left work and saw Mark with Elle on her way home, followed them, and saw her opportunity when Elle got into the taxi. Maybe she just meant to confront him. Maybe he tried to assault her, and she pushed him hard, knocking him off balance onto the step. Then she could have beaten and kicked him, not realising he was already fatally injured."

"Perhaps she felt angry when she saw him with another young woman," Steph said, "another potential victim. She seems to see it as her duty to call out men like Mark and to protect the women they prey on. Ordinarily, her blog would be her weapon of choice."

From his silence, Steph inferred that Elias wasn't buying it. "What? You think that unlikely?"

"It's not that. Obviously, we have to count her as a suspect. But then, if Lottie killed Mark, who killed Kylie Bright? And who attacked Ryan Brown? Someone else entirely?"

Steph didn't answer. They walked along in silence for a bit. Then, unexpectedly, Elias said. "Thanks for coming to the play the other night. Did you enjoy it?"

Steph shrugged. "The plot was ridiculous. You were good though. Did you ever think of becoming a professional actor?"

Elias looked surprised. Probably because she seldom asked about his private life. Steph backtracked. "You don't need to answer. It's none of my business."

"No. No. I was just taken aback. You aren't known for . . ." He seemed embarrassed.

"What? Showing an interest in other people?"

His voice quiet, Elias said, "I know it's not that you don't care."

Steph flushed with anger. She was about to ask how he knew what she cared about when he got in first. "Yes. I did consider it for a time. I took a year out after school to tour the country with a travelling theatre group. It was great fun, but it made me realise I didn't want to act for a living. I've kept up with acting by being involved with amateur groups. It's hard to fit rehearsals around the job sometimes, but there's always someone else ready to jump in if I can't make a performance. It's fun. A great way to de-stress. You should try it."

"I don't think I'd be much good at it." Steph's sudden anger had abated. *I'm always acting.* As far as she was concerned, she'd had enough drama in her life.

That night, she started awake from another nightmare. Cal, eyes on fire, telling her he'd just killed Marketa and she was going to be next.

"But I'm still here, Cal," Steph whispered into the darkness. "Where are you?"

She knew the answer. He was where he always was. Right inside her head.

CHAPTER TWENTY-THREE

Thea took the dogs out for a last walk before setting off to meet Stacey. She'd miss them when her brother arrived to take them away. She made a big fuss of them before she left, giving them extra treats. She felt bad about leaving them at home, but at least they had each other for company. Thea felt abandoned.

She didn't miss her parents. Not really. It was more the idea of them that she missed. Her brother, Hugo, was supposed to be checking up on her from time to time, but he lived in York and his calls were infrequent.

Thea thought of what her mother had said to her as she kissed her goodbye and got into her brother's car beside her father. Hugo was driving them to the airport. "You'll be fine, won't you, darling? You're all grown up now." She'd barely turned sixteen.

It had seemed exciting at first. A big house all to herself, no one to tell her what to do. As the weeks passed, however, she felt her enthusiasm wane. Being on your own with two non-humans for company wasn't as much fun as she'd anticipated.

Stacey had stayed over a few times but she didn't like being away from her family. 'Gotta go check in with my family,' she'd say, as if they couldn't manage without her.

Thea was glad of Jane Bell's visits. Jane was of an age with her mum but they were quite different. Jane had spoken of setting boundaries for her two children. Thea's parents had set few boundaries for her and Hugo. They'd encouraged them to be 'free spirits,' to 'find their own way in life.' Thea now thought that all of this loose parenting had just been a way for their parents to shrug off their responsibilities, letting their kids bring themselves up.

She had understood early on that her mother's shows of affection were superficial, brought out for show in front of other people. As for her father, he didn't even bother to pretend.

That's why she was becoming so attached to Jane Bell. When Jane asked Thea how she was feeling, she actually cared about the answer. It was also why she didn't want Jane to speak with her parents. Jane would have to be straight and tell them their daughter didn't need any more private tuition, she'd more than caught up.

Thea had been hoping that she could help Jane with the murder investigation. Maybe even help her get reinstated as a special. It was so unfair that she'd been suspended. That DI Warwick had seemed okay when they were talking outside the stage door. Who'd have thought she was such a bitch? Jane hadn't done anything wrong. She'd hadn't ordered that murdered girl — what was her name, Kylie — to do anything dangerous. How could DI Warwick be certain that Kylie had been murdered because of Jane? It could have been a random stranger waiting for an unsuspecting woman to walk up those creepy steps. Thea shuddered at the thought.

The dogs settled, Thea changed and left the house at a run and just made the Lincoln bus. Missing it would have meant a whole hour's wait for the next one. She could probably walk into town in less time than that.

Stacy was waiting for her at the bus station and waved as the bus pulled into the stance. They hugged, Thea's first human contact for a while.

"How's life in the mansion in the sticks?" Stacey teased. She lived in a pleasant residential area a short walk from the cathedral. Her parents were both health workers at the County Hospital on Wragby Road and were able to walk home after a late shift.

"It's just a modest six-bedroomed family home in a quiet village location within easy reach of the city of Lincoln."

"With four acres of land!"

"A good-sized garden. And life's a bit lonely sometimes, if you really want to know. Do you want to come over for a sleepover soon?"

"Yeah, why not? My parents would never agree if I told them you lived by yourself. Shame you can't come stay at ours, but I know you can't leave the dogs." Stacey gave Thea a friendly punch. "So, where do you want to hang out? There's a vintage and craft market on over at the university this morning. It's in the hall where they have the music gigs. Karina's going with some of her mates from uni."

"Cool."

It was a short walk to the university from the bus station. Stacey hugged her sister when they met. She chatted to Karina's friends, whom she'd obviously met before. Thea stood back, feeling shy and awkward, unused to being around a lot of people.

There were the usual sorts of stalls to browse in the events hall. Thea bought a pretty silver ring. Stacey tried on some dresses from a vintage clothes stall but decided none of them suited her. After a while, Karina suggested going for lunch in the Student's Union bar. Her friends didn't join them.

"My treat," Karina said. "I got paid yesterday." Karina worked part time in a shop on the High Street. The pay probably wasn't that good, so it was generous of her to offer to pay. Thea felt guilty. Her parents gave her a big allowance, but she didn't want Stacey and Karina to know how well off she was. It was embarrassing. Stacey had been to her house and knew her parents had to be rich, but Thea always tried to play it down.

"Just some fries for me," she said, but Karina insisted she add a burger. Karina returned from the bar with three cokes. "So, did my little sis tell you what I found out about Mark

Ripley and his mates' business venture, and did you pass it on to your police friend?"

"Yes, and yes. Thanks."

"I know what he did to Kylie was horrible, but he didn't deserve to be murdered," Stacey said.

"Well, it's certainly got the whole campus in hysterics, and I don't mean the laughing kind. Everybody's terrified we've got a serial killer on the loose."

"Neither of them was murdered on campus," Thea pointed out.

Karina made a face. "They were both students here. That can't be a coincidence. I was stopped by a journalist earlier in the week. He asked me if I felt unsafe."

"What did you say?" Thea asked.

"I said I was okay, but nowadays we go out and about in small groups after dark."

"Mum and Dad are glad you're living at home," Stacey said. When Karina raised her eyebrows, she added a hasty, "Me, too." They smiled at each other in a sisterly way and Thea felt a surge of envy.

"Did you know Mark or his friends?" Thea asked.

"Not before all this blew up. Now every time I look around, I seem to see either Adam Eades or Phil Lavin. It's not that they're around more, I'm sure, just that I've got better at spotting them." Instinctively they all looked around. All three exclaimed at once, "Oh my God."

"Talk of the Devil," Stacey said.

"See what I mean?" added Karina.

Adam and Phil were playing pool on the far side of the bar. Thea tried not to stare. Despite not having seen them since that time at the café at Hi! To Fitness she recognised them instantly. She squinted. "Who's that with them?"

"One of their mates, I think. He's with them a lot."

"I've seen him before somewhere. But I don't think I'd have realised that if he hadn't been with them."

"Well, you've only seen them the once, haven't you?" Stacey said. "That time at the fitness club."

"Yes." Thea thought back to when DI Warwick had asked her if anyone else had been with Mark and his friends in the café that time. Only a couple of members of staff had been there.

Stacey scrutinised the man over the rim of her glass. "Oh, I've got it! He's one of the exercise coaches there."

She was right. Now Thea could picture him in her mind. "I must have seen him around the leisure centre and made the association with Mark and the others. I think I remember seeing him there when we went swimming once."

"We could be planting a false memory." Karina was studying psychology.

"No. I definitely recognise him. Seeing him with those two must have triggered my brain to remember. He was talking to someone else, another member of staff, but I can't picture him. I think he had his back to us." She looked at Stacey, who shook her head.

"Nope. Does it matter?"

"I suppose not," Thea said. But somewhere in the back of her mind, a little voice sounded, telling her that it did.

"What are you guys doing later?" Karina asked. "There's a gig on here this evening. It's a student band, but they're pretty good."

"If we go, will you get us some drinks?" Stacey asked.

"A couple, but no more. I don't want to have to answer to Mum and Dad for getting you pissed."

Again, Thea envied the knowing smile that passed between them. There was no one to answer to if she went home drunk. No one to worry if something bad happened to her.

"Cool. I'm in. How about you, Thee?"

"Will you sleep over at my house afterwards? We can get an Uber."

"Sure. It'll be a fun night." They bumped fists.

CHAPTER TWENTY-FOUR

Thea had to go home to feed and walk the dogs before returning to Lincoln in the early evening to join Stacey and Karina for the gig. She'd changed into a little black dress that she'd found in her mother's wardrobe, and put on some make-up, but when Stacey saw her, she shook her head and offered to give her a makeover. The effect was to transform her from a youngish looking sixteen-year-old into someone who could pass for eighteen. "You still can't go anywhere near the bar," Stacey told her. "You need to look twenty-five or they'll ask for ID."

Stacey managed to talk Karina into ordering them cocktails. Thea had hit her parents' drinks cabinet a couple of times in their absence. She'd sampled gin, brandy, tequila and scotch and found them all disgusting, but the cocktail tasted sweet and fruity and not at all alcoholic. She wondered if Karina had brought her a mocktail, hoping she wouldn't be able to tell the difference. Then, a few sips in, she began to experience a warm glow of contentedness.

"Is this what tipsy feels like?"

Stacey giggled. "Hell, yes!" She was sipping her drink through a long, striped straw. She nudged Thea, who followed her gaze down to Stacey's open handbag. There, nestled between her make-up bag and her shiny black Ted Baker purse, was a half-bottle of vodka.

"Fancy a top up?" Stacey scanned the bar before surreptitiously lowering her glass and tipping in a generous measure. "Quick, before Karina gets back from the loo."

Thea held her glass under the table. It felt like everyone in the room was looking at her with disapproval.

"How did you get that through the bag search?" she asked.

"There's a sort of secret zippy part at the bottom to keep your umbrella in. They didn't notice it." Stacey's eyes widened. "Well, look who's just arrived."

Over by the door, Adam Eaves, Phil Lavin and the man who'd been with them earlier strolled into the bar. With them, hanging back slightly as though unsure of himself, was another young man, who stuck closely to the exercise coach.

"They've just seen us looking at them. Don't stare."

"I'm not!"

"Are they still looking this way?"

"You said not to stare at them!" Thea sneaked a look. "No, they're going to the bar."

Karina returned, accompanied by the two friends she'd been with earlier in the day. "You baby girls alright?"

"Sure," Stacey said, "Guess who's here? Adam Eades, Phil Lavin and friends."

"So?" Karina sounded bored. "Why wouldn't they be? I think one of their mates is the bass guitarist. Look, I'll get you two another drink, then we're going to join some friends from my psych class. Will you be okay?"

"'Course," Stacey assured her. Karina moved off to the bar. "Look at her acting all cool with her friends. She was only saying earlier that Adam and Phil should be suspended until the police either arrest them or someone else for the murders."

"They didn't actually do anything that bad, did they? It was their mate, Mark, who treated that Kylie Bright badly. And it was Mark who asked us to go to the pub with him.

Adam and Phil must have realised we were a bit young for them. I don't think they're murderers."

"Why? Because they're hot?" Stacey giggled.

Thea laughed. "I wonder who the other not-so-hot guy with them is."

All four young men were clustered around a small standing table, holding pints and talking. The one Thea described as 'not-so-hot' seemed slightly aloof from the others, as if with the group but not really part of it. Thea knew that feeling. Her parents had moved around a lot and she'd been the new girl at school too many times. Moreover, she could never say how long she was likely to be sticking around for, and no one wanted to invest time in someone who was going to be moving on. It had been a lonely childhood.

Thea was right in one thing. He wasn't hot. While his companions were relaxed, he stood hunched, self-consciously arranging and rearranging his face into the right expressions to suggest he was following and enjoying their conversation.

Thea recognised the signs. She'd practised them herself in situations where she'd felt socially excluded. Smiling, nodding, raising her eyebrows. Saying yes and no as appropriate. It should have made her feel drawn to him, but it didn't.

Her head was reeling by the time she'd knocked back her second vodka-laced cocktail. But it felt good, sort of buzzy, exciting. Stacey kept topping their glasses up until the bottle was empty. Then the band came on stage.

The music was shockingly loud, she felt the bass pounding in her chest. It made her feel alive, bursting with boundless energy. Thea danced uninhibitedly, joyfully, soaking in the pulsating beat, the electric atmosphere, the rhythm of bodies around her dancing as one.

"Watch out!" Stacey shouted. "You're crashing into everyone!"

Was she? Thea didn't care. She didn't care about anything but the music. It was exhilarating and she never wanted it to stop.

She was startled when Stacey took her arm and tried to pull her off the dance floor. "I need to pee!"

Thea shook her off. She didn't want to miss a moment of the band's performance. What was up with Stacey, anyway? Surely, she didn't need her hand holding to go to the loo? She pulled away from her friend and sank, laughing, into the press of people around her. It was liberating to be alone in the crowd. On and on she danced, oblivious now to everything.

The music stopped suddenly. The band left the stage. Thea looked around in confusion. The room was spinning. Her hearing was muffled. Without the music, she felt disoriented. Everyone around her started going crazy, shouting, and stamping their feet. She looked about her, searching for Stacey. A surge of panic threatened to overwhelm her.

"Are you okay?" a concerned voice asked amidst the chaos. "Take my hand. I'll help you outside for some fresh air. You look as though you need it."

It was true. She was feeling nauseous and dizzy. Sooo dizzy! She groped for the hand and grasped it, grateful for its steadying strength.

The music was starting up again. This time it sounded like screaming. Thea covered her ear with her free hand as she allowed herself to be led through the jostling crowd towards the exit.

CHAPTER TWENTY-FIVE

Jane checked her calendar. Yes, it was book group that evening. They were fitting in an extra session because a well-known author was giving a talk in Lincoln the following week and they'd decided to read her book and discuss it before the event. Jane hadn't expected to be going out this evening. She should have been doing a shift but since she was no longer a police officer, she was now free. She had confided in Allie about her suspension and Allie had told the other members of the group that Jane would be attending because her Saturday evening shift had been cancelled. Jane supposed she would have to tell everyone eventually.

She sighed. She wasn't a fast reader and she was only halfway through the book. Perhaps she'd just find a summary of the plot somewhere, read a few reviews. She suspected that's what Karun did most of the time. Or maybe he and Frieda read half each and filled each other in on the details. It didn't matter. The group was as much an opportunity for a catch-up with friends as a literary exercise. The books chosen were never too challenging.

Jane hadn't seen Ed Shipley since he'd walked home with her after Yvonne's birthday party more than a week ago. She wondered if something might have happened between them that night had her mood been more upbeat. Ed had told her that he had an early appointment the following morning but she'd sensed he'd made that up when she hesitated over inviting him in. She was glad nothing had happened. If she ever did begin a romantic relationship with Ed, she didn't want their first date to be linked forever in her mind with the murder of a young woman.

Allie called to remind her about the book group. Her attentiveness since the assault had begun to grate a little. She meant well, but Jane didn't like to be fussed over. "I hadn't forgotten," she said. "It's on my calendar."

"I just thought after everything that's happened, it might have slipped your mind."

"Well, it didn't. Stop treating me like I'm a . . . Oh, Allie. I'm sorry. I know you mean well. I'm lucky to have such a great friend." The instant apology worked its magic on Allie. She wasn't the type who bore grudges. Jane promised to knock on her door later so they could walk to Veganbites together.

She called Thea. There was no answer, so she texted her. Kylie's murder had made her more protective of her student. It was a Saturday. Perhaps Thea was doing something with her friends.

To tell the truth, she'd been worrying about her a bit since the day she'd sat in on DI Warwick's interview with her. A moment or two later, Thea texted back to say that she was in Lincoln with Stacey and her sister. She was planning on going to see a band at the university in the evening. At the end of the message there were a series of exclamation marks to show how excited she was about the gig, followed by a smiley blowing a kiss. It made Jane smile. She texted her kids often but their replies were sometimes too brief. She was lucky if she got more than a 'yep,' or a 'nope' out of Patrick. But that was okay. They were used to their mum being interested in their lives. They took her for granted, whereas Thea probably wasn't used to an adult caring about what she was doing.

To her surprise, she managed to finish the book in time, following an intensive reading session. It was a straightforward read, strong on character and plot, which in Jane's opinion was what storytelling was all about.

At 6.55, she called at Allie's house. Dudge was first to greet her and pushed past Pete to give her an enthusiastic welcome. "Hello, my little hero," Jane said, never forgetting, despite his overexcited slobbering, that Dudge had done her a good turn, maybe even saved her life.

It was an unspoken rule that they didn't discuss the book on the way to the meeting, not even to hint whether they'd liked or disliked it.

They puffed and panted their way up the Steep Hill to the Bail. Allie stopped to take a breath. "I swear this bloody hill gets steeper every year. Any news about your suspension, Jane?"

"No, sadly. That DI has really got it in for me. Not that I don't deserve it."

"Come on, Janie, we've talked about this. There's no way you were responsible for that young woman's death. She was the one who suggested trying to find the man in the restaurant who harassed her. She'd probably have gone ahead even if you'd actively discouraged her."

"There's a part of me that wants to believe that. Do you think it's selfish of me? I've been thinking, he could have been stalking her for a while before he followed her into that restaurant. Then, when she rebuffed him, he resolved to kill her."

"No, I don't think that's selfish. I think it's a very likely explanation. He was absolutely consumed with jealousy after seeing her talk to Ryan Brown and went after him first. Then he came back for Kylie as soon as an opportunity presented itself."

"Even if she didn't die because of her conversation with me, the fact remains I should have discouraged her from taking any sort of action that might put her at risk. There's no getting away from that, is there? In DI Warwick's eyes I'm forever guilty. She'll never allow me to be reinstated."

Allie put her arm through hers. "Well, maybe it won't just be up to her."

They saw Karun looking out of the window when they arrived. Allie indulged him with the secret knock. He beamed at her as he unlocked the door.

The little tealights on the coffee table, around which comfy seating had been arranged, reminded Jane of the evening of Yvonne's birthday party and the terrible news of Kylie's murder. She took a deep breath.

"Lovely and cosy as always," Allie said. "Would you like some help with the drinks?"

"All under control. And this evening, we also have cake. My new recipe. I need some guinea pigs to try it out on before I put it on the menu. Can you let the others in when they arrive, while I assist my lovely wife in the kitchen?"

"They're such great hosts. I feel guilty that it's always them doing all the running around," Jane said.

"Well, we all chip in to cover the cost of drinks and biscuits, but it's kind of Karun to bake for us. I don't believe for a moment that he needs to try his cake out before serving it up in the café. He's incapable of making anything that isn't delicious." There was a tap on the window. "Oh, look, Ed's not last, for once." Allie got up to let him in.

Ed and Allie greeted each other with one of those embraces that was somewhere between a hug and a continental greeting. Jane wondered when people started doing that in reserved Britain. Once upon a time, hugs had been kept specially for close family. She stood up to welcome Ed and they enacted the same exchange, though with a little less extravagance. What did that mean? That he didn't like her, after all?

Ed sat down next to Jane. It seemed to be expected these days. Jane had purposefully avoided the sofa, thinking that a single person on a two-seater sofa might look a bit desperate. Also, she'd wished to avoid presenting Ed with a potentially awkward choice.

When Jan and Yvonne arrived, there were more hugs and kisses. Jan and Yvonne settled into the two-seater sofa together, and Jan pulled out a dog-eared copy of the book. He and Yvonne always shared a single copy. It was rather sweet.

Frieda brought out a tray of hot drinks. Green tea with lemon for Jan and Yvonne, Yorkshire tea for Ed, and coffee for everyone else. Karun made a bit of an entrance with the cake, raising it to shoulder-height. "Ta-da! Frosted coffee walnut layer cake adapted from a recipe by the wonderful Mary Berry!" Everyone clapped.

Karun loved Mary Berry, bless him. Jane couldn't remember the last time she'd baked anything. Probably when the children were younger, before they both became calorie conscious. She didn't miss it. All that measuring and beating and folding wasn't for her, still less the clearing up afterwards. However, she did enjoy the results, and Karun's sponges were legendary. Perhaps if she'd managed to produce such wonders the effort would have seemed worthwhile.

It was customary for Allie to give a brief introduction to the author of the book they were reading that month. Afterwards, a lengthy discussion ensued, which left the group pretty much in agreement about what they'd thought of the book. Pity. Jane always thought it more interesting when a book divided opinion.

"How many stars then?" Allie asked when they'd all run out of things to say.

"Five from me," said Jan. "I like a good page-turner."

"Four," Yvonne said.

"Four from me," Frieda said.

"Same." Karun always agreed with his wife.

"Jane?"

"Four."

"Ed?"

"Four."

"And I'm a five. It's a while since we've all been roughly of the same opinion about a book. Anyone got any suggestions for next time?" Frieda suggested a book by a well-known crime writer. There were no objections. Allie set a date for the next meeting. Then she said, "Pete's thinking about coming along next time. Is that okay with everybody? He's not a great reader but he'll definitely have strong opinions."

Great, Jane thought. That would mean she and Ed would be the only singletons in the group. Was this another ploy on Allie's part to pressure them into coupling up?

After the discussion they often stayed for a while, chatting and catching up on news. Inevitably, Jane was again asked about the murders. It was time to come clean. "Actually, I don't know. I've been suspended. And as a humble special constable, I wouldn't have been working the case anyway." There was a shocked silence.

"Suspended? Since when?" Frieda asked.

"Since the day after Yvonne's birthday party. The police questioned me about the second murder, remember?" Their startled faces prompted her to add, "I'm not a suspect!"

"What happened? Why were you suspended?" Ed looked and sounded concerned.

Allie echoed Jane's earlier words. "Because that pompous DI Warwick's got it in for our Janie. The murdered girl volunteered to try to find out the name of someone who'd harassed her. Jane didn't forbid this outright, though she never encouraged it, but Warwick assumed Jane had asked her to do it. She thinks Jane caused that poor young woman's death."

"No!" Frieda looked shocked. "That's absurd. Jane would never let someone risk coming to harm for her sake."

"I totally agree," Yvonne said, while the others nodded.

"Thanks, guys. I appreciate your faith in me. And your support, but the fact is, I didn't expressly ask her not to, which as a police officer, was the first thing I should have done. It's my job to protect people, not to encourage them to put themselves in harm's way. *Was* my job, I should have said."

Karun offered her the last piece of cake, which she refused. It wouldn't taste as good now. Jan and Yvonne moved in for a hug, which prompted the others to follow suit. Ed hung back until last, then enveloped her in his arms, making her feel giddy. It was almost worth being suspended for.

"Aaw, thanks for all the love, guys."

A date was set for the next meeting and everyone began to disperse. Jane would have liked a chance to speak with Ed, but he was already walking towards his car when she and Allie came outside.

"That was some hug Ed gave you. Looked like he wanted to hold onto you for ever."

Jane reddened. "Shush, Allie! He'll hear you!" Indeed, at that very moment, Ed turned and waved.

"I won't say another word."

Jane thought Allie would never manage it, but she did. Ed's name wasn't mentioned all the way back to Danesgate.

She and Allie stood and chatted on the pavement outside Allie's house for a few minutes, until the bitter night air drove them to seek the warmth of their respective homes.

Ed was waiting for her at the bottom of the steps leading down to her front door. Jane saw him from street level in the glow of the light from the hallway. She wasn't at all surprised at seeing him there. It was like coming home and finding an old friend waiting on your doorstep.

"Hi," Ed said. "Is it too late for a nightcap?"

She smiled at him. "Not for me. Don't you have a client first thing in the morning?"

"Not this time." Ed smiled back shyly. She liked that. He was unsure of himself. How could he be after that hug? Suddenly, she was unsure of herself too. Had she been the only one to feel a jolt of electricity in their embrace?

He followed her into the kitchen where she poured them each a glass of red wine. They went into the sitting-room. Ed sat on the sofa. Jane considered the chair, until Ed patted the empty space next to him. They sipped their wine in silence for a moment or two. It seemed they couldn't stop smiling. Until they kissed.

"Stay the night," Jane said.

She checked. Ed was still smiling.

CHAPTER TWENTY-SIX

Only the tips of the cathedral's three towers were fully visible behind a scrim of freezing fog. The rest of the building's hulking mass was a looming presence, felt rather than seen. Like a huge object exerting a gravitational pull on the people in its orbit.

Steph was one of them. She made her way to the station at Newport, where she found Elias at his desk, pen in hand, phone clamped to his ear. She could tell it was an important call by the way he looked at her, grave-faced and eager for it to end so he could talk to her. It would have to be something mega if it were going to lift her mood that morning.

"Lottie Purdey's in interview room two. She's asking to speak with us about a girl she thinks went missing at a gig at the university last night."

"Go on."

"That's all I know."

"What now?" Steph gave a sigh and motioned for Elias to accompany her.

The blotched face and red-eyed stare of the young woman sitting next to Lottie struck Steph as alarming. Lottie Purdey, by contrast, was fresh-faced and attentive, if a little tired looking around the eyes.

"How can we help you?" Steph asked.

"She's not feeling great," Lottie said.

"I can see that."

"Is it alright if I speak on her behalf?"

"That depends," Steph said. She looked at the girl. "You okay with that?" The young woman gave a nod. "All right. Unless I need to hear it from her."

"She went to the gig with her friend. They were drinking. I saw her friend dancing alone and felt concerned for her. Adam Eades and Phil Lavin were there with a couple of mates. One of them seemed to be taking a lot of interest in them."

The mention of Adam and Phil's names banished any remnant of Steph's enervated mood. "Which one?"

"I don't know his name. He was a medium-sized guy, dark hair. I didn't really pay too much attention to him. He had a beard, I think."

"Go on," Steph said.

"I stepped in when she got a bit . . . disoriented. The band had gone off stage and everyone was making a lot of noise, you know, trying to get them to come back and do an encore. I think it threw her a bit. She looked like she was about to fall over, so I took her by the arm and led her outside for some fresh air."

Steph looked at Thea, slouched in her chair, eyes on the floor. She was impatient for Lottie to get to the point, if there was one, which she assumed there must be. Lottie wouldn't have dragged the wretched girl all the way to the police station just so someone could tell her off for underage drinking.

"As I said, she went to the gig with her friend. At some point, the two got separated." She stopped as Thea emitted a strangled sob. Lottie patted her arm. "It's alright, sweetheart. We don't know if anything's happened to her yet."

Steph and Elias exchanged glances. Steph looked at Thea. "Who are you talking about? Stacey? The friend who told you about Adam and his mates?" Thea bit down on the knuckles of her right hand. They'd get nothing from her. Steph looked urgently at Lottie.

"Yes. I waited outside with Thea until the gig was over. Stacey was supposed to be going back to Thea's for the night. We waited until everyone came out, then went back inside to check if Stacey was in the loo or something, but we couldn't find her."

"There would have been a lot of people streaming out all at once," Steph said, "and it must have been quite dark. Are you sure you didn't just miss her?"

For the first time, Lottie looked uncertain. "I've never actually met Stacey, but Thea showed me a selfie she'd taken of them earlier in the evening, when they were getting ready to go out."

"Right. I still think you could easily have missed her. It's not that easy to recognise someone from a selfie, and I'm assuming Thea was in no state to concentrate. Couldn't Stacey simply have gone home? Have you checked?"

"I rang Stacey's house this morning, pretending to be one of her friends." I didn't want to worry her mum and dad by saying she was missing, you know, until . . ."

Alarm bells were ringing in Steph's head. "What about her sister, Karina? Have you checked if she knows where Stacey is?"

Lottie nodded. Steph hadn't expected anything less of her. "Karina went back to her mates' hall after the gig. They had a party in the communal kitchen. Karina stayed over."

"Did you tell Karina her sister was missing, or didn't you want to worry her either?"

"Thea called her. She said Stacey had lost her coat at the gig and asked if Karina had maybe picked it up. Karina would have said if Stacey was there, wouldn't she?"

"Not necessarily. If she'd been partying half the night and you woke her up at the crack of dawn." Steph looked at Thea. "Call her, now."

The look of dismay on Thea's face didn't get her off the hook. "We need to know if this is a false alarm," Steph said sternly. "Turn it up so we can all hear."

The phone shook in Thea's hand as she made the call. "Hello? Karina? It's Thea Martin."

"Thea? Oh, yeah, Thea. Stacey's friend. Did you call earlier, or did I dream that?" She yawned.

"Is . . . is Stacey with you?"

"No. Wasn't she supposed to be going back to yours last night? Did she change her mind? Isn't she answering her phone? Typical! It's only ten o'clock, mind you. Stace never gets up before half ten on a Sunday. Try her again in half an hour, okay? I need to go to the bathroom. Byeee!"

So that was that. Still didn't mean any harm had come to Stacey.

Yeah, right. The warning bells in Steph's head had gone silent, but they'd been replaced by another, equally alarming sound: her own heart, pounding wildly in her ears.

CHAPTER TWENTY-SEVEN

Ed had left early. It was Sunday, but he was driving out to Louth later on, to make a delivery to a client. "Come with me. We can have lunch in a cosy pub somewhere deep in the Lincolnshire Wolds." But Jane passed. She needed a bit of time to process the events of the past few hours.

Ed had looked disappointed. Then he'd reassured her. "There's no rush." That was all he said, but the words meant everything.

She'd expected the house to feel different after he'd gone. It did, but in an unexpectedly good way. There were reminders all around that she hadn't just imagined the past nine hours. Two toothbrushes in the bathroom (Ed had borrowed one of hers), two wine glasses on the coffee table in the sitting-room (both half full). When she took them to the kitchen, she found Ed's scarf (cashmere, tartan) draped over the back of one of the chairs. Possessions left behind meant that their owner had to come back.

Jane picked up the scarf and held it to her cheek. It smelled faintly of Ed. She smiled, wrapped it around her neck, half wishing she'd accepted his offer of a trip to the Wolds. *Idiot. Acting like a lovesick schoolgirl.*

She felt restless. It would have been a good day to be wearing her uniform, either out on the streets or in the patrol car. She wondered how the investigation into Mark and Kylie's death was progressing, as she did every day. She hadn't heard from Warwick since she'd turned up to interview Thea.

The look on Warwick's face when she walked into the sitting-room at Thea's house and saw Jane sitting on the sofa! Priceless! She'd barely been able to acknowledge her presence. Not that she'd behaved much better. She hadn't exactly jumped up and embraced Warwick.

Jane's phone rang. A number she didn't recognise.

"Hello. You don't know me. My name's Lottie Purdey. I'm with your friend, Thea Martin."

"Thea! Is she okay?"

"She's fine, but she's a bit upset. We've just been talking to the police. I was going to get her a taxi home, but she says she'd rather go to your house — if that's okay with you?"

Jane was pretty sure her heart rate had just quadrupled. "Of course. Where are you right now?"

"About a minute from your front door."

Jane rushed to her door, still holding her phone. She hurried up the steps to the pavement, looked right and left. A young woman waved to her from a short distance away. Thea was by her side.

Thea ran to her. "Oh, Jane! Something terrible's happened."

"Let's go inside. It's freezing out here."

Lottie was included in the invitation, but she shook her head. "Now that I know Thea's okay, I'll head back to the uni. I've got a seminar on Monday that I need to prepare for."

Jane led Thea inside and sat her down at the kitchen table. "Whatever it is, I'm pleased you've come to me," she said. "When that young woman called and said you'd come from the police station, I was afraid something bad had happened to you."

"I wish it had! Then I wouldn't feel so terrible."

"Come on. Tell me what's up."

"Stacey's gone missing."

"When? How?" Jane listened while Thea gave her a run-down of the events of the previous evening. It was an effort to stay calm and not interrupt until she'd finished. When she had, Jane fired out one question after another. "What did DI Warwick say? Did she take it seriously? Is she going to investigate? What did she say when Lottie told her Adam Eades and his mates had been watching you?" She paused. "Sorry, Thea. I shouldn't be bombarding you with questions."

"It's okay. I just want someone to do something. I don't trust that DI Warwick."

That's my doing. "She knows her job."

"I don't care. I trust you."

"Thea, I'm suspended from duty, and even if I weren't, there wouldn't be much I could do. I don't — didn't — have the authority or the powers of a detective inspector. And I can't wear the uniform while I'm under suspension."

"People don't know that you're suspended, do they? Anyway, you don't need a uniform. You can investigate without one. Private detectives do."

Jane couldn't think of an appropriate reply to that. Private detective. Hmm. She turned the idea over in her head and liked the images the words conjured up.

Without the uniform, as she'd pointed out to Thea, she'd have no authority, no additional powers over an ordinary citizen. On the other hand, as a PI she would have the freedom to investigate a case without being hampered by her rank as a special. No more being constrained by her lowly status in a hierarchy in which she couldn't, at her age, hope to progress much further. Best of all, she wouldn't have Warwick at her back. She had to admit it was an attractive fantasy. But fantasy was all it was.

"Jane? Are you okay?"

"What? Yes, I'm fine. I was just thinking about what you said."

"You'd make a brilliant private detective, Jane. You can get people to talk to you. I bet they don't open up to that tight-arsed DI Warwick. You can start by finding Stacey."

Thea's faith in her was touching. Jane smiled at her apt description of Warwick. "I'm not sure I know where to start." She sighed. "What if I make us some coffee and we go over what happened last night again? You might remember some more details."

A few minutes later, bolstered by a frothy cappuccino, Thea recounted what she remembered. "It's a shame I was so drunk. It really does give you blank spaces in your memory, doesn't it? I'm never touching alcohol again."

Jane smiled. She'd said that plenty of times herself, and every time she'd believed it.

"Karina only got us two cocktails each, but Stacey had sneaked in some vodka in her handbag. She kept topping us up."

"So, would it be fair to say that Stacey was as intoxicated as you were?"

"Probably. Maybe she wasn't as completely out of it. I wish I'd gone with her when she asked. I wouldn't normally just abandon her. It's just . . . the music seemed like it was alive inside me. I couldn't pull myself away." She sipped her coffee. Jane waited. She could see Thea frowning, as though trying to remember more. "Come to think of it, there is something I didn't mention to DI Warwick."

Jane leaned in closer. "It's probably not important. I forgot to tell her that I'd met up with Stacey earlier in the day. We went to one of those vintage craft fairs at the uni, then we had lunch at the Savvy Swan with Stacey's sister, Karina. Adam Eades and Phil Lavin were there with another man. I recognised him, but only because he was with Adam and Phil. You know how a memory is sometimes triggered by something sort of associated with it?" Jane nodded. "I realised I'd seen him at the leisure club. Stacey said she thought he was one of the exercise coaches there, so that would explain it. He's probably a student too."

"You didn't tell DI Warwick any of this?"

"I only told her about the evening. She knows Adam and Phil were at the gig with two other men. One of them was the guy who'd been with them at the Swan. I didn't recognise the other man. My head was still a mess when Warwick questioned me, and I forgot to mention we'd seen them earlier in the day." She smiled at Jane. "See. You are a great detective. You got me to remember something that DI Warwick didn't."

"This other man, the one you said you didn't recognise. Was he the one Lottie told the police was taking a lot of interest in you and Stacey?"

"I think so."

"And you definitely didn't recognise him?"

"No. Sorry. He seemed to stick close to the guy from the leisure club. The one Stace said was an exercise coach."

"Can you describe him?"

"Medium-sized, bulky, brown hair and bearded. He wasn't hot like Adam and his mates. I wouldn't even have noticed him if he hadn't been with them. He was sort of . . . *meh*, if you know what I mean."

Jane did. Meh was her son's favourite word. He used it in response to her questions about everything from how he was feeling to what his latest girlfriend looked like.

"He was just kind of ordinary." Thea looked at Jane. "Maybe he works at the club too? That would explain why he seemed to keep close to the exercise coach guy." Thea looked pleased with her deduction. She sat back and sipped her cappuccino.

Her theory sent a creeping sensation up Jane's spine. The associations with Hi! To Fitness seemed to be stacking up. Mark, Adam and Phil had all been there. Now it appeared that at least one of the men accompanying them the previous night worked there.

Other memories began to stir, as though triggered, like Thea said, by association. She recalled Kylie's description of the man who had harassed her in the restaurant. A man of average height, heavy-set, with dark hair and a beard. Mr Generic. It was almost word for word how Thea had just described the man at the Savvy Swan.

"Right." Jane said nothing more. She needed some time to absorb what Thea had just told her.

The man who abducted Stacey might also be connected with the leisure club in some way. Adam, Phil and Mark were regulars there. The friend who'd been with them last night worked at the leisure club. The other man had stuck close to him. Was he another student? Or a colleague at the leisure club, as Thea suggested.

Jane thought of the description Thea had given her of the man she'd described as hot. Things began to fall into place. She was pretty sure that he was Chase, the good-looking young man who'd shown her around Hi! To Fitness the day she'd gone there to get some information on Adam and Phil, under the pretext of being interested in taking up membership.

"Oh, something else has just popped into my head," Thea said. "I must be sobering up. When he was stretching across the pool table, his shirt gaped open across his stomach a bit and I could see he was really hairy."

Jane stared at Thea, another memory by association forming in her mind. It seemed like the confirmation she needed. "I think I know who they both might be."

Chase's handsome features and blond hair had remained in her memory, precisely because it wasn't every day that you were introduced to an Adonis. In contrast, she could scarcely recall a single feature about the other young man she'd met that day. The one who'd been more interested in ogling the young women in their bikinis than telling her about the pool. When she tried to summon up an image of him in her mind, all that she could come up with was a vague impression of hirsuteness, and not a lot else. The reason? He had been quite ordinary. Unmemorable. Indistinguishable from hordes of other young men his age. He was Mr Generic.

"Jane?" Thea said. "Who are they?"

"The exercise coach is called Chase."

"And the other one?"

"His name is Dale. He's a pool attendant at Hi! To Fitness."

CHAPTER TWENTY-EIGHT

Steph would have liked a double gin laced with ice and tonic. Instead, she had to settle for making herself a cup of coffee in the station kitchen. She'd known it was going to be a long, long day the moment it was confirmed that Thea Martin's friend, Stacey, had not gone home, or to her sister's after attending the gig at the university. Any hopes that she might simply have left with another friend, or someone she'd met at the gig, dwindled as the day wore on and the usual missing persons protocols failed to uncover her whereabouts.

Now Steph had Stacey's guilt-stricken and anxious sister and her worried parents to deal with. She'd sent a family liaison officer round to their home to keep them up to date with any developments, and if she were being honest, to keep them off her back. Add to all this the pressures of two ongoing murder investigations. She was beginning to feel overloaded.

Karina Ashworth had last seen her sister when she arrived at the venue for the gig. She confessed to having bought Stacey and Thea a couple of drinks each. Cocktails. She should have known better. Steph made sure she was aware of it.

Thea had told them Stacey had smuggled in a bottle of vodka. No wonder Thea had looked so delicate when Lottie brought her to the station that morning. It was a wonder she hadn't needed to be rushed to the hospital to have her stomach pumped.

Steph allocated a couple of officers to carry out a foot search of the local area, check for CCTV opportunities and collect details that would allow a missing person's report to be collated. She also ensured that someone contacted the COMPACT missing person system to see if Stacey had gone missing before or was on the system, just in case. She wanted to make sure that full information was recorded in case a statement was needed at a later stage.

Lottie Purdey and some of her friends, including Tristan and Ivy, were mounting their own search for Stacey, showing her picture around campus. They had also posted requests on social media with pleas for anyone who'd seen Stacey at or after the gig to come forward. This had already resulted in a message being relayed to the police that Stacey had been seen in the Ladies toilets about ten minutes before the band went off stage. That was when Thea had slipped off into the crowd to continue dancing. The witness had confirmed that Stacey seemed very drunk, on ecstasy, or both.

A little later, Lottie contacted the station again to say that she'd heard from two female students who'd been stopped by a young woman fitting Stacey's description. She'd asked them if they'd seen her friend. They claimed to have seen the same young woman stopping other people, presumably asking them the same thing. This had been after the band returned to the stage to perform their encore of two more songs. The same time that Thea had left with Lottie.

Steph recalled what Lottie had said that morning. She'd been concerned about Thea because she was obviously very drunk. She'd also mentioned that Adam Eades and Phil Lavin had been at the gig and that one of their friends had been taking an interest in Thea. Could it have been Stacey he was really interested in? He could have kept an eye on Thea, thinking Stacey would re-join her at some point. Then, when Lottie led Thea outside, he would have had to have changed his plan and gone looking for Stacey. If he'd abducted her before the end of the gig, that would explain why Lottie and Thea didn't see her leaving the venue. Had he spotted Thea and Lottie as he left the area? They hadn't seen him.

It was possible Stacey had approached Adam's group seeking information about Thea, and he'd seen his opportunity. Maybe he'd even followed her and offered to help her find Thea.

Steph shared Lottie's latest information with Elias. "We need to interview Eades and Lavin again. Let's go."

* * *

The house across the street from Adam and Phil's had had a new window fitted, Steph noted. The planks of wood that had been used to board over the broken glass were lying on the street outside the front door.

Adam didn't seem surprised at seeing the police on his doorstep. "Is this about that missing girl? We don't know anything about that. What is this? A case of rounding up the usual suspects?"

Steph stuck Stacey's picture under his nose.

"Still don't know anything about her," Adam said.

"All right if we come in and ask you some questions?"

Adam sighed. "Sure." As they passed the stairs, he shouted up, "Phil! Cops are back." Phil joined them in seconds.

"So, you've seen the reports about Stacey Ashworth going missing then?" Steph said.

"Hard to miss. It's all over the student forums," Adam said. "Lottie Purdey's getting everyone riled up about it."

"You object to that? She's concerned about Stacey's welfare. As are Stacey's family and a lot of other people, DS Harper and I included."

"Sure. We're concerned too." Phil agreed with Adam. As always.

"You two were at the gig last night?"

"Yep. We were. So were a lot of other people. Are you going to be questioning all of them?"

Steph ignored the question. "Stacey was with her friend, Thea. Did you see either of them?"

"Nope. I only know what Stacey looks like because of the pictures that are being posted everywhere. Never met either of them. How about you, Phil?" Phil shook his head.

"You have seen them before."

"Not that I'm aware of."

"They were in the café at the leisure club on Outer Circle Road, Hi! To Fitness, a few weeks ago. You two were there with Mark Ripley. They were at the table next to you. Ring any bells? Sometimes we remember better with a bit of context thrown in."

Adam shook his head but Phil looked thoughtful.

"Phil?"

"I'm not sure. I do remember a couple of girls messing about taking selfies. It seemed like they were trying to get our attention. One of them looked pretty young, maybe fourteen or fifteen? The other was a bit older."

"You didn't speak to them?"

Phil hesitated. "No. Why would we? They were school-kids. We aren't into young girls."

"Did Mark speak with them?"

Phil frowned. "Not that I remember."

"Actually, he did. As you were leaving, he hung back to ask if they'd like to meet him later for a drink."

"No kidding?" Adam grimaced. Phil looked uneasy. "He was probably just playing around with them."

"We mentioned before that Mark encouraged Tristan Morley to approach underage girls."

"And I told you, not on my watch. We were really strict on that." Beside him, Phil nodded vigorously. "Tristan Morley must have heard wrongly. It can be pretty noisy out on the street. Like I said, Phil and I would never do that, and I feel we can vouch for Mark, seeing as he's not here to defend himself. Right, Phil?"

Steph didn't even glance at Phil to confirm his response. "Do you remember Stacey and Thea now, Adam?"

"I can vaguely remember some kids giggling and being a pain, but I didn't pay them much attention. As for the gig, if they were drunk, any bloke in his right mind would steer well clear of them for fear of them crying 'rape.'"

Steph didn't comment. "Who were the other two men with you at the gig last night?"

"One of them's a mate. He's Phil's cousin. The other was just someone from the leisure club he works at."

"Names?"

"My cousin's called Chase Gilbert," Phil said. "He's a student here too. Works part time at Hi! To Fitness. Who was that lad he brought along with him again, Adam?"

Adam scratched his head. How hard could it be to remember the name of someone you'd been with the previous evening? "I can't remember offhand. He wasn't a very memorable bloke, was he, Phil?"

"I don't think I spoke to him all night, actually," Phil said.

"We've been informed that one of the men who was with you at the gig last night was taking quite an interest in Thea Martin and Stacey Ashworth."

"Well, that wouldn't be Chase. Chase bats for the other side." Adam smirked.

Phil glared at Adam, clearly displeased with his description. "My cousin is gay." So, he was capable of standing up to Adam after all. Who'd have thought it?

"Right. So, neither of you remembers the name of the person who was with Chase. Was he a student?"

"No idea. Chase might know. Want me to call him?" Phil said.

Steph nodded. *Get on with it already.* "Tell him we need to talk to him."

Phil's call was answered immediately. "Hey, Chase, how's it going, cuz?" A pause. "Good, good, man. Yeah. Great news." Steph drummed her fingers on her arm. "Can

I stop you a minute, mate? We've got the police here asking about that girl who went missing last night. They want to talk to that dude you brought along to the gig. You in your room?" Another pause. "Yeah, yeah, that's right. Anyway, they want to talk to you. I know, I know, mate, but it is what it is. Thanks for that, cuz. See you Wednesday for training, right? Cheers."

Elias handed him a pen. Phil wrote Chase's contact details on the back of a torn brown envelope that was lying on the coffee table.

"Chase says you're on the wrong track if you think the guy he brought along last night approached this girl, or her friend. Apparently, he's very shy when it comes to women. Never had a girlfriend. Probably never hit on a girl in his entire life, according to Chase."

Steph signalled to Elias that it was time to leave. It took about ten minutes to get over to the university and another five to locate Chase's accommodation. He met them at the door to his room, which was located at the end of a corridor through a set of fire doors that someone had propped open with a Meerkat toy. It reminded Steph of Jane Bell. She kicked it out of the way.

A lemon-scented mist hung in the air in Chase's room. A can of air-freshener missing its top sat on his desk next to an open laptop, the screensaver displaying a rainbow LGBT logo. The bed was unmade, dirty clothes had been heaped into a pile in a corner, three empty pizza boxes and half a dozen empty coke cans lay on the floor next to an overflowing wastepaper bin. Steph didn't judge. It looked like her place most days of the week, and she had a lot more space.

"Phil said you wanted to talk to me about the missing girl."

Elias showed Chase the selfie of Thea and Stacey.

"I've seen them at the leisure club where I work, but I've never spoken to either of them."

"Do you remember seeing them at the gig last night?"

"Yes. Together at first." He pointed at Thea. "Then she was on her own. I saw her leave with another girl. Have you spoken to her?"

"Yes. She was concerned about Thea and took her out for a bit of air. We think Thea's friend Stacey came looking for her. Did she approach your group? Ask whether you'd seen her?"

"Yes. She was pretty drunk."

"Okay. I'd like to ask you some questions about the man who accompanied you to the gig."

"You mean Dale? Dale Lister?"

"Yes. How well do you know him?"

"He's not really a friend, just someone I know from work. He's a lifeguard and pool attendant. I work in the gym. Also, we work shifts, so our paths don't cross very often. Mostly I see him in the staff kitchen when I'm on a break. I don't normally socialise with him out of work. Last night was the first time, if I'm honest. I'd been talking to him in the kitchen the previous day, and I felt a bit sorry for him."

"Why?"

"He was saying how he'd been on various dating sites and wasn't having much luck. The girls he was attracted to weren't interested. He got a bit agitated about it to tell the truth. Started going on about how girls are too fussy, and they only go for the best-looking guys."

"The alpha males."

Chase looked at Elias in surprise. "That's exactly how he put it. And how guys like him don't get a look in, and it wasn't fair that some guys can get any girl they want while others are stuck with being celibate whether they like it or not."

Steph exchanged a look with Elias. "He used that exact word? Celibate?"

"Yeah, you know. Like a Catholic priest."

"You said he was agitated. Was he angry, do you think?"

Chase thought about it. "Could have been, I guess."

"And you felt sorry for him?"

"I did think he was wallowing in self-pity a bit but sure, I felt sorry for him." Chase rubbed his nose. "Look, don't get me wrong. I talk to everyone, but Dale is kind of negative, like he can suck all the good energy out of you. Do you know what I mean? A couple of the female staff at the gym told me he creeps them out. I sort of know what they mean. He can come across as charmless."

"Anything else?" Steph sensed he was holding back.

"I don't know, but I got the impression . . . the way he was talking about women and the whole dating thing. It came across a bit like he thought he was entitled to have a girlfriend. Almost like the girl shouldn't have a say in the matter. If he wanted her, he should be able to have her as a right. It came across as misogynistic. I don't agree with any of that stuff."

"Why did you feel sorry for him then?" Elias asked.

"I suppose because I know how it feels to be the outsider. It's not easy growing up gay. The only person I told before I came out was my cousin, Phil. He was great about it. Not everyone was."

"Did you ever mention Adam, Phil and Mark's pick-up group to Dale?" Steph asked.

"No. But he might have heard us talking about it at the club."

Steph thought, suddenly, of Dominic Tickle. He had learned about the group from overhearing conversations about it at the gym. Had it been the same one? "Go on."

"I remember this one time we were all discussing their group in the changing rooms. Dale was hanging about in there. I think he was checking the lockers, making sure the keys fitted or something."

"Was Mark Ripley there at the time?"

Chase cocked his head to one side. "Yes, he was. He was usually there with Adam and Phil. Not sure what they liked about the guy, being honest. I'm sorry about how he died, but I never rated him. The group was all his idea. You know that, don't you? Phil's heart wasn't really in it, but he's easily influenced by Adam. Adam can be a real dick."

"We'd noticed," Steph said drily. "Tell us more about that occasion. What was the conversation about, exactly?"

"They were talking about the group and the strategies they use, but mostly Mark was boasting about how many girls he'd slept with. How easy it was to get them to go to bed with him. Next thing, we hear a loud bang." He clapped his hands together, making Elias start. "It was Dale. He tried to make out he'd had to bang a locker door because it wouldn't close properly, but it was obvious he'd just hammered it with his fist. His knuckles were bleeding."

He was angered by Mark's words. Steph felt a chill. She pictured Mark lying across the bench, bleeding into his brain.

"I hope I've not landed the guy in trouble telling you this. You don't really think Dale has something to do with that girl going missing, do you? I think he's got a lot of anger and resentment in him but he's too shy to approach women." He paused. "And I can't really see any woman going off with him unless she was really drunk." He seemed to realise what he'd just said and uttered a quiet, "Oh!" He looked at Steph, then at Elias, made another connection. "You think he killed Mark too, don't you? But why?"

Because Mark was one of the alphas, the one with all the gifts, and Dale was a loser. Unattractive to women. Charmless. Invisible to men like Adam and Phil, who couldn't even remember his name after spending an evening in his company.

Had he found his niche by going online and encountering other men who shared his feelings of resentment towards men who could attract any woman they wanted, and who reinforced his misogynistic views?

"Did Dale leave the hall at the same time as you and the others last night?" Steph asked.

"No, he left before the end. When the band came back on." A pause. "Oh God."

"It's important that you do not get in touch with Dale, Chase. And don't discuss the conversation we've just had with anyone. Do you understand?"

"S . . . Sure." Chase bowed his head, ran his fingers through his hair. "I wish I'd known you were interested in Dale when I spoke to that other detective. Maybe that girl wouldn't have been killed, or the other one gone missing."

Steph and Elias exchanged a look. "What other detective?" Steph asked.

"The one who came to the leisure club asking about Adam and Phil. Jane something? Sorry, I forget her surname. My supervisor would know. She was her teacher at Ollie Granger's."

Steph stared at him, astonished. "Jane Bell?"

"Yes, that's it."

"Right." Steph suppressed her anger with some difficulty. "Well, I doubt it would have made any difference."

"Thanks." Chase looked unconvinced.

They thanked him and left his accommodation. Immediately, Elias said, "This Dale fits our profile of the killer."

Steph was silent. She agreed, but that wasn't what was uppermost in her mind. Elias looked at her. She hoped he wouldn't say it, but of course he couldn't stop himself. "I'm guessing you're even more angry at Jane Bell now."

Angry doesn't cover it. But now wasn't the time. She needed to focus.

"We need to trace Dale's whereabouts, fast," she barked.

Elias began stabbing numbers into his phone, then spoke with the manager of Hi! To Fitness, Dale's supervisor. "He called in sick this morning."

Another call, this time to the station, and Elias had Dale Lister's address.

"He lives on Walter Street. That's near the Lincoln Imps stadium at Sincil Bank, isn't it?"

Steph didn't answer. She was already running towards the car.

CHAPTER TWENTY-NINE

The girl was drunk, but not as drunk as her friend. She was wearing the slutty satin top she'd been admiring in that shop in the Riverside Centre that time he saw her there. It looked good on her. She kept glancing over, but he knew it was the others she was interested in, not him. Adam. Phil. Chase, even, though she wouldn't bother with him if she knew what he was.

Even if she had noticed him, he was sure she wouldn't remember. He'd walked right past her at the pool once and she hadn't batted an eyelid. Guys like him were invisible to girls like her.

He liked the sexy way she moved to the music. He'd noticed her in the bar at lunchtime too. One of the girls she was with looked just like her. An older sister? He shut his eyes, imagining what that would be like. The two of them. He was already hard, but the image made his cock feel like a column of solid concrete.

"You alright, mate?" Chase asked. He'd asked that earlier too, in the bar when he was talking to his friends. The alphas. Chase had introduced them but they obviously didn't find him interesting enough to include in their conversation. Chase was the only one who bothered to check if he was okay.

"Yeah. Great, man. Cool band." He clutched his plastic beer glass so tightly, it crumpled like cardboard. Good thing it was empty. Chase hadn't noticed. He'd already turned back to Adam and Phil.

He looked for the girls. Where were they? What the fuck? He scanned the crowd and finally picked out the younger one dancing — if you could call what she was doing that — she looked like she was possessed by a devil. He waited. Minutes passed. Where the hell had her friend gone? It couldn't take that long to piss.

The band stopped playing. He kept his eye on the girl. She was totally out of it, staggering about, eyes half-shut. What a state! For a moment he considered how easy it would be to get her to go outside with him.

She wasn't as sexy as her friend. Small tits, skinny as fuck. But she was there for the taking. He hesitated. A beat too long. Another girl came up to her out of nowhere and took her hand. He watched them weave through the yelling, stamping crowd towards the exit at the back of the hall.

He wasn't that bothered. She wasn't the one he wanted. He was going to wait for that other bitch to show up. She'd rejected him once. He'd sworn he'd make her sorry.

His eyes roved the room. There she was.

CHAPTER THIRTY

Jane suggested that Thea have a lie-down. There was a bed in the spare room.

"It's so pretty! Your whole house is lovely. I wish I lived somewhere like this instead of in that big, soulless, modern monstrosity. This place has so much character." She beamed at Jane. "I like old things." Jane hoped she was still referring to the house.

"I might pop out for a bit," she told Thea. "If I'm not back before you wake up, there's some leftover lasagne in the fridge. Warm it up if you're hungry."

Thea looked at the bed, stifling a yawn. "I'm tired, and my head feels like a giant's punched it, but I know I won't be able to rest again until I know if Stacey's okay."

"They'll find her." Jane noted the dread in Thea's eyes. Both of them understood that finding Stacey wouldn't necessarily mean a happy outcome. She gave Thea a hug.

"Find her, Jane. Please? I know you can do it." Her voice sounded small, like a child's. Jane left her to rest. She checked on her after ten minutes and was relieved to see that she was fast asleep, cuddling a teddy bear that had once belonged to Norah. For some reason, her daughter had never taken to it. It had escaped the charity shop because Jane liked its silky fur and smiley face. Bears should never have unhappy faces. 'It' was now a 'she,' and her name was Sylvie, because the name Sylvie made Jane think of woods, and woods made her think of bears, probably because of the song, which was in her head as she descended the stairs.

She was glad Thea hadn't asked where she was going. She wouldn't have felt comfortable lying to her. She suspected Thea would sleep for several hours. She'd had a shock, and her body was still dealing with the effects of unaccustomed drinking. At first, she'd been worried about the dogs until Jane suggested that she give her keys to Allie so that she could pop round and attend to their needs. Still, Jane moved around the house as quietly as she could.

Her car was parked in a designated space a few minutes' walk from her house. She could have gone to Hi! To Fitness on foot, but it would take at least half an hour, and time was of the essence. Moreover, there was a possibility that she might have to drive somewhere else afterwards. More a probability than a possibility, really. If she was right, and Dale really had taken Stacey, he was unlikely to be at work. In that event, Jane was counting on capitalising on Clutterbuck's indebtedness to her old teacher to find out where he lived.

There were a few spaces left in the car park at the club, mostly ones that were difficult to manoeuvre into, or too far from the entrance. Jane opted for one of the more distant spaces. No point stressing over parking when there was no need.

There were three members of staff at the reception desk but Jane didn't recognise any of them. She went up to a ginger-haired woman arranging swimsuits on a rail. "Excuse me. I'm looking for Crystal Clutterbuck. Is she on duty today?"

"She's on her break, Officer." The woman took in Jane's uniform. "I'll just give her a call."

"Thank you." Jane felt her cheeks burning. She really was justified in feeling like an imposter now. She had no right to be wearing the uniform while under suspension.

A moment later, the woman returned, accompanied by Crystal.

"Mrs Bell . . . oops, sorry, Officer Bell. Would you like to come to my office?" She glanced at the ginger-haired woman. "We can talk privately there."

She closed the office door behind them. "Have you come about the break-in?"

"Er . . . No, actually. It's about another matter."

"That's a shame. Still, I only reported it this morning. Wasn't really expecting anyone this quickly. Lucky if anyone turns up at all, really, these days." She covered her mouth. "Oh, sorry, Mrs Bell. That wasn't a criticism of you personally. I meant the police are so short-staffed, that's all. All those cuts you keep hearing about."

"It's okay," Jane said, suddenly remembering what an annoying student Crystal had been. "I need to speak to a member of your staff about an incident."

"Is he or she like a witness or something?"

"Something like that."

"Who is it? I'll check if they're on duty."

"His name's Dale. He's a pool attendant. I met him the day Chase showed me round the club. He was at a gig at the university with Chase last night."

Was it her imagination or had Crystal winced slightly upon hearing the name? "You don't like him?"

"Is it that obvious? I shouldn't really say so, but no, I don't. I was off the day he had his interview. I doubt he'd have got the job otherwise. I was never much of an academic, but I have good instincts when it comes to people," she said pompously. "It's like a kind of radar, actually. I can tell what a person's like within minutes of meeting them."

"Oh." Jane was doubtful. Surely, success in an interview should be based on a person's suitability for the job, not on the interviewer's subjective feelings. But she wanted to keep on Crystal's good side, so she said, "That must be a good skill to have."

"You'd better believe it."

"What was it about Dale that, er, put him on your radar?"

233

As she'd expected, Crystal was a bit vague about her special talent. "Just a feeling, I suppose. He's, I don't know, a bit off. I'm not the only one who thinks so either, he's not popular with the rest of the staff." She lowered her voice. "Especially the women. I've had complaints about him."

"What kind of complaints?"

"Nothing concrete, otherwise I could probably have had him on a disciplinary. It's more that he's kind of funny around women."

"Funny?"

"Yes. For one thing, I don't think he likes women telling him what to do. He never says anything, it's just his manner. Plus, I've had female swimmers complain that he stares at them when he thinks they're not looking."

"Have you challenged him on that?"

"Of course. He denies it, says it's his job as a lifeguard to be observant. Which it is, I suppose. But there's looking and *looking*, isn't there?" She lowered her voice even more. "There was a rumour that he catfishes. Do you know what that is?"

Jane nodded. "It happened to my daughter a couple of years ago. She turned up for a meeting with a man she'd met online. He looked nothing like the pictures he'd posted. He was about thirty years older for one thing. When she changed her mind about spending time with him, he bombarded her with obscene and misogynistic verbal abuse."

"Right. I don't have any proof, but a club member, a young woman, came up to me and said that Dale Lister looked a bit like a man who'd catfished her. Like your daughter, she'd been getting to know him online and agreed to meet up with him. She noticed immediately that he didn't look anything like his profile picture but she went for a coffee with him anyway, just to be polite. She wasn't attracted to him, so she told him she didn't want to see him again. He turned nasty."

Crystal took a breath. "I'm not going to repeat the things she told me he said. I would have confronted him, but the young woman didn't want me to. She said it had happened over a year ago and she couldn't prove anything. She said Dale looks kind of like a lot of other guys. It was hard to be certain they were the same person, and even if we did accuse him, it would be her word against his. She just wanted me to be aware of the kind of person I might have working for me. Needless to say, she hasn't been back since."

"I see." Jane wondered how much of Crystal's 'instincts' about Dale had kicked in after her conversation with this young woman. She pondered over what Crystal had told her and decided to chance her luck. "Crystal, I can't give you any details as its part of an ongoing investigation, but . . . I can say that it's very important that I find Dale Lister as soon as possible."

Crystal's eyes widened. "How can I help?"

"I need his address."

Crystal was hesitant. "I'm not supposed to just give out addresses. You know, because of data protection. We've been told that even the police need a warrant for personal information."

Jane considered Crystal's indecision a good sign. "I know and I wouldn't ask, except it's really urgent."

If Crystal asked why if it was that urgent, she hadn't obtained a warrant already she'd have no answer. But she didn't. Just as she hadn't questioned why Jane, whom she had been led to believe was a detective, was in uniform. She drew her computer keyboard towards her and brought up a database. She tilted the screen in Jane's direction, gave her a knowing look, then stood up and crossed to the window.

Jane smiled. She knew that she was on shaky ground in obtaining Dale's address this way. But it didn't matter. She intended to alert DI Warwick as soon as she found out whether Dale was responsible for Stacey's disappearance. Warwick would have no problem obtaining the information via the official channels.

"Thanks, Crystal," she said.

"What for?" Crystal winked. "See you soon, Mrs Bell. You get some sessions booked soon to get the benefit of your membership, okay?"

"Oh. Yes. I will. Thanks for the reminder, Crystal. And, next time you see me, call me Jane, okay? We're not at school anymore."

"Thanks, Mrs Bell."

Jane smiled. She hadn't written Dale's address down, but it was emblazoned in her memory. Eleven Walter Street. She pulled out her phone and considered calling Warwick. Then she imagined the DI's sneering disbelief and pocketed it.

Before she contacted her, Jane needed more proof. Her mind made up, she got in her car and headed for Sincil Bank.

CHAPTER THIRTY-ONE

Dale Lister lived in a mid-terrace house on Walter Street, one of a maze of identical residential streets in Sincil Bank. The last time Steph had been this way was six months ago when she took a visiting cousin to a football match at the Lincoln Imps stadium just around the corner from Walter Street.

They parked on nearby Henry Street and walked the rest of the way. Steph rapped loudly on the door of number eleven. They waited. Elias looked, discreetly, through the window and signalled to Steph that there was no sign of Lister in the front room.

Then the door opened a crack, taking them by surprise. "Police. Are you Dale Lister?" Steph flashed her ID.

"Dale's my brother. What's up?"

"We need to speak to him urgently. Is he here?"

"He doesn't live here now."

"You sure about that?" Steph asked.

"I'm sure."

"Then you won't mind if we come in and see for ourselves."

"Be my guest." He threw the door wide and stood aside. "Where do you want to start?"

"Let's start with you telling us your name."

"Walter Lister. Dale moved in with his girlfriend about a month ago."

Elias smirked. "Walter of Walter Street. That's a coincidence."

"Is what it is, mate."

"I'm going to check upstairs," Steph said. "My colleague will keep you company while I'm gone."

"Sure. What's Dale supposed to have done, by the way?"

By then, Steph was halfway up the stairs. She didn't stop to answer. On the upstairs landing she was confronted with black-painted walls, a crimson carpet and three doors, one of which, wide open, led to a bathroom. She turned the knob on the first door and looked inside. It was small, one wall painted a garish red, the others white. There was an attractive cast iron fireplace, a single bed, a side table, a rack of clothes. Nowhere that anyone could be hiding.

The second bedroom was larger, three white walls, one deep purple, more sparingly furnished than the first. Again, nowhere Lister could have Stacey hidden away.

Steph moved to the window, looked outside. Directly under her was the kitchen, a single-storey extension projecting into the back yard. There was a small, stone outbuilding, probably once used as a coal house, at the end of the yard. Yard backed onto yard all along the terrace, separated on three sides by brick boundary walls. Steph's gaze was drawn to the coal house. It had a door with a padlock.

There was a creak on the stairs. She turned sharply, ready to reprimand Elias for leaving Lister alone downstairs, but it was Lister, not Elias, who stood in the doorway.

"Satisfied?"

"Where's my colleague?" Steph felt a prickle of unease.

"Downstairs."

She was standing with her back to the window. Dale took a step towards her. His right arm was behind his back, his left in his pocket. *He shouldn't be up here. Something's wrong.* Steph took a step back. "Show me your hands! Now!"

He was on her before she had a chance to react, dragging her away from the window, slamming her hard against the wall.

Steph gagged as some rough material was stuffed into her mouth and shoved right to the back of her throat. She blinked, saw Lister's face morph into Cal's, blinked again and Lister's bearded face was inches from her own.

"Don't struggle." He showed her the knife he'd had concealed behind his back. "It'll only make it worse for you." He looked her in the eye. "And for your friend downstairs."

Steph nodded, still gagging. She felt like she was suffocating. She had to calm herself, try to regulate her breathing, or she'd go under. Not easy with adrenalin shooting through her veins. She focussed on Elias. On Stacey. For their sake, she had to hold it together.

Lister. Dale Lister — for that's who he had to be — forced her over to the bed and shoved her, face down, onto the mattress. Panic surged through her. *He's going to smother me!* But when she turned her head to the side to gasp for air, he did nothing to stop her. She struggled again. He straddled her, knees on her arms, his body weight pinning her to the yielding mattress, making movement all but impossible.

Steph strained to lift her head. Lister grabbed hold of her hair and slapped her, hard, across the face, bringing tears to her eyes. She heard the unmistakeable sound of tape being ripped from its roll. He used it to secure her gag.

That done, he opened a drawer in the bedside table and took out some twine. It cut, cruelly, into the skin of her wrists and ankles as he pulled it tight, then tighter.

If he's tying me up, it means he's not going to kill me, right? Then a terrifying thought struck her. Had he already killed Elias?

At last, he was done. He got off her. Steph's legs prickled as some feeling began to return. Lister crossed to the window, looked out. She wondered if he was looking at the coal shed, whether Stacey was in there, similarly bound and gagged. Or worse. He'd already killed at least twice. The chances of any of them cheating death seemed non-existent.

It must have occurred to him by now that tying up two police officers wasn't the smartest move he could have made. Was he panicking too? Going over his options? He had to realise they were all bad. If not for the gag, she'd be negotiating with him right now, telling him that there was no way forward other than by giving himself up. But he'd silenced her. He didn't like his victims to have a voice.

She strained her neck, cricking it painfully in an effort to twist round to see what he was doing. He was still at the window, head bowed, no longer looking out. Seconds ticked by. Minutes. He seemed frozen. Good. That might mean he had no clue what to do next.

Steph almost smiled at the irony of her situation. This was nothing like the scene that had played out between her and Cal more than a dozen years ago, yet here she was again, at the mercy of a dangerous man.

His indecision made her anxiety surge again. After a while she began willing him to do something. Why? As long as he remained frozen, she was safe. But the longer he delayed, the more she began to lose her grip on reality. She closed her eyes, opened them and didn't immediately recognise her surroundings. When she did, it was with a sense of *déjà vu*.

"Stephanieee!" The radio stopped abruptly. He'd crept into the kitchen while she was absorbed in chopping carrots, humming along to a song with a catchy tune. Startled, she turned around.

"How did you get in?"

"You were careless."

"No, I wasn't. How did you get in?"

"You let Marketa have a key. Moving back in, was she? I saw the boxes in the hall at her place all packed up and ready to go."

Steph shivered. "Marketa? What . . ?"

He shook his head. "Dead, Steph. It took longer than I thought. She was a fighter, your friend, I'll say that for her. But we got there in the end."

"That's not funny, Cal." She still hadn't got it. Even after everything. His words were so repugnant that she thought he was making a sick joke. He'd always hated Marketa.

He waved the keys in front of her eyes. Marketa would never have surrendered them to him willingly. It was true! He saw she believed him at last, and a slow smile spread across his face.

"Open your eyes!"

Steph didn't understand. Her eyes were already open. Was he speaking metaphorically? She made to rub her eyes and found that she couldn't because something was stopping her arms from moving.

"Open your eyes!"

The voice didn't sound right. She blinked in confusion. The face bearing down on her wasn't Cal's.

"What's wrong with you? Are you deaf or something?"

She tried to speak, but something was stopping her mouth from opening. No words came out. Her throat felt constricted. It was hard to breathe.

"Hey! Police bitch!" Suddenly, she was jolted back to the here and now. It was Dale Lister, not Cal, looming over her. "Is anyone else coming?"

Steph nodded. That's why he'd been standing by the window for so long. Checking for back-up.

"Better be quick then." He turned her over, roughly, reached for something behind her. When she saw what it was, Steph shook her head frantically. She pleaded with her eyes for him to reconsider. He slapped her. "Stop it!" The pillow closed in on her face, covering her nose and mouth. Steph gave in to panic as she felt it pressing down, squeezing out the last breath of air.

Step by step, Cal was closing in on her from the other side of the table. She couldn't move. Her mouth was dry, her throat constricting so that she could scarcely breathe. He was on her now, backing her up against the sink. He grabbed her wrist. The vegetable paring knife she'd been clutching dropped from her hand, landing with barely a sound on the cushioned vinyl floor.

"It needn't have been like this, Stephanie. You have no idea how much I loved you, babe. We could have just gone back to how it was before if you hadn't . . ." He turned his face away as though tortured by some unspeakable memory.

Her chest was tight, her lungs burning. The palm of Cal's hand closed over her nose and mouth.

It took longer than I thought. She was a fighter, but we got there in the end. Cal's words echoed inside her head. She thought of poor Marketa, fighting, just like her, to draw a breath in the final, terrifying moments of her life.

The more you struggle, the longer this'll take. Who had said that? She didn't think it was Cal. Who then? She was confused. It really was impossible to breathe. Then, nothing.

CHAPTER THIRTY-TWO

Jane could have found her way to Walter Street blindfolded. It was practically around the corner from the Lincoln Imps' home turf at Sincil Bank. She, Sam and the kids had cheered the Imps on at dozens of matches there, strolling back afterwards, elated or, more often, downhearted, through the rows of terraced streets towards the car park. She must have walked right past Lister's door countless times.

She didn't have much of a plan of how to proceed once she got there. Doubts flooded her thoughts. Should she alert the police now, in case her suspicions about Dale Lister were correct? If she called 999, they could be here in moments. In the end, she decided to wait, at least until she'd checked the house from outside.

Unless she could find some excuse for being admitted to a neighbour's garden, from where she'd have a good view of the rear windows of Lister's house, she'd be restricted to looking through the window facing onto the street.

She found a space to park and was about to get out of her car when her attention was drawn to two people walking along on the other side of the street. She stared at their backs, then ducked down, even though they'd already gone past without seeing her. Her mind was in turmoil. If Warwick and Harper were here, it meant she was right. She took no pleasure in the realisation. The fact that they had all converged on this one street seemed to confirm that a young woman's life could be in danger.

It was a slight shock to see Lister answer the door to Warwick and Harper. She wished she could hear what they were saying. More than that, she wished she could go into the house with them. It was frustrating to do nothing but sit and wait while she longed for a piece of the action. As the minutes ticked by, impatience set in, then a creeping sense that something was wrong. She got out of the car.

Warwick would be furious with her. She had no right to be here. Moreover, she was in uniform while under suspension. If she had an ounce of sense, she'd get back in her car and drive away, leaving the professionals to do their job.

But they had been in there for such a long time. Jane walked towards the property. *Just a quick look in the window.*

She saw a sitting-room and dining-room separated by an archway. An opening in the dining area provided a view of a seemingly empty kitchen.

There was something odd about the fact that the downstairs appeared so quiet. Where was everyone? It was tempting simply to knock on the door. But what if she interrupted something? For all she knew, Warwick and Harper might be involved in a sensitive operation.

Jane considered her options, then walked to the end of the terrace, turned right into the next street and knocked on the door of the house that backed onto number eleven's garden. A woman who looked no older than Thea answered, a plump baby balanced on her hip.

"Oh! What a beautiful baby," Jane began, hoping the compliment would make the woman more receptive to her proposal. "I'm sorry to bother you. I can see you've got your hands full. I'm Special Police Constable Bell. The occupant of number eleven Walter Street has put in a complaint about some damage his neighbour has done to his garden wall. I need to take a look at the rear of his house from your back garden, and he's not answering his door. I just need a quick look to check the full extent of the damage."

"First I've heard of it," the woman said.

"Oh, that's probably because it only happened this morning. I was asked to check up on it as I was sort of in the area anyway."

When the young woman didn't react, she asked, "So, would it be alright for me to access your garden?"

"S'pose so."

"Thank you so much." Jane followed behind her, noting the layout of her house, which would probably be the same as number eleven's. The door to the sitting-room was open, giving a glimpse of a playpen and some baby toys scattered over a worn, grey carpet. They walked through the back room to the kitchen. Unlike at number eleven the front and back rooms had not been knocked into one. The woman pointed at a door in a small lobby outside the kitchen.

"You're welcome to use the bathroom if you need to."

Jane hadn't been expecting that. Of course, in these Victorian terraced houses, the bathroom was downstairs.

"Are you okay looking around by yourself? I just need to finish feeding Theon and get him to burp before I put him down for a nap."

"Of course. I'll let you know when I'm finished."

"Sure. Take as long as you like."

Jane thanked her and went outside. There wasn't much of a garden. The only green thing was a sad-looking round plastic table missing a leg, and some chairs. A small stone outbuilding with a splintered door stood at the end of the uneven, concrete yard. It was about half a metre short of the height of the boundary wall. Probably an old coal shed.

Jane pulled one of the green chairs up to the wall and stood on it. Save for an area of neglected, peeling decking, number eleven's back yard looked identical to the one she was in. She had a clear view of the rear of Dale's house. Someone was standing with their back to one of the windows. Jane squinted. It looked like DI Warwick. No sign of DS Harper. Perhaps he was inside the room, concealed from view.

Jane turned her attention to the other window. No one there. No sign of Dale. Were they all huddled together in one bedroom?

A sudden movement pulled Jane's gaze back to the first window. Warwick was no longer there, but Jane had a blurred sense of her pitching out of the frame as if she'd been rammed at speed by a violent force.

Something's wrong. Warwick hadn't just fallen over, she'd been pushed. Hard. She'd dropped out of sight in the blink of an eye.

Jane looked at the wall separating the garden she was standing in from Dale Lister's. Maybe if she'd made more use of her gym membership, it wouldn't look so much like Mount Everest. Her feeble upper-body strength obliged her to look around for an alternative to heaving herself up and over.

The roof of the coal house was lower than the height of the wall. Jane dragged the plastic chair over to it and climbed up. The chair wobbled dangerously on the uneven concrete path. Bit by bit, she managed to hoist herself onto the roof. From there, it was easy to get on top of the wall. The drop to the ground on the other side looked daunting. The easiest way was to lower herself down, gradually, then let go. Pain shot, jarringly, through her knees and lower back as she landed.

The frosted glass of the bathroom window barred any clear view of the inside, but Jane made out enough to know what she was looking at. A dark shape, lying on the floor between the bath and the toilet bowl. DS Harper.

The window was locked. She looked around for something to break the glass and found a brick. It was slightly disquieting to realise that she had something in common with a serial killer. Dale Lister used a brick to weigh down the lid of his wheelie bin. She grabbed it, shielded her face with her arm and smashed the pane.

There wasn't time to clear all the glass away before she clambered onto the sill. A stray shard, razor sharp, ripped through her left trouser leg and tore a gash in the flesh of her calf. "Aaargh!" Even with her hand over her mouth, her yell must have been heard two streets away.

"Mmmmm." DS Harper lay bound and gagged, on the yellowed linoleum. Ignoring the pain from her cut, Jane dropped to the floor beside him.

"Mmm . . . mmm."

"Sorry. This is going to hurt." The duct tape sealing Elias's mouth came away along with a sizeable amount of facial hair.

His eyes watered. A grey sock was stuffed in his mouth. Jane pulled it out. His tone was urgent. "Can't move. Leg broken. Warwick's upstairs . . . Back-up's been delayed."

Jane stood up. "I'm going to help her."

"No! Wait! It's too dangerous."

"I have to."

Jane curled her hand around her truncheon and crept into the hallway, hyper alert. A muffled sound drifted down from upstairs. It sounded like the noise Harper had made trying to communicate through his gag, only more stifled. It stopped, followed by an ominous silence.

Jane grasped the square cap of the newel post, feeling the rough finish of the varnished wood on her sweating palm. The first step creaked under her weight. She stopped, held her breath, her stomach churning. Then, she moved, swiftly but lightly, feet barely touching the treads, to gain the upstairs landing.

There, she stopped for a moment, listened. Laboured grunting noises came from a room with a half-closed door. Heart pounding, she stepped towards it. The gap was just wide enough for her to squeeze through without making a sound.

Lister sat astride Warwick. He was pressing a pillow to her face. Warwick's legs, bound at the ankles, thrashed out ineffectually, then slowed to a stop. Jane watched in horror as Lister leaned in with all his weight and pressed down harder.

Finishing the job. His determination to carry on after Warwick's struggling stopped was shocking. It roused Jane out of her inertia.

"Police! Step aside! Now!"

She was surprised at the authority in her voice. It was, she realised, the tone she had reserved to blast her worst-behaved students at Ollie Granger.

In other circumstances, Lister's startled-schoolboy look would have been comical. Jane held her baton up in front of her to show she meant business. The fingers of her left hand curled around her PAVA spray. Her eyes flitted to Warwick, unmoving on the bed. Lister had loosened his grip on the pillow, and it had slipped sideways, revealing part of Warwick's face. But Jane couldn't tell if she was breathing. *Please don't let it be too late!*

Lister hadn't moved. Jane took advantage of his momentary confusion. "I said, step aside. Get off the bed and put your hands against the wall. Do it! Now!"

"All right, bitch, I'm doing it!" Lister rolled off the bed, crossed to the wall, pressed his palms against it. But his posture didn't indicate surrender. It suggested muscles tensed and ready.

You can do this. Jane's heart, pumping alarmingly, disagreed. She advanced towards him, trembling slightly, acutely aware that his compliance was everything. If he resisted arrest, *And why wouldn't he? This is insane,* she wouldn't be able to restrain and cuff him alone.

Lister knew it too. Head tilted to look over his shoulder, he watched her, cold-eyed, a cornered beast waiting to strike.

Jane advanced another step, truncheon raised. Lister's hands slid from the wall. He swivelled . . .

"Mmmm . . .Mmmm."

Startled, Jane's attention switched to Warwick. The momentary distraction was all Lister required. He barrelled across the last remaining distance between them, knocking Jane to the floor. Then he flung the door wide and bolted.

"Mmmm . . . Mmmm." Warwick had managed to shake the pillow off. Her bloodshot eyes stared into Jane's, full of accusation.

Jane struggled to her feet and crossed to the bed. For a split second, she was tempted to untie Warwick before removing the duct tape. Anything to keep her quiet a little longer. Then, she yanked it off.

Warwick looked a mess. The lower part of her face was raw from the tape. Her lips were variegated — pale blue and pink. Jane reached two fingers into her mouth and pulled out a grey sock, a match for the other.

Her voice hoarse, Warwick rasped, "What the hell are you doing here?"

"Saving your bloody life!"

"You let him get away!"

"I did not!"

"Untie me. Hurry!"

As soon as she was free of her bindings, Warwick got to her feet. Jane worried she'd keel over from shock, or lack of oxygen, or numbness in her legs, but Warwick proved that she was made of sterner stuff. She headed straight out the door.

She took the stairs three or four at a time, calling out, "Where's Elias?"

"Tied up in the bathroom downstairs. He's okay, but he has a broken leg."

"Stay with him."

Jane caught up with Warwick at the bottom of the stairs. She grabbed her arm. "What about Stacey? Is she alive?"

Warwick shook her off. "I don't know." She looked around. "He didn't go out the front door."

They raced through the kitchen and out to the back yard. Warwick raised a hand. "Go back! Stay with Elias. That's an order!"

Jane stared past her to the outbuilding at the bottom of the yard. "Oh no!"

Steph followed her gaze.

Lister was at the door of the coal store holding up a red petrol container. The lid dangled loose. He held the container at arm's length and tipped it upside down to show that it was empty.

"He's got Stacey in there," Jane said quietly. She looked at Warwick and was surprised to see her blink three, four times in rapid succession. She seemed confused. "DI Warwick? Did you hear what I said? I think Stacey's in the shed. We need to keep Lister away from it."

Warwick didn't seem to hear. It was as though, in her mind, she was somewhere else. Jane hoped it was merely her way of focussing, preparing herself mentally for the coming confrontation with Lister. She was relieved when Warwick began to walk, slowly, towards him. Jane followed, a beat behind.

Warwick stopped abruptly. She called out something to Lister. It sounded like a name. Cal? What did it mean?

Close up, Jane could see that Lister's clothes were drenched. The reek of petrol coming off him was so strong she could taste it.

Lister held something up. Jane's heart lurched when she saw what it was. A red, plastic safety lighter, the kind used to ignite a gas ring on a cooker. Beside her, Warwick muttered something. That name again. Cal.

"No! Cal!" Whatever Warwick said next was drowned out by the sound of sirens. Lister started. He took a step backwards towards the shed.

What's wrong with Warwick? Why doesn't she do something? Who the hell is this Cal? Where does he come into it? Jane took matters into her own hands. "Please. She's just a young girl . . ."

"Stay back, bitch!"

Warwick stepped forward level with Jane. "Please, Cal."

Jane stared at her. She moved forward, positioning herself between Warwick and Lister. She no longer had any faith that the DI knew what she was doing. She opened her mouth to plead with Lister again, but before she could utter a sound, he held the lighter against the leg of his trousers.

Warwick screamed. "No! Cal! No!"

There was a clicking sound. The tip of the lighter sparked red. Lister's trousers flared instantly. Within seconds, the lower part of his body was ablaze. He beat at the flames, only spreading the fire upwards to engulf his upper torso. Flames shot up into the air above his head.

The sound of his screams made Jane sick with horror.

Suddenly, Warwick ripped off her jacket. She rushed to Lister and began beating at the flames, repeating her mantra. "No! Cal! No!"

Jane rushed to help her, but it was obvious that it would take more than beating with jackets to extinguish the conflagration. Suddenly, the sleeve of Warwick's jumper flared.

Jane swallowed, ran to her and tried to pull her back. Warwick pushed her away. Jane grabbed her around the waist, heaved with all her strength and the two women went tumbling backwards. Jane threw her jacket over Warwick to smother the flames, then rolled her on the concrete path. Warwick struggled to break free.

Suddenly, Jane broke. She hoisted Warwick upright and slapped her across the face. "Warwick! Look at him. He's not Cal, whoever the hell that is. He's Dale. Dale Lister. It's too late. You can't save him!"

Warwick went limp in her arms. She blinked, looked across at Lister.

He was a human torch.

CHAPTER THIRTY-THREE

A calm voice behind Jane said, "I've got her." A firefighter.

As soon as she was certain Warwick wouldn't be able to throw herself at Lister again, Jane scrambled to her feet and made for the coal shed, only one thought in her head now.

"Stacey!"

The young woman was trussed up, legs bent to her chest in the confined space, but she was alert, eyes wide with fear.

"It's alright, Stacey. You're safe now. I'm Jane Bell. I'm a friend of Thea's." Stacey nodded. Her eyes shone with tears. Gently as she could, Jane removed the tape covering Stacey's mouth, untied her and led her out of the shed.

The small back yard was abuzz with people — uniformed police, firefighters and paramedics. Jane indicated that she was unharmed and left Stacey in the hands of a couple of paramedics. There was no sign of Warwick. She must have gone inside to check on DS Harper.

Jane wasn't sure what to do next. She wished for nothing more than to slip away unnoticed. Unfortunately, this was out of the question. She averted her eyes from the sight of the charred, blackened shape lying on the concrete. How had it come to this? Why would a young man with his whole life ahead of him set himself on a course leading to murder and suicide? Jane hoped he was dead. If not, he was in for a world of pain. She didn't want to feel sorrier for him than she did already.

"Love it when the bastards pull a stunt like this to avoid facing justice." It was one of the PCs. Jane ignored the comment. People were entitled to their opinions.

She found Warwick inside the house being treated by a paramedic. Her arms were bare, revealing red inflamed skin. Jane was in time to hear the paramedic reassure Warwick that the damage was superficial.

"I owe you a new jacket," Warwick said without looking up. Jane guessed this was as close as the DI was likely to come to thanking her.

Without thinking, she said, "It was police issue." Not that that would have escaped DI Warwick's attention. "How is DS Harper?"

"Broken leg, like you said. He'll be fine. They've taken him out to the ambulance already. Stacey?"

"Shaken, but unharmed. Her parents have been informed."

"What about Lister?"

"I don't know. It looked bad."

"Speak to someone and give a brief statement. You'll need to make a full statement, but it can wait. Go home." Warwick's tone was different from the one she'd used to dismiss Jane from the scene of Mark Ripley's murder. Maybe it was because she was exhausted, or in pain. This time, Jane didn't need to be told more than once.

But as she turned to go, Warwick called her back. She asked the paramedic to leave them alone for a few minutes.

As soon as he'd gone, Warwick cleared her throat. Her voice was hoarse. "I . . . er . . . lost my bearings for a moment out there. I think it must have been something to do with my brain being starved of oxygen when that bastard tried to smother me. I thought Lister was someone else. No need to mention it when you give your account of what happened. Just tell them I went to his assistance and my sleeve caught fire."

When Jane said nothing, Warwick added. "Thank you for what you did. Given your heroics this afternoon, I'll do what I can to see that you are reinstated when your case comes up."

Their eyes met. Jane nodded.

* * *

A few days after the horrific events at Walter Street, Jane sat opposite DI Warwick and DS Harper in Warwick's office on the top floor of the recently built police station on Newport. On the wall behind Warwick was a framed photograph of the steel spire of the International Bomber Command Centre on Canwick Hill, glinting in a frosty sunlight. The height of the spire, Jane knew, was exactly the wingspan of an Avro Lancaster bomber. This was another fact (like the 'tanks for Mesopotamia') that Jane suspected was bound to come up at a quiz night at her local sooner or later.

The centre had been built to commemorate the men and women who had served or supported bomber command during WWII. Jane had visited it soon after it opened. She'd learned that the average age of the young airmen who had died in action was twenty-three. Almost the age of her son now.

Thinking of the young lives lost made her forget her irritation with DI Warwick, who'd barely acknowledged her when she walked into her office.

Jane had only a vague sense of why she'd been asked to attend the meeting. She'd been informed it was to help resolve some issues concerning the investigation. It was probably too much to hope that Warwick might share some information with her about how the case had progressed. She didn't even know for certain that Dale Lister had been responsible for both murders, and she had no real sense of what might have impelled him to kill two people and take his own life in such a violent fashion. There were gaps in her knowledge, and she was desperate for them to be filled.

"Let's get started, then." Warwick's tone was surprisingly neutral. "Why don't you begin by explaining, again, how you came to be at Walter Street, Ms Bell."

Jane explained how she had put two and two together when Thea told her about the two men who had been at the gig with Adam Eades and Phil Lavin.

"Thea had told me previously about Mark Ripley approaching her and Stacey in the café at Hi! To Fitness. She told you about that too, remember, the day you interviewed her at her home?"

"Yes."

"You asked her if anyone else was in the café that day. Thea mentioned that there were a couple of members of staff there, but no other customers."

Jane made sure to mention all this, for she suspected that Warwick would rebuke her for not bringing the connection with the leisure club to her attention.

"I remember."

"So, when Thea mentioned that she thought both of the men worked at Hi! To Fitness, I asked her to describe them to me." Jane chose her words carefully. "I'm a member of that club and it suddenly clicked with me that I knew who she was talking about. Chase Gilbert showed me around when I went to the club to enquire about membership. He introduced me to Dale Lister, who was on duty at the pool that day. The way Thea described Lister put me in mind of Kylie Bright's description of the man who'd harassed her in the café. She described him as 'Mr Generic,' the sort of person you would overlook because he wasn't memorable. I know it was a bit of a leap—"

"We saw him too," DS Harper said, earning a stern look from Warwick. "In some CCTV footage from Starbucks, where Mark Ripley went with a woman called Elle Darrow on the day that he was murdered. Lister approached her table when Mark went to the toilet. He was clearly asking if the seat opposite her was free. Elle hardly looked at him."

Jane nodded. How Lister would have disliked being dismissed so casually. "Do you think he was watching them, that he followed them and killed Mark?"

"We believe so," Warwick said. "We'll be double-checking the CCTV footage from the day of the murder to see if he shows up elsewhere. We'll never know if Mark was his first choice of victim that night. If Elle hadn't gone off in a taxi, perhaps he would have chosen her instead."

Warwick cleared her throat. "We know that you didn't go to the club to enquire about membership, Ms Bell. You went there to make enquiries about the men Thea Martin saw with Mark Ripley. You led the staff to believe that you were a police detective."

"I . . . didn't exactly say I was a detective. They sort of made that assumption and—"

"You didn't bother to correct them."

"I suppose I didn't. I thought I might be able to discover more about Mark by finding out about his friends. That's why I went there."

"You went there again to find out Dale Lister's address. Your former pupil, Ms Clutterbuck, alleges that she 'just happened' to have his details on the screen when you were in her office."

Jane looked down at her hands. "I saw Lister's details on her screen, yes." She was aware of Warwick's penetrating gaze but avoided meeting her eyes.

"Hmm. Quite the coincidence." There was a short silence. Then Warwick said, "Why on earth did you go charging off to Lister's house on your own? Didn't it occur to you to contact the police?"

"I didn't think you'd believe me if I told you my suspicions about Lister. As I said, it was a bit of a leap to connect him with the man Kylie described."

"Indeed," Warwick said. "A leap in the dark."

"I didn't have any proof that Lister was the killer. I had no proof and no idea about why he would have killed Mark, or Kylie. Or why he'd abduct Stacey. I was planning on contacting you immediately if I found some sort of evidence, or if I got to Lister's house and suspected Stacey Ashworth was being held there. When I saw you and DS Harper walking towards the house, I was going to just wait in my car to see if you made an arrest, but you were in there for a long time, and I started to wonder what was going on."

"Your behaviour was reckless and stupid. It was good, solid, investigative police work that led us to Dale Lister's door. Not gossip from teenage girls. Or abusing the trust of an ex-pupil to obtain information illegally. I don't know what you thought you were trying to accomplish, or how you intended to find this proof you were talking about."

Jane said nothing. She had an idea Warwick was enjoying telling off a former schoolteacher. Maybe she'd had a bad experience with one as a child.

"DS Harper, perhaps you'd like to enlighten Ms Bell as to how we too ended up on Lister's doorstep."

DS Harper heaved his plastered leg onto a spare chair. "Do you mind, boss? It's aching a bit." Warwick waved a hand.

"So, quite early in the investigation, we interviewed a young man called Jason. He'd been caught on CCTV footage of the Riverside Shopping Centre, observing Mark Ripley. Jason told us that he'd been trying to pick up some tips on how to approach women. Mark had previously approached Jason in a pub and tried to talk him into joining the pick-up group he was running, but Jason couldn't afford Mark's fees, so he did what he thought was the next best thing. He followed Mark when he spotted him going into the centre."

"Did he tell you about Adam Eades and Phil Lavin?" Jane asked. She'd assumed they had known about their involvement before her and was surprised to learn that they hadn't.

"No. We didn't hear about them until Kylie's friend, Lottie Purdey, contacted us after Kylie's death. It was Lottie who told us that they ran the pick-up group with Mark."

"I found out their names from Chase Gilbert the first time I went to the club, but I didn't know anything about the pick-up group until much later, the day DI Warwick came to my house to find out what I knew. I'm sorry. I should have mentioned them to you, but I didn't know they were involved in anything. As I said, I just thought I could talk to them as a means of finding out a bit more about Mark."

There were no harsh words of criticism from Warwick. But Jane had no illusions that they were best buddies now.

"When we interviewed Eades and Lavin after Stacey's disappearance," DS Harper said, "we asked them about the men who were with them at the gig on Saturday night. That led us to Chase, who told us the other man was a colleague of his at Hi! To Fitness, Dale Lister. Lister fitted the profile that we'd formulated of our killer. Chase told us Lister left the gig earlier than the others, just after the band returned to the stage. We decided to interview him. The rest you know."

Jane listened. As Warwick had probably intended, DS Harper's description of their methodical approach to the investigation highlighted that, though it had led them to the same conclusion as Jane, it had been conducted quite differently. The difference, as Warwick had so kindly pointed out, lay in their method — not hunches and what Warwick had referred to as 'gossip.' Jane preferred to think of Thea's contribution as serendipitous, but she also appreciated that there was more to a murder investigation than chance and intuition. Still, a small part of her believed she was owed some credit for her investigative work.

"Don't look so downhearted," Elias said. "You saved DI Warwick's life and probably mine and Stacey's too." Jane didn't dare look at Warwick.

"I hope you don't mind me asking, but what did you find when you searched Dale Lister's house? Were you left in any doubt that he killed Mark Ripley and Kylie Bright?" she said.

"We found plenty on his laptop after only a cursory look," Warwick said. "It's with our digital forensics team now and I'm sure they'll come up with plenty more. Dale Lister was a very troubled young man. He had low self-esteem and his lack of success in forming romantic or sexual relationships with women drove him to seek advice on the Internet. Unfortunately, or perhaps inevitably, he entered the Manosphere, where he encountered people with deeply misogynistic views. It's very likely that they encouraged him to believe that his failure to attract women wasn't his fault, but that of women who always selected the best-looking men for their mates, leaving men such as him at a gross disadvantage. Once on that path, a descent into violence was, sadly, always a possibility."

Jane nodded. "I've read about this sort of thing. Presumably, it's why he went after Mark. He saw him as one of these 'best-looking men' who were depriving him."

"Yes. We're hoping that forensic evidence will support our theory. We hope to be able to match trace evidence from both murders to Lister."

Jane nodded, aware that it was often possible to obtain samples of DNA from a badly burned body.

"You might be interested to learn that it wasn't Lister who attacked you in your garden that night," Warwick said.

"You found out who that was? Was it a burglar?"

"It was Dominic Tickle."

"Tickle? Why on earth?"

"He was questioned a couple of days ago in relation to a sexual assault on an ex-girlfriend in Skegness. It took place the night of the attack on you. You were his alibi. The sexual assault took place at the same time as he was bashing you over the head with a brick. He confessed that he didn't intend to hurt you. He was planning on breaking into your home and giving you a scare, apparently to teach you a lesson after you and PC Sterne messed up his date with Holly Carpenter. Then you came outside, and he panicked."

So, Warwick had been right in suspecting that the attack had been perpetrated by someone she had come into contact with while on duty. As if reading her mind, Warwick said, "It's very rare for something like that to happen. I wouldn't worry too much about it happening again."

Not much chance of it happening at all while I'm on suspension. Jane didn't say it aloud. Instead, she thanked Warwick for letting her know.

Warwick cleared her throat. "Regarding your suspension. I've made it known that I was possibly a bit hasty in proposing that you put Kylie Bright's life in danger. I'm now satisfied that you did nothing to actively encourage her to approach Lister."

A jug of water stood on the table. Warwick poured herself a glass, while Jane waited, impatient to hear what else she had to say. Finally, Warwick said, "I have also made it known that your prompt action in distracting Lister from his attempt at smothering me probably saved my life."

Probably. Jane smiled inwardly at Warwick's wording. She waited for Warwick to mention that she had also acted promptly in pulling her away from Dale Lister in time to save her from going up in flames with him, thus saving her life twice over. She did not, of course.

"I am confident that you will be reinstated in your duties as a special constable directly after the hearing, which I believe is next Monday."

Jane nodded. A silence of several moments ensued. Jane assumed the meeting was over and made to get up. Warwick looked at DS Harper. "There's something I'd like to discuss in private with Ms Bell . . ."

"Right. I'll be off, then, boss." He gave Jane one of his theatrical bows and left the office.

As soon as Harper had hobbled out of the room, Jane braced herself for another ticking off. She noticed Warwick slip two fingers under the neck of her jumper, as if to let in some air. Her top lip glistened with moisture. She fiddled with some notes on the table in front of her. After some loud throat-clearing, she finally met Jane's eye and said, "That matter we spoke about at Walter Street. Can I continue to count on your discretion?"

Jane considered what she was being asked. She thought Warwick owed her some sort of explanation for her behaviour. She wanted to ask who Cal was and why Warwick had seemed willing to literally walk through fire for him, but now wasn't the time. She looked Warwick square in the eye and said, "Yes, ma'am."

There was no mistaking the relief in Warwick's tone when she said, "Good. Let's go over our reports now, shall we? We need to make sure our accounts match up."

CHAPTER THIRTY-FOUR

Frieda and Karun insisted on inviting everyone to Veganbites to celebrate Jane's reinstatement as a special police constable. It was the first time they had all been together since the Walter Street incident, and everyone was eager to hear Jane's story.

"You're such a hero, Jane," Allie began. "Really, you saved that DI's life twice, didn't you? Once when Lister was smothering her, and again when he tried to burn her with him. She could have been his third murder victim." There was a general murmur of agreement.

This was the version of events that Jane and Warwick had agreed upon during their private 'chat.' Warwick had gone to Lister's aid, only for him to try to draw her into the flames with him. Jane had succeeded in pulling her free. It showed them both in a favourable light.

Jane knew that she had not only saved Warwick's life, but possibly her reputation also. Warwick would have had a lot of explaining to do if she'd confessed that in a moment of crisis, she'd completely lost her sense of reality and mistaken Dale Lister for someone called Cal. At the very least, she would surely have had to submit to some sort of psychological evaluation to determine whether she was competent to perform her duties.

Even after a lot of reflection, Jane had lingering doubts about whether she'd done the right thing in agreeing to keep quiet about Warwick's 'episode.' What if it happened again? Was she putting lives in danger if she didn't report Warwick's behaviour? For she was sure that under some circumstances, a slip such as she had witnessed that day could have potentially catastrophic consequences. Surely Warwick had to know that? As for the excuse about her brain being starved of oxygen, Jane didn't give that the time of day.

No doubt Warwick believed that Jane had consented to keep quiet because of her generosity over the matter of Jane's reinstatement. One good turn deserves another.

The thought bothered Jane. She had no wish for Warwick to believe that she could be bought so easily. Nor was she comfortable with the fact that Warwick's generosity in having her reinstated probably had more to do with self-preservation than gratitude toward Jane for saving her life.

After a lot of soul-searching, she'd come to a decision. She would seek a second opinion. She would speak with Elias Harper. At the very least, he needed to be aware that in a stressful situation, he might not be able to rely on his colleague.

Karun proposed a toast. "Here's to our Jane." Everyone joined in.

Jane smiled modestly. "I was only doing my job." She glanced at Ed. He'd heard her story already. She'd called him soon after all the drama was over and her adrenalin rush had subsided. He'd come at once.

He was looking at her now with an expression that would have been easy to interpret if anyone had been looking. Fortunately, all eyes were on her. Jane bathed in the warm glow of love and friendship.

"Talking of DI Warwick, she was here this morning," Frieda said. "For her morning coffee. That makes three times this week she's been in. She says our coffee is the best in town. I always make a point of talking to her. I think she's lonely."

"I wouldn't have thought she'd have much to say," Jane said.

"Not on her first few visits, but this morning she was quite chatty."

"So, had you heard all about Walter Street from her already?"

"Oh no. She said she would leave you to tell the story yourself if you felt up to it. But she did say that the only reason she was still alive was because of your courageous action, and she was truly thankful to you."

Jane thought she'd misheard. "She said that?"

"Yes. I remember because she was quite emotional when she said it."

"Emotional?" Jane was astonished. "Tearful emotional?"

"Not quite, but her voice shook. She was very sincere."

Jane wondered at what she had just heard. Warwick must have known that anything she said to Frieda would eventually get back to her. Had that been her intention?

Under the table, Ed slipped his hand into hers.

Jane put Warwick out of her mind. After all, there was little chance of their paths crossing again.

THE END

ALSO BY JANICE FROST

WARWICK & BELL SERIES
Book 1: MURDER AMONG FRIENDS

DETECTIVE AVA MERRY SERIES
Book 1: DEAD SECRET
Book 2: DARK SECRET
Book 3: HER HUSBAND'S SECRET
Book 4: THEIR FATAL SECRETS
Book 5: DIRTY SECRETS
Book 6: MURDEROUS SECRETS

STANDALONE
THE WOMAN ON THE CLIFF

Please join our mailing list for free Kindle crime thriller, detective, mystery, and romance books and new releases, as well as news on Janice's next crime thriller!

www.joffebooks.com

FREE KINDLE BOOKS

Please join our mailing list for free Kindle books and new releases, including crime thrillers, mysteries, romance and more, as well as news on the next book by Janice Frost!

www.joffebooks.com

Thank you for reading this book. If you enjoyed it please leave feedback on Amazon, and if there is anything we missed or you have any questions, then please get in touch. The author and publishing team appreciate your feedback and time reading this book.

www.joffebooks.com

Follow us on Facebook, Twitter and Instagram
@joffebooks

We hate typos too but sometimes they slip through.
Please send any errors you find to
corrections@joffebooks.com.
We'll get them fixed ASAP. We're very grateful to
eagle-eyed readers who take the time to contact us.

Printed in Great Britain
by Amazon

54988086R00163